KEEPING KIERA (A MFM MENAGE ROMANCE)

TARA CRESCENT

1

KIERA

When I was a child, I had an imaginary best friend, an old dragon named Rhun. It was Rhun's voice I heard when Lenny Johnson offered me twenty bucks if I would carry a backpack to Mr. Garcia. *He's a bad man. Don't do it, Kiera.*

It was Rhun that I played with. Rhun that kept me safe in the night when my mother was out with her newest boyfriend. Rhun was my constant companion, even after my sister Bianca came along.

Then I grew up, and Rhun melted away into the shadows. Real-life, draining and stressful and often terrifying, took over. My mother died from an overdose. Greg Dratch took an interest in my fifteen-year-old sister. I tried to break them up, with disastrous consequences. People died. My life shattered. There was no room left for childish things like imaginary friends.

Years later, I have a small dragon tattoo on my right arm, a larger one on my left, and a third that hugs my left thigh and curls around my hips, but I have just one remaining memory of Rhun. His eyes, brown, piercing, and wise.

The man in front of me has the same eyes.

He's tall. Six-feet-something. Broad shoulders tapering to a narrow waist. His face is framed by a neatly trimmed beard. His dark hair is long enough that he's pulled it back into a knot. I didn't think I was attracted to guys with long hair, but the butterflies in my stomach are very real. He's dressed more casually than most of the patrons. His jeans are faded, and he's wearing an olive-green t-shirt. From the lines on his face, I'd peg him in his thirties.

No wedding ring, either, though that doesn't mean anything.

"What's your pleasure?" My voice comes out huskier than I intended. The words sound like a come-on, and in a place like Club M, where sexual energy fills the air and lust laps at me from every direction, that's a bad idea.

The stranger's lips tilt up. His eyes rest on me, and his scrutiny freezes me in place. A shiver goes up my spine. Is it fear or desire? I can't tell. *No one can recognize you, Kiera Lynne,* I remind myself. *It's been eight years. You're far away from home. Vladimir Sirkovich is still in jail, serving a life sentence, and his organization is in shambles. You're safe.*

"My pleasure..." His voice, deep and self-assured, sends something twisting inside me. "An intriguing question to ask in a place like this."

My cheeks heat, which is a bizarre reaction, all things considered. I work as a bartender in a sex club, for fuck's sake. Right now, in the corner of the main floor, a masked guy is kneeling on the floor, his head between the legs of a woman. He must be good at what he's doing, because her expression is filled with bliss, and her moans are increasing in volume. In the center of the room, on the raised stage, a dominant is dripping wax on his clearly aroused submissive. Just another Friday night at Club M.

I've barely registered any of it. You learn to tune it out.

I don't blush easily, but this man has me red-cheeked and stammering. With effort, I reach for composure. "What can I get you to drink?"

His lips stretch into a slow smile. "Rum and Coke, please."

I fix his drink and set it in front of him and then make myself move away. I don't understand my reaction. It's as if he's a magnet that I'm drawn to. Only one other man makes me feel this way.

Speaking of the devil… Caleb Reeves enters the club.

Farid, the other bartender working tonight, nudges me. "Incoming," he says under his breath, a grin forming on his face. "I'd ask Mr. Reeves what he'd like, but I already know the answer."

Oh, dear God. Caleb Reeves, the guy I've had a massive, unrequited crush on for the last six months, strides purposefully toward the bar and settles next to the stranger. Of course. There are only two guys I've felt a frisson of attraction for in the last eight years, and they clearly know each other well, because the universe has a twisted sense of humor.

I drag my attention back to Farid. "You do?"

"Mhm. You."

Caleb Reeves wants me? I shake my head to dispel that fantasy. "Mr. Reeves flirts with every woman in this place, Farid. Besides, I like my job. The hours are reasonable, it comes with benefits, and the customers tip well." I'm a bartender at Club M. Caleb Reeves is a member. That's a chasm that cannot be crossed without serious consequences.

Farid gives me a sly smile and moves away to take care of some people. I make my way to the two men on shaking knees. "Mr. Reeves, good to see you. What would you like?"

Caleb Reeves is lean and tightly muscled. As always, he's impeccably dressed in a suit that probably costs more than I make in six months. His dark hair is mussed, and his green-gray eyes are amused. "For starters, you could call me Caleb."

I've moaned out his name plenty of times in my fantasies. I give him my best professional smile. "You know I can't do that, Mr. Reeves. What would you like to drink?"

Once again, I feel the stranger's scrutiny on me. "It was worth a shot," Caleb says, shrugging disarmingly, as he always does. "I'd like a Dempsey, please."

Club M doesn't have a cocktail menu. We have a crazily well-stocked bar, and in deference to the outrageous sums of money the guests pay to become members, we're expected to make whatever they want.

Caleb Reeves does his best to stump me by asking for obscure drinks. This is a game the two of us play, the only one I allow myself. For the last few weeks, it's been pre-prohibition cocktails, and I've had to buy a book or two to bone up on them. Today, it's the Dempsey.

So far, I've never failed to make him his drink, something I'm absurdly proud of. Today's not going to be the day I fail, either. I search my memory for any reference to the Dempsey, and at first, I draw a blank. Caleb raises an eyebrow. "Want help?" he murmurs.

Ah. I've got it. I grin back at him. "No need, Mr. Reeves. Is there a brand of gin you'd like me to use?"

"I'm entirely in your hands, Kiera."

Banishing that unlikely image—Caleb Reeves is a dominant through and through—I start making his drink. Both men watch me, and it's all I can do to tune out their gazes.

Gin, Calvados, absinthe, and grenadine go into my shaker. I give it a vigorous shake and then strain the contents out into a chilled glass, which I carry over to Caleb. He takes a sip. "Thank you. It's delicious."

"Fancy cocktails, Caleb?" The stranger's voice is coated with laughter. "Really?"

Caleb's eyes remain on me. "You know me, Nolan. I enjoy games."

And there it is. The definitive reason I can't ever let myself fall for Caleb Reeves. The man is rich and handsome. He's used to getting whatever he wants. To him, I'm a challenge, interesting only as long as I resist. If I let him in, he'll tear my world apart, and he'll leave me to pick up the pieces.

I've already picked up the pieces once. Bianca is gone, lost forever. My mother is long dead. I have no family, no real friends. Once Vladimir Sirkovich went to jail, I got a nose job, changed my last name, and entered witness protection. At the start, I moved around a lot, terrified that the *bratva* was going to find me. It's only in the last three years that I've put down tentative roots in this quiet part of Pennsylvania.

My peace of mind is hard-won. God knows Caleb is gorgeous, but I can resist his appeal, because to him, I'm a game. Like I told Farid, Caleb Reeves flirts with everyone. I'm not stupid; I don't think I'm special.

The stranger—Nolan—is saying something to Caleb, his voice too low for me to pick up the conversation. As much as I want to linger, I force myself to leave.

These men aren't good for me. I cannot forget that.

2

CALEB

Kiera moves away, and Nolan turns to me. "Am I getting in your way?"

Yes. No. I don't know. "Don't be ridiculous."

His expression turns amused. "I don't think I am." His gaze tracks Kiera. "How long have you been flirting with her?"

I dip my voice in ice. "I flirt with everyone, Nolan."

He takes a sip of his rum-and-coke. He's almost done with his drink. Soon, he's going to raise his hand, and Kiera's going to come back here, her hips swinging, her lips curled into a ready smile, the pink highlights in her hair glistening under the bar's lights...

I groan silently. Fuck. I really have it bad for this woman.

Nolan laughs. "I've known you for a long time, Caleb. I assure you, I know the difference between casual flirting and genuine interest. Have you asked her out?"

"No." Damn Nolan and his curiosity. "She works here. She works for tips. If I asked her out, I'd put her in an incredibly awkward situation, and I'm not going to do that."

"Xavier's not going to fire her if you ask her out, and she

declines." He takes a sip of his drink. "Or if she accepts. Have you looked her up?"

I run a computer firm specializing in cyber-security. While Nolan does flashy stuff like stopping black-market weapon deals and rescuing women held captive in the slave trade, I stay in the background and provide him the information he needs to get stuff done.

Nolan's at the forefront of the action. I used to do that once upon a time. There's a part of me that still misses the thrill, the adrenaline rush that comes with being in the field. There's a part of me that's envious of Nolan's relative freedom. But I have adult responsibilities, ties that anchor me to Myersburg. I don't begrudge them. If I were traveling the world, I wouldn't find time to visit Club M.

Or to play cocktail-games with Kiera.

Nolan can be like a dog with a bone. "No," I reply shortly. "She's entitled to her privacy."

His eyebrows creep up. "You look everyone up," he says. "You really like this woman. Ask her out, for fuck's sake."

"Nolan, you have a vivid imagination." I change the subject. "What brings you to town? I thought you were in Mexico City."

"I'm looking for someone." He glances at the ceiling, at the cameras dotted through the club floor. He drains his drink and gets to his feet. "Let's chat somewhere more private."

Kiera's talking to a couple of guys at the far side of the bar. She's laughing at something they're saying. I fight the urge to march over to her and growl possessively. *She works for tips, asshole. Let her do her job. Leave her alone.*

3

KIERA

Everyone on the club floor seems to want a drink. For thirty minutes, I drown in activity, pouring beer, mixing cocktails, rushing from one well-dressed customer to another.

Finally, the rush dies away, and I inch next to Farid. "Who is he?" I ask.

Farid gives me a blank look. "Who is who?"

"The guy at the bar earlier, the one talking to Caleb."

He gives me an amused look. "Caleb, huh? Not Mr. Reeves?"

My cheeks heat. "He keeps asking me to call him that. So, who's the guy? I've never seen him here before. Is he a new member?" Farid's been working here forever. He knows everyone and everything. In a club where most of the men scream of power and dominance, Farid, with his tousled, curly hair and friendly smile stands out as a non-threatening presence.

It works for him. I swear he's been propositioned by every female member in the club. Some men too.

Farid's smarter than me. He never crosses the line. He

doesn't even tiptoe to the edge. Members are, to him, an alien, forbidden species. Unlike me, he doesn't waste his time entertaining useless fantasies about well-dressed, billionaires who enjoy games.

"Nolan Wolanski," he replies. "No, he's not a new member, he's been here from the start. He's good friends with Mr. Leforte. He doesn't come around very often. Did he make a pass at you?"

I wish. "Just some subtle innuendo. Nothing creepy. Why, is he married?" I really hope not, though I know it happens. I'm in a sex club. I've seen everything.

Farid chuckles. "You have no idea who he is, do you? No, Nolan Wolanski isn't married. He's loaded, he's good-looking, and he's single."

"What does he do?"

"Nothing, Kiera. He's a billionaire. Family money, lots of it. He doesn't need to work. He owns stuff. An investment bank, a castle in Scotland, a villa on the banks of Lake Como. As far as I know, he bums around the world, and gets photographed with models and actresses." He gives me a kind smile. "Billionaires. They're not like us."

He's warning me away, but it's not necessary. I'm a bartender. I make decent money at Club M, but I'm working class, through and through. I already know that the members here are out of my league.

A trio of men walk up to the bar, and I paste a smile on my face. Time to put Caleb Reeves and Nolan Wolanski out of my mind.

KELLIE TAKES over for me at midnight. Sighing in relief, I head upstairs to the break room and change into my regular clothes, shorts and a t-shirt. We're in the grip of a hot, humid spell. Inside the club, the central air is working overtime, but if today's like every other day this week, the moment I step outside, I'm going to be drenched in sweat.

Amy, one of the club floor monitors, is in the corridor outside the break room. She takes in my attire. "No air conditioning in your car?"

I shake my head. "The mechanic said it'd cost a thousand bucks to fix. Even worse, my window AC broke. My apartment is a sauna."

"Ouch," she says sympathetically. "The Walmart sells window units."

I make a face. "I called around. Every store in a hundred-mile radius is sold out. Ah well. Such is life. You working tomorrow?"

She nods. "Yeah, an eight-hour shift. You?"

I pick up all the extra shifts I can, not just at the bar, but also at the restaurant, and I save every bit of money I get. It's the smart thing to do when you need to be prepared to run at a moment's notice.

Tomorrow though, I'm only working the bar. "Just the evening. I'm going to the community pool in the morning, hopefully, before it gets too crowded. I've got my swimsuit in my car and everything."

"Good call. See you tomorrow."

I wave to Amy and head toward the rear elevator. As I pass Xavier Leforte's office, the door opens. "Kiera," Caleb says. "Can you come in for a minute, please?"

4

NOLAN

I probably shouldn't mess with Caleb. But the truth is, it's really good to see him give a shit about something.

After Theo died, after Joha's depression and subsequent suicide, Caleb has withdrawn into a shell. On the one hand, he's doing all the right things. He's running a successful business. Along with his parents, he's raising his niece Nala, providing her with the stability that she needs. Hell, he even coaches Nala's soccer team.

But it comes at a cost. Caleb used to be a fun-loving, devil-may-care kind of guy. Back in the old days, he would've never thought twice about asking Kiera out. Now? Things are very different.

He's told himself that the reason he hasn't made a move is because Kiera works at Club M. He's told himself that by asking her out, he'll put her in an awkward spot.

That's bullshit. The truth is, Caleb's running scared. Theo and Joha's deaths have scarred him. He lost people he loved, and it's made him gun-shy. I've talked to Xavier; I've heard the rumors. Caleb will occasionally play at the club, but he hasn't had a meaningful relationship since Theo died. Hell, I don't even think he's gone out on a date in the last five years.

Maybe it's wrong for me to push. Maybe I'm being a jerk. But when I hear Kiera talk to someone in the corridor, telling them that her apartment resembles a furnace, an idea strikes me. My lips twitching, I get to my feet and head toward the door.

Caleb's recognized Kiera's voice too. He lifts his head. "What are you doing, Nolan?"

My smile widens. "My hotel has a pool. I'm going to invite Kiera to join me for a swim tonight." I turn toward him, my eyebrow raised. "You don't mind, do you? Like you said, you flirt with everyone."

Caleb shoots me a dark look. "You're going to ask her out?"

"Is that a problem?"

If looks could incinerate, I'd be nothing but a pile of dust and ash on Xavier's antique Persian rug. "Why are you doing this?" he grinds out through gritted teeth. "She's a good person, Nolan. Don't play games with her. She deserves better than you and me."

"I'm not doing anything. It's a hundred degrees outside, and I have access to a pool. Besides," I add, my smile fading. "You shouldn't lump yourself in with me. You're the CEO of a multi-billion-dollar company. You take care of your niece. You're loved by your family. If something were to happen to you, you'd be mourned."

Caleb's expression sharpens, and I clamp my mouth shut. *Fuck. I've said too much.* Yes, I'm lonely as fuck. Yes, I sometimes wonder if anyone would miss me if I were killed in a gunfight. Last year, I'd been wounded in Mogadishu. I'd laid in a hospital bed for six weeks, and I've been struck with a painful realization. I've made a difference in peoples' lives, but it's not personal. People like me. People are grateful to me, but no one loves me.

But I've made my choices. I've always held myself aloof. It's what I've needed to do. My life is too dangerous; I have no business dragging someone into it.

Theo Reeves, Caleb's brother, thought he could have it all, but when he was killed, his wife Joha had been so broken-hearted that she'd withdrawn into herself. She'd self-medicated with alcohol and drugs, and eventually, she'd overdosed. Their daughter Nala, who had just been two at the time, had been so traumatized that she hadn't talked for over a year.

I shake my head to clear my thoughts. I need to keep my eyes on the prize. I've been hunting for Luis Fernando Martinez for three years, and I've never been closer to finding out who he is. All I have to do is locate Gregory Dratch and let the former IT guy of the Kitai Bratva take me right to his boss. I've no doubt Dratch will cooperate; the guy's a fucking coward who's already faked his death once to hide from the *mafiya*.

Club Ménage can be a pleasant diversion, a way to blow off steam for a day or two. But it cannot be anything else.

Caleb's giving me a searching look. "Somalia was a shit show," he says, accurately pinpointing the problem. "I came to see you in the hospital, but you weren't accepting visitors. Alexander tried too; Ellie and Alexander flew all the way from Paris, and you pushed them away."

Damn it. I need to distract Caleb before he launches full force into psychoanalyzing me. "If you have a problem about me inviting Kiera to the pool, why don't you do something about it?" I taunt.

"Fuck you, Nolan."

"Suit yourself."

I'm almost at the door when Caleb jumps to his feet and cuts ahead of me, muttering a curse under his breath. Wrenching Xavier's office door open, he steps out into the hallway. "Kiera," he says. "Could you come in for a minute please?"

5

KIERA

My first reaction is to almost jump out of my skin. I even yelp a little.

Caleb's lips tilt up. "Sorry," he says. "I didn't mean to scare you."

"You didn't," I lie. "I was just surprised. Mr. Leforte is away for a few days. I didn't expect to see anyone in his office." The stranger—Nolan Wolanski—is standing behind Caleb, and I study him with narrowed eyes. "Are you breaking and entering? Because if you are, I will call Security."

Nolan's brown eyes laugh at me. "That's very admirable of you." He fishes a black keycard out of his wallet, and waves it in front of the lock. The light turns green. "I'm an old friend of Xavier's. I have a standing invitation to use his office when I need privacy." His smile widens. "I don't always want to be on camera, and this is the only place in the club that isn't on the security feeds."

My cheeks heat. "That's good to know." I feel like a fool. It's not as if Farid didn't warn me that Nolan and Xavier are old friends; he did. It's just that, face to face with these two impossibly good-looking men, it totally slipped my mind.

I don't always want to be on camera. Just like that, my fantasies veer into X-rated territory. Caleb shrugging off his jacket. Loosening his tie. Ordering me to cross my wrists and tying them tight with the scrap of silk. Nolan taking off his t-shirt, those massive muscles flexing as he gets undressed. Stalking toward me, his dark eyes filled with heat. *What's your pleasure, Kiera?*

Caleb clears his throat, pulling my mind out of the gutter. I turn to him, pasting a polite smile on my face. The kind of smile that says I wasn't imagining him naked. "What can I do for you, Mr. Reeves?"

"You're leaving early. Don't you work late on Fridays?"

"Not this week. Kellie's got family visiting next week, so we switched shifts." Yes, I know I'm babbling.

Nolan shifts his weight from one foot to another. "Oh, for fuck's sake, Caleb, get to the point."

Caleb gives the taller man a withering look. "Nolan, you have all the subtlety of a bull in a china shop. Shut up." He turns back to me. "We overheard your conversation. Your air-conditioner is broken, and you're planning to wake up early to use the community pool?"

I lift my chin in the air. It's not a crime to be poor. "Yes. What about it?"

"I have a pool," he says. "Nolan and I were headed over to my place for a swim and a beer. Want to join us? If you'd like, you can spend the night, and hang out by the pool all day tomorrow. You'll have the house to yourself; I'll be at work."

My mouth falls open. Is he inviting me to sleep with him? Is this how billionaires proposition the help? One beer, a couple of laps in the pool, and I'll be ready to jump into Caleb Reeves' bed?

Be honest, Kiera. He wouldn't even need to buy you a beer.

Caleb sees my expression and winces. "Ah, I should have worded that better. I have four guest bedrooms. You're welcome to use one of them."

Oh, okay. That's good. I'm not disappointed. Not even a little.

Behind Caleb, Nolan grins. "Don't worry, Kiera. I'll come along and play chaperone."

A giggle bursts out of me before I can help myself. "You're a long-time member of a sex club, and you're going to act as my chaperone?"

"Is that a yes?" Caleb smiles at me, his eyes crinkling.

I hesitate. Earlier tonight, I drew the line at calling Caleb by his first name. I have no business going to his place and swimming in his pool, even if the idea of a dip sounds like heaven. "I can't," I say reluctantly. "I should go home. I'm binge-watching every Bourne movie on Netflix."

Caleb smirks. "I've been told I have a massive..." He pauses for a second. "...TV."

Someone slap me. I feel the heat creep up my cheeks. When I'm working, I can let the double-entendres slide off me. Even better, I can give back as good as I get.

But I'm not in my Club M uniform. The armor is gone, stripped bare. In my street clothes, I'm a blushing, stammering fool.

"Do you want a dip?" Caleb asks directly.

"Yes."

"Are you afraid I'll make a pass at you?"

I'm afraid I'll want you to. "No."

"Are you worried that Xavier will disapprove of you socializing with me?"

"A little."

Nolan shakes his head. "Kiera, I've known Xavier since college. I've been a member of this club since it was founded. I promise, you won't get into trouble."

Caleb's gray-green eyes rest on me. "Please join us."

I swallow. I'm tempted. *So tempted.* It's so hot that even Xavier's air-conditioning isn't up to the task of cooling the club. My t-shirt is sticking to my back. A pool sounds like bliss.

That's not the only reason. For all his flirting, I don't know a damn thing about Caleb. I know he owns a computer company, but that's it. I don't know where he lives. I don't know if he works in New York or DC, and commutes to this part of the world on the weekend, or if his company is based in the area. Caleb hides it well, but he's extremely private, and this is my one chance to learn something about him.

Have I mentioned I've had a giant crush on him for the last six months?

Guys get to think with their dicks, but women always have to be responsible. Fuck it. I want to cut loose for one night. Do something just because I want to, damn the consequences.

I did all the right things in life, and so far, that's backfired spectacularly on me. I tried to get Bianca out of Greg Dratch's clutches, and it ended up with both of them dead. Greg's boss, Vladimir Sirkovich killed two men in front of my eyes. The FBI convinced me to testify, but they forgot to mention that the mafia doesn't like snitches. Now, I'm in hiding, in witness protection, always looking over one shoulder, always ready to flee at a moment's notice.

Screw doing the right thing for once. Call me superficial, but I want to ogle Caleb and Nolan in their swim trunks.

I can take my own car. I don't have to drink. Besides, I trust Caleb. For six months, I've noticed the way he behaves. Caleb treats everyone with respect. Not just the members. He treats the employees well too. The club monitors, the floor staff—they all like and respect Caleb. It's part of the reason I'm attracted to him.

Nolan's a wild card, but hey, I grew up in a rough neighborhood. I can take care of myself. If it comes down to it, I have mace in my purse, and I'm not afraid to use it.

I throw caution to the wind. "Thank you. I'd love to."

6

CALEB

I could happily strangle Nolan.

Yes, it's true. I am attracted to Kiera. Who wouldn't be? She's a beautiful woman. The pink highlights in her hair, the dragon tattoos on her arms, her bright, cheerful smile—she stands out from everyone else. In a world of black and white, Kiera is a rainbow.

But being attracted to her is one thing. Doing something about it is an entirely different matter.

When Keira had first started working at the club, more than one member had taken note. Most guys flirted a little, but when their interest wasn't returned, they got the message.

Then there was Brett Fisher. He came on to her, constantly and unrelentingly. He sent gifts. He made pass after pass at her. He kept asking her out. He just wouldn't give up.

The thing about Kiera? She's always pleasant. Always smiling. She's cheerful and talkative.

But after watching her for a while, I've learned something. Her surface bubbliness hides a deep well of privacy.

Whatever Kiera is really thinking or feeling, she keeps it well hidden.

Had I thought that Fisher was seriously bothering Kiera, I would have intervened. But I hadn't been able to read her. I didn't know if she welcomed the attention, but I didn't think she minded it too much.

I was very, *very* wrong. She'd felt badly harassed by Brett Fisher. Worse, she felt that because she was just a bartender and Fisher was a long-time member, she had to stay quiet and tolerate the harassment.

It finally got so bad that she walked into Xavier's office one day, four months after she started, and told him she was quitting.

I still remember the look on Xavier's face when he told me about their conversation. His eyes were dead, and his voice was flat. "I should have realized what was going on," he'd said. "This is my fault. This is my club. I approved Brett Fisher's membership."

He'd thrown a vase against the wall. The gesture had been shocking in its unexpected violence. Xavier Leforte never lost his cool. "It's even worse than that," he'd continued, his voice a monotone, as if shards of seventeenth-century pottery didn't litter the floor. "I created an environment where Kiera didn't feel safe. Where she was afraid to approach me because she thought I would take Fisher's side, not hers."

I'd moved the antique glass paperweight on his desk before it could meet the same fate as the vase. "Twelve years after Lina's death, and I'm still making the same mistakes." He'd taken a deep breath. "The world hasn't been kind to Kiera. It was my responsibility to be better, and I've failed."

Fisher's membership had been swiftly revoked. New club policies had been drawn up.

The incident is in the past, but Xavier's words have stayed with me.

The three of us walk to the parking lot. Andrei is waiting for me, leaning against the car, his jacket off and his shirt sleeves rolled up. When he sees me, he snaps to attention and hurries to open the passenger door.

Kiera stops dead in her tracks. An odd expression flashes over her face. "You have a driver. A driver who's waiting for you at one o'clock in the morning outside a sex club."

I can hear the judgment in her voice. "That Dempsey packed a punch," I respond mildly. "And I don't like to drink and drive."

"Right." She shuffles her feet. "Maybe this wasn't such a good idea..."

Damn it. She's pulling away.

"Changing your mind?" Nolan drawls. "Afraid we might bite?"

Her shoulders stiffen. "Where do you live? I'll follow you in my car."

She's thinking about her safety, and I can respect that. I give her my address. "Do you need directions?"

She pulls out her phone and punches it in. "No, I'm okay."

She's as skittish as a colt, and I don't want to push. I don't want to be another Brett Fisher. "See you in a bit."

We wait for her to start her car, and then I slide into my own seat. "Kiera will be following us, Andrei. Can you keep her in sight?"

"Of course, Mr. Reeves."

Nolan gets in as well. "You're so jumpy around her. What gives?"

I give him a deeply exasperated look. It's obvious what

Nolan is doing. He's not the only person who thinks that Theo's death has changed me. They all think that the reason I'm not dating is because I'm still dealing with my brother's untimely end.

They're wrong. Yes, it had been devastating to lose Theo, but his death was quick, and he'd gone out doing something that mattered to him.

It's not his death I'm broken up by. It's Joha's. I didn't have to see my brother suffer, but for a year and a half after it happened, I watched Joha grieve, and there was not a damn thing I could do about it. As much as I wanted to, I couldn't help her.

It's not loss I'm staying away from. It's the feeling of helplessness you get when someone you care about is hurting, and you are powerless to do anything about it.

"Kiera's been harassed at the club before," I say shortly. "And she felt that she couldn't do anything about it. I would really like to avoid repeating that experience."

"Whoa." Nolan raises his hands. "I'm not going to do anything that she is uncomfortable with. You know that."

I do. That's not who Nolan is. "Kiera is a bartender who probably lives paycheck to paycheck. You are not only enormously wealthy but also good friends with her boss, so much so that you have a key to his office. We've both been members of the club since it opened. Consider the optics."

Nolan's expression turns serious. "You're right. I wasn't thinking." He lapses into thought. "She kept looking at you," he says at last. "She's at least a little interested."

She did? "Brett Fisher probably thought the same thing."

Nolan makes an impatient noise in his throat. "In that case," he says bluntly, "He wasn't paying enough attention to what she was and wasn't saying. Unless you've changed dramatically since the last time I saw you, you're not going to do the same thing."

"Even so. Nothing's going to happen. I'm warning you, Nolan. I'm dead serious about this."

Nolan stares at me for a long time. "You're a good person, Caleb," he says. "Your concern for Kiera is admirable. But you're so worried that you won't hear her saying 'no' that you're going to miss it when she says 'yes.'"

I'm attracted to Kiera. I've been attracted to her for quite some time, yet I've had the sense to keep my interest in check. Then Nolan comes along, and in the space of one conversation, all my good intentions have gone flying out of the window.

Outside, the car eats up the miles. It's a full moon night. The air shimmers with possibilities.

Could Nolan be right?

7

KIERA

I'm allowed to look, I tell myself as I drive through the quiet country roads. *Just not touch.*

No matter how much I want to.

The moon is big and silvery. Marvin Gaye is on the radio, his voice low and sexy, singing that he wants to get down with me.

It's been a while since a man touched me. Too long.

Behave yourself, Kiera.

Caleb lives forty-five minutes away. We pass a golf course and a country club on the way, and when I turn into his driveway, I brace myself for a mansion.

It's not a small house, by any means, but it's also not obnoxiously large. If I were to channel my inner Goldilocks, I'd say it's just right. I don't know anything about architecture, but Caleb's house looks old. The walls are stone, and there's a rounded turret on one side. *Magical.*

Andrei, Caleb's driver, parks to one side of the driveway. I pull up beside him, and Caleb opens my door. "Welcome."

I smile at him, butterflies dancing in my stomach. "Thank you. Your house is lovely." I grab my backpack, the one with my swimsuit, from the backseat, and get out of the car. *You're just here for a swim. No need to freak out.*

"You haven't seen the inside yet." He switches his attention to his driver. "I'm done for the night. Thank you, Andrei."

The older man smiles cheerfully. "You're welcome, Mr. Reeves. See you on Monday."

Nolan stretches lazily. His t-shirt rides up, exposing a sliver of his abs, and the butterflies flutter harder.

Two gorgeous guys. *What the hell am I doing here?*

"Come on in." Caleb unlocks his front door before my nerves give way. "The pool's in the back."

The inside of Caleb's house is beautiful as well, open and spacious. The ceilings are high, with exposed wood beams. On one wall, there's a massive fireplace, and above it, the just-as-massive TV that Caleb promised. Shelves overflow with books, and paintings hang on the wall.

Also, there's a half-eaten bag of chips on the coffee table.

Billionaires. They're just like us.

Caleb follows my gaze and looks embarrassed. "Sorry about the mess. My housekeeper took the day off."

Okay. Strike that. They're not like us at all.

"There's a bathroom through there." Caleb gestures in the direction of a hallway. "If you're spending the night, the guest bedrooms are..."

"I'm not," I cut in. "I have to wake up early tomorrow."

It's a total lie, but he lets it slide. "Okay."

Nolan ambles out of sight and returns with two beers. He hands one to Caleb. "Kiera, you want one?"

A cold beer sounds like bliss. "I probably shouldn't, I'm a complete lightweight," I confess. "It's embarrassing, really. One beer and I'm giggling like a fool."

A light sparks in his eyes. "Really? I'd like to see that."

A gorgeous man is flirting with you, Kiera. Say something clever.

My brain goes blank. I open my mouth to reply. Instead of a witty retort, a squeak comes out. *Lovely.*

Caleb clears his throat, sparing me any further mortification. "So, the pool? Nolan, there's a spare pair of swim trunks in my closet. Come on; I'll grab it for you."

By the time I change into my swimsuit, Nolan and Caleb are already in the water.

Ogling thwarted.

Caleb's swimming restless laps. Nolan is too, but he pulls up to the side as I walk up. Drops of water cling to his broad chest and trail down his abs, and I fight not to stare.

He knows it. His lips quirk up, and his eyes twinkle. "There's food if you want it," he says, waving to a platter of bread, cheese, and fruit on the patio table. "And the water is glorious."

I wade into the pool. The water is indeed glorious, cool and refreshing. Climbing roses trail up the back of the house, and the air is scented with their fragrance.

Caleb waves to me but doesn't come over. Nolan goes back to swimming. For a few minutes, I tread water and allow my mind to drift aimlessly. Farid's going to Spain for a week of vacation soon; he's been saving up for the trip for two years. He's an architecture buff. He probably would know at a glance what kind of house this is.

"Penny for your thoughts."

I almost jump out of my skin. I hadn't heard Caleb approach. "Sorry," he says. "I didn't mean to startle you. What were you thinking about? You had a wistful expression on your face."

"Farid," I answer automatically.

Caleb's expression shuts down. "Farid. I didn't realize the two of you were dating."

My brain catches up with my mouth. "We're not." I touch his arm; I can't help myself. "He's going on vacation to Barcelona. He's a Gaudi nut." Caleb's incredibly fit. His suits can't hide it completely, but half-naked, those yummy lean muscles on display, the way he feels, strong and powerful...

Oh God, I'm petting him. I snatch my hand back from his bicep, my cheeks flaming.

"Gaudi. Ah." Caleb sounds a little hoarse. I want to look at his face to see if he has a reaction to me touching him, but I chicken out. "Barcelona is a beautiful city. Have you been?"

I shake my head. Before I can tell him I haven't been anywhere at all, Nolan pulls himself out of the water and wraps a towel around his waist. He's big and broad and solid, and once again, I can't stop drooling.

"Kiera," he calls out. "Can I get you something to drink? Water? Pop? Caleb, you want another beer?"

"Yes, please." Caleb keeps his eyes on me. "Kiera, what would you like?"

You. Both of you.

I blame Club Ménage.

There's a tightness in my belly. My nipples are hard and pebbled. I haven't had anything to drink, but I feel drunk with desire. It's almost two in the morning. It's as if the walls I've built around myself are crumbling.

"Could I have a beer too?"

If I have a drink, I won't be able to drive back home. I'll be spending the night. I know that. Nolan knows that. Caleb knows that.

There's a split-second pause. "Of course."

8

NOLAN

She's got a tattoo of a dragon on her hip, half-hidden by her swimsuit. It's taking everything in my power not to reach out and touch the ink. Not to trace my fingers over her smooth skin, to curve around her soft inside thighs...

Get your head out of your ass, Wolanski.

Caleb is right about one thing—actually, to be fair to him, Caleb is right about most things, but I'm not going to give him a chance to be smug about it—Kiera is off-limits. Not just because of the power mismatch, and the potential for misunderstandings—though that's a pretty damn good reason to keep my hands to myself—but also because of the first rule of hookups.

Don't pee where you eat.

Club M attracts the rich and the powerful. Over the years, it's been a valuable source of information. The people in the club see and hear things, and I need access to them.

Kiera is hot. Small and curvy and lush, with an ass I want to sink my teeth into, but at the end of the day, she's a complication.

My brain knows all the reasons not to be with her.

Then she pulls herself out of the pool, water sluicing down her thighs, glistening in the golden lights that bathe the backyard, and my cock goes hard, and my brain stops working.

She's saying something. Something about a beer. Caleb's looking at me with a strange expression, and I...

Caleb. *Fuck.*

Caleb likes this woman. Likes her enough that the shell he's encased around his emotions is starting to crack. And fuck me, I cannot get in the middle of that. I might not be the best friend in the world—both Stefan and Lina are dead because of how terribly I fail my friends—but the least I can do is keep my dick in my pants around Kiera.

Caleb's watching me, his eyes narrowed. "Beer," I repeat, mentally shaking myself to clear the fog. "Got it."

She wants a beer.

She didn't want one earlier, and she wants one now.

I'm not going to think about what that means.

Not going to do anything about the speculative interest in her eyes.

Nothing.

9

KIERA

Nolan returns with a drink for me. "Thank you."

"No problem."

He's not bare-chested anymore; he's put his t-shirt on. It's subtle, but I'm not the clueless girl from a trailer park in San Diego anymore. I've learned to pick up cues.

Ever so slightly, Nolan's pulling back. Should I do the same thing?

All evening, I've been winging it. Ignoring the voice of caution in my head. Acting on instinct. But I'm not a child; I'm a grown woman. It's time to answer the question: what do I want to happen tonight?

Drink me, the beer in front of me invites. Drink me, and you'll fall down a rabbit hole into Wonderland. Drink me, and adventure awaits.

I used to go on adventures with Rhun, my imaginary dragon. I was a princess, but I had a sword, and I knew how to use it. I'd climb on his back, and we'd fly into the sky. I'd rescue villagers from bandits. Ships from pirates.

The air smells like roses. Music is playing in the background. Drumbeats throb, low and insistent, and I feel their pulsing in my core. The moon shines down, glowing and silvery and magical, and damn the consequences, I want to have another adventure.

They're looking at me. Caleb leans back on the couch, the picture of relaxation, but the expression in his eyes gives him away. It's intent. Focused. Predatory.

This is a side of Caleb Reeves I haven't seen before. Dominant. In charge.

I want to see more of it.

I sit down on the couch as well, a safe distance away from Caleb. Nolan sits across from us. "How do the two of you know each other?" I ask, partly to postpone the moment of reckoning, but also because I'm curious. "Did you meet at the club?"

"No, we went to college together."

"That's nice." *That's nice?* Argh. Not winning any prizes for conversational skill here.

A brief smile crosses Nolan's lips, one that doesn't reach his eyes. He gulps down his beer and places the empty bottle on the table in front of him. "It was, until it wasn't."

"What does that mean?"

I don't expect either of them to answer. I'm being terribly nosy, after all. "Two of our friends died right before we graduated," Caleb responds. "Stephan and Lina scened together, and Stephan enjoyed pushing boundaries. We thought Lina liked it." His voice is steady, but his eyes are far away. In a different place. "Maybe she did. I don't know; it's too late to ask her. One day, they went too far. Lina died in a breath control scene gone wrong. Stephan shot himself. And ever since then, we've wondered how we missed the signs."

Oh wow. I place my hand on top of Caleb's. "I'm sorry."

He squeezes my fingers. "Nolan had it harder. Stephan was his roommate."

I turn to Nolan, who lifts his shoulders in a shrug. "It was a long time ago." His voice sounds casual, but it carries a hard edge. His muscles are tense. His fingers grip the empty beer bottle so hard I'm afraid it'll shatter. "Life moves on."

This is a very personal conversation. I don't belong here, but I can't pull away. Nolan looks haunted, and so does Caleb, and I understand only too well how they feel. I've spent eight years hiding. Every single one of those days, corrosive guilt has eaten at me. Every single one of those days, I've obsessed over the what-ifs. What if I told my mother the first time Bianca met Greg? Could I have tried harder to break them up? What if I'd never gone to the Rose and the Crown that fateful Thursday night, looking for Bianca? Had I not seen Vladimir Sirkovich shoot two people in the head, would he have set the bar on fire? Would Bianca still be alive? Was it my actions that caused her death?

Eight years of keeping secrets. Eight years of searing regret. I can't—shouldn't—tell them any of that. "My sister Bianca died almost a decade ago. It still aches. Sometimes, it's impossible to move on."

Caleb's grip on my hand tightens. "I'm sorry," he says, an echo of my own words.

I don't want their pity tonight. I want something else. "Let's change the topic."

Nolan props his legs up on the table in front of him, just as ready as me to shift the conversation away from the minefields. "Is Nala living with you now?" he asks Caleb. "Is that why the house is such a mess?"

Nala? Hang on. I thought Caleb was single. *He isn't?* What the hell is he doing then, stroking my palm with his thumb, each pass sending a concentrated burst of heat through me?

Caleb shakes his head. "She had some friends over for a sleepover," he says. "She wanted access to the pool." He turns to me. "Nala's my seven-year-old niece. She lives with my parents, but according to her, their house is less interesting than mine." He rolls his eyes. "The real reason she likes to hang out here is because my parents make her pick up after herself, and my housekeeper, Soledad, is far too nice to crack the whip."

His niece. Relief floods through me, and I take a sip of my beer to disguise it. "And what about you, Mr. Reeves?" I tease. "Do you crack the whip?"

Caleb and Nolan snap to stillness. The silence stretches. I start to second-guess myself. Wonder if I've read the situation very, *very* wrong. I open my mouth—undoubtedly to put my foot in it again—when Caleb leans forward, his eyes fixed on me. "That's a loaded question."

"Are you going to answer it?"

Nolan stirs in his seat. "I should head to bed." It's phrased as a sentence, but there's a question in his voice.

"You don't have to," Caleb answers. "Kiera?"

He gives me an inquiring look, and the subtext of the conversation crashes into me. Nolan and Caleb are asking if I want one of them. Or both.

I can pretend I don't understand what's happening. I can flutter my eyelashes and be coy and giggle. But that's not me. When I like someone, when I want someone, I don't want to play games.

Tonight, I'm throwing all the rules out of the window. "Stay. Please."

Nolan eyes me with a speculative look, and then he nods. Caleb stares at me. "What do you want, Kiera?"

Cue my deer-in-headlights look. He's being so *direct,* and I don't know how to respond. "Umm," I stammer. "Are you always so blunt?"

Nolan makes a choked off sound. He sounds like he's struggling not to laugh. Caleb doesn't look amused. "Two words," he bites out. "Brett Fisher."

Oh. Comprehension washes over me. That's what this is about. "This isn't the same thing," I murmur. "I'm here because I want to be." My fingers worry the label on the bottle. The beads of condensation have weakened the glue, and I peel back the edge as I think about how to answer.

Both men are dominants. They probably value open communication. If I give them clear guidelines on how far they can go, they'll respect it. All I need to do is open my mouth, swallow the lump in my throat, and tell them what I want.

Only problem? I don't know what that is. I mean, I'm not a total idiot. I want them. I want to do something with the delicious sexual tension that's building in my insides. I want to be kissed. Touched.

But I don't know if I'm ready to sleep with them this very second. There's two of them, and I've never done anything like this before. Most of me is tempted, but there's a small part of me that's very nervous.

"You're not talking," Nolan says. "You have a very strange look on your face."

I gather my courage in both hands. "If I say stop, would you?"

"Yes." There's no hesitation in either of their voices.

I believe them. I take one last sip of my beer and set it on the coffee table. Anticipation blazes through me. "Then let's play."

Heat sparks in Caleb's eyes, but he doesn't move. "I like to be in charge."

"Hello, Captain Obvious. I work at Club M, remember?"

Nolan laughs softly. Caleb looks amused, but underneath, the heat's still there. The lust, the need. It's like fuel to my arousal. "So much sass from that pretty little mouth." He drains the last of his beer and puts the bottle on the floor. "Stand up, Kiera."

I hear the command in his voice, and desire punches me in the gut. I rise on unsteady legs, obeying him. Is this wise? I don't know; I don't care. The world has shrunk to this moment. I'm cocooned in a snow globe, and everything else is outside. Guilt, fear, stress—the emotions I carry with me on a daily basis—they can't touch me tonight.

"Come here." He indicates a spot between his legs. I move there, and he smiles at me, warmth touching his expression. He lifts his hand and traces the dragon on my thigh. "All night, I've wanted to touch you here," he murmurs. "Spread your legs for me."

I obey again.

My tattoo is a work of art. A powerful, ferocious dragon snarls, his claws gripping my hip, his face near my waist, his mouth erupting fire over my stomach. His tail curls around my left thigh.

Caleb traces the tail with his fingers, and goosebumps erupt on my skin. "Are you cold?"

I'm burning up. "No."

Nolan's watching me. He reminds me of a tiger. One second, relaxed, languid, even lazy. The next, uncoiled, unleashed, erupting into action.

Is he going to join in?

Caleb's thumb strokes my inner thigh. So close. Just

move it up a bit, push aside my swimsuit... "I'd like to see the rest of this tattoo."

Another shiver wracks me. "I'll have to get naked."

There's no give in his expression. "You say stop, we stop. Until then, you follow instructions."

So serious. I grin at him. "I know how this works, Mr. Reeves. If you say jump, I ask how high."

A half-smile curls on his lips. "If I say jump, you don't stop to have a conversation about it, baby." He tilts his head to one side, challenge sparking in his eyes. "You just jump."

So arrogant. I should give him the middle finger and storm off. My fingers move, instead, to the straps on my shoulders. *See, Caleb? I'm obeying.* "You're wearing swim trunks. Nolan's fully dressed. This doesn't seem fair, somehow."

Caleb chuckles. "Life's very rarely fair, Kiera. Besides, I'm half-naked."

Yes, he is. And if I squint hard at the shadows, I can see the thick outline of his cock tenting his shorts. Screw the mood lighting; I want this place flooded with light so I can see him.

"And you've been looking all night," Nolan quips. "At both of us. Like what you see?"

My cheeks flame. "You're not supposed to notice," I grouse, mortified. "Even if you notice, you're not supposed to call me out."

"I rarely do what I'm supposed to do," Nolan replies. "Pretending we don't want each other is not a game I want to play."

"What kind of games do you want to play?" I sound exactly how I feel. Breathy. Needy.

Caleb reaches for me. His hands grip my hips, not painfully, but hard enough for me to be very aware of him.

"You're stalling," he says, his voice coated with steel. "Do you want me to stop?"

His touch inflames me. "No."

"Then get naked, or there will be consequences, and you will not like them."

I'm going to explode; I'm wound so tight. The instant one of them touches my clit, I'm going to erupt like a firecracker. It's going to be the Fourth of July in here.

"Will you spank me?"

His expression sharpens with lust. "Not tonight. Tonight, if you don't behave, I'll lay you out on this table." His gaze holds mine. "I'll spread your legs, and I'll taste you."

I swallow hard. "That sounds pretty good to me, Mr. Reeves."

His smile grows feral. "I'll take you to the edge, over and over, and I won't let you come. No matter how much you beg."

I want to be defiant and tell him that I won't be begging, but those words are a lie. Already, need is clawing through me. If he follows through on his threat, I will die. "Take off my swimsuit," I manage. "Yes, Sir. Jumping now."

Nolan just laughs. *Jerk.*

My fingers are shaking. I slide the straps off my shoulders and push the suit down to my waist. Caleb takes over from there, thank heavens, because my courage's on empty. He rolls the swimsuit past my hips, down my legs, to the floor.

I step out of the pool of fabric.

His growl is pure male need. Primal satisfaction spreads through me. Women flirt with Caleb all the time at Club M. Gorgeous women, beautiful, perfect, and model-thin. But tonight, I'm the one standing in front of him, soaking in the heat of his gaze. *I'm the one he wants.*

"Come closer."

I inch toward him. He catches me, pulls me to him. One hand encircles my waist, the other traces a gentle line over my hip, outlining the delicately shimmering wing of the dragon. "Beautiful," he murmurs.

"It took three sessions and hurt like a bitch."

"I wasn't talking about the tattoo."

His lips touch me, his tongue glides over the ink. Glides over my skin. Tendrils of desire writhe over my body, enveloping me in a raging cocktail of need and lust and heat. "Please," I whimper. "Caleb..." He lowers his mouth to my mound, and my voice dies. Oh God, yes. So much yes.

Out of the corner of my eye, I catch Nolan shift in his seat. He pulls out his cock. Another jolt of pure lust runs through me. He's watching Caleb touch me, and he's fisting himself, and I've never been as turned on as I am right now.

Then Caleb pushes me back on the coffee table. His big hands part my thighs, and his eyes rake over my naked body. He smiles, cocky and confident. "Want me to stop?"

"I will kill you."

He bends his head. His laugh resonates in my core. Then I stop noticing anything, because his mouth is back on me, and my fantasies about Caleb Reeves—hot and vivid though they were—have nothing on reality.

At first, it's slow, almost meditative. He licks me, one long swipe of his tongue between my folds. I arch my hips, hoping this is the first, pleasurable, prelude, but he chuckles and moves away. "I've wanted to do this for at least the last six months, Kiera," he says, his voice vibrating against my core. "I think we can both hold on for just a little longer, can't we?"

"Speak for yourself," I manage.

He laughs again. He kisses my inner thighs, his hands on

my hips, holding me in place. He'll get to my clit when he feels like it, and there's nothing I can do or say that will make any difference. *Argh.*

Nolan's hand moves over his cock. His eyes are on me, and his expression is raw. I watch him watch me. I watch the way his muscles tighten as he strokes himself. The way his face clenches. The tiger's woken up, and he's on the prowl, and I'm the prey.

Hot arousal knifes through me.

Caleb finally decides to stop torturing me. He licks me, careful to avoid my throbbing clitoris. Again and again, his tongue swipes through my folds, and every single time, my clit is left aching and needy. My hands form fists. I throw my head back and groan. I'm ready to scream in frustration...

Then Caleb thrusts two fingers into me, and I arch off the table as pleasure shoots through my body.

I'm lost. His mouth plunders me, restraint gone now. His tongue dances over my clit, hard, fast, raw. Every muscle of my body clenches as I hurtle toward climax.

"Ask for it." Nolan's voice slices through my haze of lust. "Ask for permission to come."

Of all the smug, arrogant things to say... I lift my head and glare at him, and he smiles as he strokes himself. "Ask nicely, Kiera."

Then Caleb sucks my clit gently between his teeth, and my defiance drains away. "Please," I gasp. My body's shaking as I struggle to hold back. "Please, I'm so close."

Caleb slams his fingers deep inside me. "Anytime you want, Kiera," he growls, just in the nick of time. The dam bursts. The fireworks explode. Shock waves hurtle up my spine. My orgasm rips through me, a tsunami of sensation. It isn't gentle or sweet. It's raw and primal and powerful.

I'm going to need a few minutes to catch my breath.

Nolan groans as he comes. For a long moment, none of us say anything, and then I lift my head. "I want to return the favor."

Caleb wipes his mouth with the back of his hand, an expression of male satisfaction on his face. He starts to say something, and the sound of a shrill ringtone cuts him off.

A phone. It's three in the morning. Who could be calling so late?

"Fuck," Caleb swears. He looks at the display and swears again, and then he answers the call. "What's wrong?"

I can hear a woman on the other side, her voice coated with stress. "Nala's had another nightmare, Caleb. She won't stop sobbing."

Caleb's hand clenches into a fist. "I'll be right there." He hangs up and turns to me. "I'm sorry," he says, his expression etched with regret. "That was my mother. Nala had a rough few years, and she's prone to bad dreams." He reaches for my hands. "There's a bedroom upstairs," he says. "Please stay. I'll be back."

"I'll drive you." That's Nolan. "It's late, and Andrei's probably fast asleep. I've had less to drink than you have."

"Thank you." His eyes search mine. "Will you be here when I come back?"

The moon's still high in the sky. The music's still playing, the notes soothing, but with an insistent undertone of pulsing drumbeats. The night's not over yet, and I'm reluctant to let go of the dream and claw back up to reality. "Yes."

Once they're gone, I make my way upstairs and claim one of the minimally furnished guest bedrooms. I expect to lie awake for a long time, but the instant my head touches the pillow, I fall asleep.

~

The sunlight is streaming in through the windows when I wake up. I grope for my phone, and yelp when I see the time. It's after ten. Crap. I hadn't meant to sleep in; I even set the alarm so this wouldn't happen. Or so I thought.

I hurry through a quick shower, brush my teeth—there's an unopened toothbrush in the attached bathroom—and finger-comb my hair. Getting dressed in last night's clothes, I make my way downstairs. Caleb said he had to work today. Is he even going to be around?

He is; they both are. I can see Caleb and Nolan in the backyard when I come down the stairs. I freeze in place for a second, wondering what's going to happen. Last night, things seemed, if not simple, then less complicated. But in the clear light of day, every one of Farid's warnings comes back to sound in my ears.

Caleb and Nolan are members of Club M. They're rich; I'm not. They're used to getting what they want; I haven't gone out on a date in years. I'm out of my league.

Nolan sees me and lifts his hand in greeting. His smile is wide and uncomplicated. No doubt he thinks we'll just pick up where we left off. But I can't. Today, my self-preservation instincts scream at me, warning me to walk away.

Come on, Kiera, I tell myself. *Put on your big girl panties and clean up this mess.*

I cross the living room. The bag of chips is gone this morning. A pair of laptops litter the surface of an ebony dining table, their screens half turned toward me.

And on one of the screens is an image that stops me cold.

Short black hair. Long nose. High cheekbones. Gray, ruthless eyes.

It's a photo of Greg Dratch, my sister Bianca's sleazy ex-boyfriend.

My heart hammers in my chest. My brain feverishly throws questions at me. Whose laptop is this, Caleb or Nolan's? Why is there a photo of Dratch on it? Is it possible that Nolan or Caleb work for Sirkovich? Are they going to kill me for putting the head of the Kitai Bratva behind bars?

Then my phone rings and my problems multiply. It's Xavier Leforte, the owner of Club M. My boss. "Kiera," he says, his voice clipped. "Can I see you in my office, please?"

10

CALEB

Cock-blocked by a seven-year-old.

Not that I blame my niece. When Joha overdosed, Nala had been with her. She sat next to her mother's dead body for an entire day until I came to check on them. She's been seeing a therapist, and she's making real progress, but that kind of trauma leaves a lasting impact. Once or twice a month, Nala will wake up in the middle of the night, sobbing her heart out, and there's not a damn thing any of us can do except hold her and be there for her.

I called my mother when I woke up this morning. Nala's up, chattering about everything under the sun, demanding her favorite sugary cereal for breakfast.

And yes, I'm a selfish bastard, because the instant I knew that Nala was suffering no ill-effects from her nightmare, my thoughts returned to Kiera. Is it wrong that I'm hoping that she'll want to pick up where we left off last night?

She spent the night; I didn't really expect her to. When I turned into my driveway at four in the morning, I'd been bracing myself for the possibility of finding her gone. Then I saw her car, and a powerful surge of relief had run through me.

There's a voice in the back of my head asking if this is wise. For the moment, I'm ignoring it. I've been listening to that voice for more than six months. Maybe Nolan is right; maybe I'm being too cautious about Kiera.

Nolan pours himself a second cup of coffee. "I feel like hell," he grumbles. "I used to be able to pull all-nighters in college. Once, I did two of them in a row."

"Last-minute paper?"

"Something like that. Let's talk about Dratch. I need to find him, Caleb. He's Martinez's former IT guy, one of the few people who can identify him. Dratch is the key to this puzzle; I can feel it. Can you put a team on it?"

Luis Fernando Martinez is scum. Arms dealing, human trafficking, he's involved in it all. Martinez has never met suffering he doesn't want to profit off. The only thing he won't touch is drugs, and that's not from any sense of virtue; he's smart enough not to interfere with the cartels.

Nolan's been chasing him for three years, but every time he thinks he has a lead, it evaporates. Greg Dratch is his best lead in months.

"I'll get my best people on it," I promise him, opening my laptop and pulling up the photo Nolan shared with me. "Megan Matuki is a genius. Everyone leaves a footprint, Nolan. Even Dratch. We'll find him."

I get a coffee refill as I dial Megan. It's Saturday morning, but my best analyst always has her phone with her. Sure enough, she picks up on the second ring. "What can I do for you, Caleb?"

"I'm sending you a photo." I hit *send*, and head outside. It rained at dawn, but the sun's out now, and it's shaping up to be a glorious day. I want to savor it. Soon enough, it'll be fall and I'll be grumbling about the upcoming winter. "The man's name is Gregory Dratch. Most recently, he worked for Luis Fernando Martinez. Before Martinez, he bounced around a lot. He's worked for the Croatians, the Colombians, the Italians, and the Russians."

"Got it. What do you want me to do?"

"Find him. To the best of my knowledge, he's in the North-East corridor. Start with DC, New York, Philly, and Boston. Oh, also Jersey."

"You've just listed off four of the top twenty-five cities by population in the United States."

"I don't pay you the big bucks for easy, Megan. He'll be using an alias."

Just then, Kiera comes down the staircase, and I swear to God, the world seems to go still.

Fuck me, I have it bad for her.

She smiles at me and makes her way toward the backyard. "It's urgent, Megan," I say into the phone, finishing my conversation. "Pull in as many resources as you need. If people grumble, tell them to talk to me."

"Yes, boss."

Kiera crosses the living room, and her gaze happens to fall on the open laptop. I'm about to berate myself for the security breach—I should have shut it down, it's not like me to be so careless—and then I catch her reaction.

Kiera freezes. Her eyes widen, and her face goes white.

"I'll call you back for updates," I say and hang up. She's reacting to Dratch's photo. She obviously knows him. *How, when, where?* A thousand thoughts batter my brain.

Nolan catches it too. He inhales sharply. "Well, well," he says. "That's interesting."

It's not fucking interesting, Nolan. Not at all.

Dratch is bad news all the way. Nolan hit the highlights

of his resume this morning, and in a sick, twisted way, it's impressive. Eight years ago, he embezzled some money from the Kitai Bratva, but he faked his own death and fled San Diego. It's a miracle he's even alive, but the guy seems to be coated with Teflon.

How does Kiera know him?

Her phone rings. She answers it, and her shoulders stiffen. I'm good at reading body language, though I don't have to be an expert to know that this phone call is trouble.

She hangs up, and moves again, not looking at the laptop. She slides open the porch door and steps into the backyard, a fixed smile on her face. "Hey."

I have a split second to decide how to play the situation. I return her smile. "Coffee? Breakfast?"

"I can't," she says, feigning regret. She doesn't meet my eyes. Her mask is back in place. I'm not getting Kiera's real smile now; I'm getting the tight-lipped, *working-for-tips-forced-to-tolerate-you* smile that she gives her least-favorite customers at the club.

I've been downgraded, and boy, does it sting.

"I can't stay," she continues. "I just got a call. I have to go into work. Thank you for last night."

Before I can ask if there is going to be a repeat, she gives me another of her forced smiles. "I'll see you at the club."

Message received. *Loud and clear.*

There's nothing I can do about it, because to refuse to accept her decision is the first step on a slippery slope that leads to me becoming Brett Fisher, just another creepy guy who can't take 'no' for an answer.

Fuck.

But this isn't about me. I might not be able to pursue her, but I'm still going to figure out what's going on. How she's connected to Dratch.

I walk her to the front door. When she's gone, I turn to Nolan. "That reaction was out of place."

He nods soberly. "I think it's time to do a background check, Caleb."

My phone rings. It's Xavier. Wonderful. The cherry on this shit-sundae of a morning. I put the conversation on speaker. If I'm about to get chewed out for asking Kiera out, then Nolan might as well shoulder part of the blame. "I thought you were in Belgium."

"I got back last night," he replies. "I reviewed the security footage from my office."

Nolan rolls his eyes. "You need to get a life, buddy. Did someone ever tell you that? Also, since when do you have cameras in your office?"

"I have cameras everywhere," Xavier says crisply. "But only I have access to the feeds from my office. Did Kiera spend the night with either of you?"

"We didn't sleep together, if that's what you're asking."

He's relentless. "But you would have, had the opportunity presented itself?"

"Yes."

"Okay, I'm about to give the two of you a lecture, so listen up. If you review your membership contract, you will realize, that according to section ten-point-five, it is not strictly against the rules to engage in sexual contact with a Club M staff member."

"That's in the rulebook?" Nolan quips. "It must make riveting reading."

"Color me unamused," Xavier snaps. "As I was saying, while it is not specifically against the rules for Kiera to sleep with either or both of you, it is absolutely against the rules for you to pressure her in any way. Don't play with shades of gray here, because if you do, I will come down on your ass so fucking hard you won't know what hit you. I have standards to uphold, Caleb. I don't care that we've been friends since college. In fact, it's just going to make me tougher on you, because my employees cannot ever believe that my friends can get away with breaking the rules."

I take a deep breath before I say anything I'll regret. "I understand. Kiera has left my house. Any subsequent move is going to have to come from her."

"Yes, I know she's left. I called her. I'm going to give her the same lecture in an hour."

I grip my coffee cup so hard my knuckles go white. "Xavier, if she's in trouble because of last night, then I'm going to lose my shit."

"She's not in trouble," Xavier says bitingly. "If anything, you are."

Nolan holds up his phone. There's a picture of Dratch on the screen. "Stop your pissing match, you two. There are more important things at stake."

"What are you talking about?" Xavier asks.

Good thinking. Xavier is paranoid about security—he has cameras in his own office, for fuck's sake—and he would have done a background check on Kiera when he hired her. I fill Xavier in on the situation. Luis Fernando Martinez, Gregory Dratch, and finally, Kiera's reaction. "Kiera definitely recognized Dratch. She might be mixed up in something, and I need to know what that is. I'm going to have my people run a background check, but if you want to help, you can turn over your files to me."

There's silence on the other end. I wait while Xavier thinks through the situation. "Okay," he says finally. "I'll email you her file. Only," he adds, "Because I know that you're more than capable of finding everything out yourself."

"Give me a high-level overview."

"She's in witness protection," Xavier replies. "Eight years ago, Kiera saw Vladimir Sirkovich, the head of the Kitai Bratva, shoot two people in the head. She testified against him. Sirkovich got life with no possibility of parole. She changed her last name, got a nose job, dyed her hair pink, and moved away from San Diego."

Wow. "How do you know all this? Even I would have had a difficult time accessing that information."

"The cop in charge of her case talked. Let's just say that he has a rather flexible moral compass. He won't take money from the Mafia, but he has no qualms taking money from everyone else."

"Reassuring."

"There's more."

Something in Xavier's voice gives me pause. "What is it?"

"They really wanted to put Sirkovich away," he says. "Kiera was their star witness. But she wasn't in that bar that night by chance. She went in there to look for her sister, Bianca. At that time, Bianca was fifteen."

My mouth goes dry.

"She was also," Xavier continues grimly, "Gregory Dratch's girlfriend."

Nolan's eyes narrow.

"Armstrong told me that both Dratch and Bianca had died in a fire," Xavier finishes. "That's the only reason Kiera testified. You don't go up against the mob if you have loved ones you want to keep alive."

My world comes to a stop. "The cop lied to Kiera. Dratch isn't dead."

Not just Dratch. There's an above-average chance that Kiera's sister is still alive.

11

KIERA

I say something to Caleb and Nolan, though I don't remember what. I get into my car and turn on the engine, put it into drive. And all the while, thoughts chase each other in my head like Formula 1 cars zooming around a racetrack.

How do Caleb and Nolan know Greg Dratch? And more importantly, why is his photo on one of their laptops? Now, after all these years. The man has been dead for almost a decade.

That thought roars out, only to be replaced by the memory of Caleb's mouth on my clit. His fingers in my pussy. Nolan watching me the entire time, his hand fisted over his cock. The white-hot, bone-shattering intensity of my orgasm.

I drag my attention back to what's important. *Forget their hotness. You could be in danger.* Are Nolan and Caleb affiliated with Sirkovich? Is my cover blown? Have they figured out who I am? Do I need to run?

Then there's Xavier's phone call. His voice, clipped and

terse, when he told me to come into his office this morning. *Am I fired?*

I'd just started at Club M when Brett Fisher put the moves on me, flat-out refusing to take no for an answer. At that time, I'd read the employee manual cover to cover. I was looking for a big 36-point font headline. Something that made it brutally clear to Fisher that employees of Club M couldn't date the members. That if I agreed to go out with him—not that I ever wanted to—I would get fired.

Newsflash: It doesn't exist. Not, of course, that Brett Fisher would have given a crap about the rules. I had turned him down, and he was determined that he would make me change my mind. I was a challenge to him, not a person.

Fisher had cornered me in a narrow hallway one night. He'd caged me against a wall, his breath reeking of booze. His gaze had been predatory, and not in a good way. He'd called me a cock tease before he stuck his tongue down my throat.

Terror was a familiar companion. I'd been in witness protection for a few years by then, and I'd grown used to the fear. I hid cash in a pillowcase in my linen closet so I could run at a moment's notice. I was wary of strangers. I spent my days looking over my shoulder.

But when Fisher touched me, it had pushed me over the edge. Maybe it took me back to San Diego, to memories of letting one of Greg's buddies paw me so he'd tell me where Bianca was. Or maybe it was because I had believed, up to that point, that I was safe inside Club M. Everyone who worked there had been clear: Xavier Leforte took care of his own.

And he had. Xavier had revoked Brett Fisher's membership, and he'd apologized to me personally. The guy is a freaking billionaire who runs a vast, global business empire. He owns half of Belgium, if I was to believe the rumors.

And despite all his power, he'd sat behind his desk, and he'd crossed his arms over his chest, and he'd told me he was deeply sorry that Fisher had harassed me. That he'd believed—incorrectly—that I was interested in the man, and he took responsibility for his mistake.

I remember what I said to him that day. "I'm not here to date the members. I'm not looking for a sugar daddy. I just want to do my job."

What's Xavier going to think now?

Best case scenario: he thinks I'm terminally stupid.

Worst case scenario: He fires me. This time, I'll only have myself to blame.

I pull into the employee parking lot. It's a little before noon on a Saturday. Not a busy time and the parking lot reflects it. Yesterday, it had been so packed that I had to park in the far corner of the customer lot and take my chances that Henri, the concierge wouldn't find out. Henri isn't a bad sort; he's just a stickler for the rules, written and unwritten. If he finds out what I did last night, I'm in for a two-hour lecture. Farid would probably join him.

Stop stalling, Kiera. I get out of the car and make my way to Xavier's office. The door's ajar. The club owner sees me before I lift my hand to knock—the parking lot has cameras too—and waves me in. "Sit," he invites. If he has a comment on my t-shirt and shorts, he keeps it to himself.

I take a seat across from him. For a long moment, he just stares at me, his fingers steepled. "Are you interested in Caleb Reeves?" he asks finally.

Last night, the answer would have been an unqualified yes. This morning, after I've seen Greg's photo, my thoughts are more muddled. *Maybe. I don't know.*

I don't reply. Xavier's eyes narrow. "Did Caleb make you feel, at any time, that your job here was at risk if you didn't go home with him last night?"

He's misinterpreted my silence. I sit up in my chair. "No. I went there because I wanted to."

"And while you were there, did either Caleb Reeves or Nolan Wolanski do anything that made you uncomfortable?"

They made me come so hard I saw stars. I shake my head again. "No."

"Are you sure?"

"Absolutely."

There's another period of silence. Xavier breaks it first. "When we last had a discussion about this, you made it clear that you weren't interested in dating any of the members." I open my mouth to answer, but he lifts his hand. "Let me finish. I know my club. I know who's up for a quick hook-up, and who isn't. I know who sneaks in after-hours to take advantage of some of the more specialized equipment. I know that Caleb comes in every Friday and orders an obscure cocktail, and you make it for him."

Where is he going with this? "What do you want me to say, Mr. Leforte?"

He frowns. "I was in college with Nolan and Caleb. I like to think I know them better than most people. Neither of them is looking for anything serious. Whatever might be going on between the three of you, it's temporary. It won't last longer than a month. I want you to be perfectly clear what you're getting into."

That's not what I thought he was going to say. *At all.* "I get it," I murmur, my hands folded in my lap. "They're very rich. We're from different worlds. I have no illusions that I'm in the same league as them."

"It has nothing to do with you," he replies. "This is on them; they don't commit. There is a smorgasbord of sex on offer at Club M. To the best of my knowledge, you don't partake. I've always assumed you wanted something more committed. If you pursue this thing with Nolan and Caleb, fleeting sex is all there will be."

Every word of his warning lands with the force of a hammer.

"Caleb flirts with everyone," he continues. "It's as natural as breathing for him. You work at the club. How are you going to feel when he scenes with someone next month?"

Once again, I open my mouth. Once again, he lifts his hand to stall me. "You don't have to answer me. That's not what this is about."

"Am I being fired?"

He looks surprised. "No, of course not. This is simply a friendly warning from someone who has your best interests at heart. As long as your relationship is consensual, I don't care who you sleep with outside of work hours. I run a sex club, Kiera. It would be hypocritical of me to expect celibacy."

I release a breath I didn't know I was holding. My heart starts to beat again.

He leans back in his chair. "If you need to talk, about anything at all, my door's open."

I hesitate. I do need to talk. I need to find the link between the two men I was with last night and Greg Dratch. I need to determine if Nolan and Caleb are connected to the hacker. Xavier Leforte has known Caleb and Nolan since college. He might have answers to the questions buzzing in my brain like angry wasps.

But the half-formed words freeze on my tongue. I've

never told anyone about my past. I cannot afford to trust people. *Not even Xavier.*

I thank my boss and leave his office, heading back to my car. Greg's face swims back into my mind, gnawing relentlessly at my thoughts. Is Sirkovich out of jail? He received life in prison, no possibility of parole, but he also had high-price lawyers who were doing everything they could to get him out. Is he free now? Instead of going home, should I just keep driving?

There's only one person who knows the truth about my past—the detective who placed me in the witness protection program. Miles Armstrong.

Even with the windows down, the car is a furnace. Sweat trickles down my back as I dial his number. My mom swore up and down to anyone who'd listen that every cop in San Diego was dirty, and maybe they were when she was growing up, or maybe that was just her daily cocktail of drugs and alcohol talking. Armstrong has always been good to me.

"Yes?"

"This is Kiera Lynne Thompson." I've been Kiera O'Leary for so long that my birth name sounds odd to my ears. A fun little side effect of witness protection.

I haven't spoken to him in more than seven years, but he remembers me right off the bat. "Kiera? Is something the matter?"

He sounds surprised, but there's something else in his voice. Caution? Wariness? Whatever it is, it makes me edgy. Beads of sweat gather on my brow. "Is Vladimir Sirkovich still in jail?"

"He got life. Where else would he be?"

I don't know, Detective Armstrong. Why don't you tell me

why you sound so nervous? "Has anyone else been looking for me? Asking about me?"

There's a split-second hesitation. "No."

Goosebumps rise on my skin. Something's wrong. For three years, I've settled in this corner of the country, on the Maryland-Pennsylvania border, and nothing has ever happened. I've felt as safe as I ever have.

Until Nolan Wolanski walked into Club M...

Nolan and Caleb are the keys to this puzzle. I've known that from the instant I saw Dratch's photo on the laptop. They want to sleep with me. I want answers. And life has taught me how to use all the weapons at my disposal.

I end my call with Detective Armstrong. With shaking fingers, I call Caleb. He answers on the first ring. "Hello, Kiera."

His voice is a warm caress. Hearing him, desire sparks through my blood and pools in my belly. "Caleb." I'm trying to sound sexy, but I just sound nervous. "You told me last night you liked to be in charge."

"I did."

NOW OR NEVER. "Will you show me? Both of you?"

He inhales sharply. "When? Where?"

"Tonight. At the club. My shift ends at ten."

Caleb flirts with everyone. It's as natural as breathing for him. You work at the club. How are you going to feel when he scenes with someone next month?

"Okay," he agrees. "See you there."

12

NOLAN

Fuck. I did not see that coming.

Caleb hangs up, a stunned look on his face. "You caught that?"

"Yeah, I caught it. I caught the part where she asked you to dominate her, and more importantly, I caught the part where you agreed. Quick question: are you out of your mind?"

My friend winces. "I wasn't thinking."

No, he wasn't. Caleb has it bad for Kiera, but he knows, as well as I do, that scening with Kiera tonight is out of the question. Kiera had a definite reaction when she saw Greg Dratch's photo. Last night, her desire was real. Tonight, it won't be. Tonight, her interest in us is tainted by the ghosts of her past.

She wants to know what we know.

Caleb crosses into the house and pours himself another cup of coffee, his fourth of the morning. I stare at my own mug. We've both had less than three hours of sleep. We're running on caffeine fumes. This is not the right time to be making serious, far-reaching decisions. "Are you going to do it?" I ask him when he walks back to the deck.

He hesitates for a split-second. "Yes."

Mistake. Then again, Caleb clearly has had a thing for Kiera for quite some time now. Which makes me ask the next question. "Do you want me to walk away?"

He lifts his eyes up and surveys me. "You heard her. She asked for both of us."

"It doesn't matter." I drain the last dregs of my coffee. "You're my friend. I'm not going to let a woman come between us. Rafael and Xavier were both involved with Layla, but I didn't think that it was anything that you were interested in. This isn't your kink of choice, is it?"

He shrugs. "I'm out of practice with women. There's only been room for casual hook-ups since I got back. Nothing with any emotional attachment. I don't know what my kink of choice is anymore."

"That's bullshit."

"Fine. You want to know the truth?" He slams the cup on the table. His eyes are furious. "Theo died, and Joha killed herself, and I started wondering if a ménage wasn't the way to go. Before I came home, I lived a dangerous life. If I was in a ménage and I died, then I wouldn't leave the woman I loved all alone."

Shock courses through my body. "Caleb, that's insane."

"No. It's a logical reason. Why are Adrian and Brody both in a relationship with Fiona?"

"I don't know," I reply. I haven't met Fiona, their new submissive, but from all accounts, she makes them incredibly happy. "They've always shared. Before Fiona, there was Sandy."

"Exactly. You don't know. I asked Xavier about it once.

You know what he told me? 'You just know when it's right.'" He rolls his eyes. "Calling it an instinct is vague and nebulous. At least I've thought through my reasons."

"And when you're in the middle of a possessive rage because I touched the woman you've been lusting after for months, are you going to use logic to diminish your feelings?"

"You were here last night. Kiera was naked. You jerked off while I fingered her. I was fine. In any case, we're getting ahead of ourselves. You're in town for what, a couple of weeks? This is not a lasting relationship we're talking about."

I let it go. Caleb's a grown man, and he's not in the habit of lying to himself. If he says he's okay, I'll take it at face value.

He's right about one thing. Lasting relationships aren't for me. I'm a nomad who throws myself recklessly into the line of fire. I don't have room in my life for anything serious.

Kiera's skin had gleamed in the moonlight, the dragon looking real enough to take flight. I'd wanted to trace each line with my tongue. I'd wanted to ask her why she chose the dragon. Was it because she wanted to grow wings and fly away? Just like me?

I suppress the strange wistfulness that accompanies that thought. "What's our plan here, Caleb? We can't scene with her tonight."

He types something into his phone. "I detest situations like this. I loathe not knowing the facts. Eight years ago, a woman named Bianca, last-name-unknown, died. She lived in San Diego. If we're going to find anything else, I need a photo."

"Social media?"

A smile ghosts over his face. "You've got it. Her first

name is uncommon, so that'll help our cause. I had to look for a John Smith once. It was hell."

"We could call the detective Xavier bribed."

Caleb shakes his head. "Only in a pinch. If the Russians are watching the cop, I don't want them alerted."

Ice trickles down my spine. "You think they're still looking for her?"

"I don't know anything right now," he replies. "I've never heard of the Kitai Bratva, have you?"

I shake my head. "I didn't think the Russians had a presence in San Diego. It's too close to the border. I'm surprised the Mexicans let them move in on their turf." Frustration runs through me. "I have a fairly good handle on who the major players are, but this isn't my area of expertise. I don't know enough about their operations in America."

"Who would?"

I run my hands over my face. Caleb's a genius at uncovering the truth. We can find out what we need to know, but it will take time. Or I can make one phone call to a man who knows more about the various elements of the *bratva* than anyone alive. "Nekrasov."

Caleb raises an eyebrow. "Anton Nekrasov? Will he talk to you?"

"Not a clue. The last time I saw him, he nearly punched me in the face."

"The two of you are supposed to be on the same side."

"We don't go about things the same way." Only one way to find out if he'll talk to me, and that's to call him. I dial Nekrasov's Moscow number, and shockingly, he picks up. "I have a date in an hour," he says, his voice clipped. "What do you want, Wolanski?"

Well, he didn't hang up. That's a win. I put the call on

speaker so Caleb can hear the conversation. "Information on the Kitai Bratva. What's it going to cost me?"

Nekrasov won't want money; he's richer than both Caleb and I put together. I'm still not going to like the price. "Your friends Lockhart and Payne are securing a site in Baku. I want them out."

Adrian and Brody are going to be pissed. "What are you doing in Azerbaijan?"

Anton makes a scoffing sound in his throat. "If you think I'm going to satisfy your curiosity, you misunderstand the nature of our relationship, Wolanski."

Caleb bites back a grin. *He thinks this is funny?* Next time, he can try talking to Nekrasov. "I'll pass on your request. But I don't control them. I can't make them do this."

"Very well. That will have to do."

Why Nekrasov couldn't have picked up the phone and called Adrian directly, I don't know. It isn't as if they haven't met before. Then again, Anton, given who he is, has to be quite cautious in his dealings. My childhood was no picnic—my parents shunted me off to boarding school when I was eight, quite happy to turn over the task of raising me to hired help—but, if the rumors are correct, it's nothing compared to what Anton Nekrasov went through.

"The Kitai OPG doesn't exist," Anton continues, using the Russian acronym for the mafia. "Vladimir Sirkovich got tired of being a foot soldier in Atlanta and tried to muscle into San Diego. He set up his own operation without permission."

Sirkovich is either very brave or very foolish.

"San Diego, as you know, used to be Italian territory, but it's now firmly in the hands of the Mexicans. Sirkovich tried to muscle into that. This is not a war the Russians want. An all-out confrontation with the Mexicans would hurt both organizations, and everyone wants to avoid that."

Foolish, not brave. "Why is Sirkovich still alive?"

"He married well. His wife interceded on his behalf. The Russians have disavowed him, but he's safe as long as he's in jail."

"A woman testified against Sirkovich," I begin cautiously.

"Yes, Kiera Lynne Thompson. She went into witness protection, I believe."

How the fuck does Anton Nekrasov remember all this stuff? The guy is a machine.

"Do the Russians have a target on Kiera?"

Anton barks a laugh. "Are you kidding me? Vasily would send her a thank-you card if he could. She took care of Sirkovich for him."

I release the breath I didn't know I was holding. Kiera's safe. She's not being hunted.

"Friend of yours?" Anton asks, his voice sharpening with interest. "Someone you're interested in?"

I roll my eyes. "If you think I'm going to satisfy your curiosity, you misunderstand the nature of our relationship, Nekrasov."

He laughs out loud. "Tell Payne and Lockhart to stay away from Baku," he says and disconnects the line.

Caleb's already typing something away on his laptop. "He gave us a last name," he says. "Thompson. I found her."

I look over his shoulder. A smiling girl stares back at me. She's got vivid blue eyes, straight blonde hair and a gap-toothed smile. She looks so very young. According to Xavier, she had been fifteen when Greg Dratch seduced her. Dratch was twenty-five. Ten years older than her. Definitely old enough to know better.

I'm going to strangle him when I find him.

"Now we search?"

"Now we search," he agrees, his face somber. "She was fifteen. Going by Dratch's track record, she was probably trafficked. Let's talk to Alexander. He might know something."

I grimace. Alexander Hamilton is probably still pissed with me because I didn't want to see him in hospital. "You call him. I've done my share of groveling for the day."

"Coward," Caleb grins. He picks up his phone and dials. "Alexander? Hey, it's Caleb Reeves. I'm emailing you a photo of a missing girl I'm trying to locate."

"I'm officially retired," Alexander says easily. "I'll have to pass it on to my contacts. Hang on, here's Ellie."

Ellie, Alexander's wife, picks up the line. "Hey, Caleb," she greets him. "How are you?"

"Good. You?"

"I can't complain." She sucks in an audible breath. "She's just a child."

"It was taken eight years ago," Caleb says. "She was fifteen then. If she's still alive, she'll be twenty-three."

"She looks familiar..." Ellie's voice is thoughtful. "I've seen her before. Gimme a second, it'll come to me."

I have no doubt. Ellie has a photographic memory. She never forgets anything. It's disconcerting.

Ellie clicks her fingers. "Got it. Cali, Colombia. Two and a half years ago. Jean-Luc was watching a Christmas party thrown by the Cali cartel. Anyone who was anyone in the narcotics trade was there. This girl was one of the attendees. She wore a Dior gown and almost a million dollars in diamonds. A girlfriend of one of the mob bosses, I think, but I don't know whose."

Caleb thanks Ellie and hangs up. The two of us

exchange a long look. Bianca Thompson could be an innocent, trapped in a world that she doesn't know how to escape from.

Or she could be a willing participant.

Fuck me sideways. "How much of this do you want to tell Kiera?"

Caleb goes silent. He doesn't know how tonight's going to play out. Neither do I.

13

KIERA

For a while after I hang up with Caleb, I sit in the car, stunned at what I've done. I can't believe I asked Nolan and Caleb to scene with me.

Some clubs forbid intercourse, but Club M isn't one of them. People don't always have sex there, but it happens often enough in the private rooms. Is that what's going to happen tonight? Is that what I want? Am I really willing to sleep with them in exchange for information?

I bang my head against the steering wheel. *Fool, fool, fool. What were you thinking?*

That's just it. I wasn't thinking. I've been freaking out ever since I saw Greg Dratch's photo this morning. All at once, the demons of the past have reared their ugly heads, and my painfully won peace of mind has been obliterated.

Run, Kiera, run, my instincts scream. *They've found you. Run and hide. Run before they kill you the way they killed Bianca. Press the accelerator and roar out of here. Hide until they stop hunting you. Hide until you're safe.*

I take a deep breath. And then another. Rinse and repeat, until my heart stops racing, and the panic recedes. I wipe my palms on my shorts. Fear isn't useful. I need to stay clear-headed.

Someone knocks on my car window. I jump like a startled cat, and Dixie Ketcham starts to laugh. "I called out," she says when I unroll my window. "You didn't seem to hear me. It's a thousand degrees in the shade. Why are you sitting in a sweltering hot car?"

Dixie Ketcham used to work with Adrian Lockhart and Brody Payne, two of Club Ménage's long-time members. Then her mother got sick, and she quit her job and moved back home to Mississippi to nurse her through years of chemo and radiation.

Cancer is a bitch. It doesn't play fair. Annie Ketcham had lost her fight with the disease a couple of years ago. For a while, Dix was numb. She operated on autopilot, took the clients that walked through her door and did the bare minimum to keep the wolves at bay.

But the wolves weren't content to be kept at bay. Dix had racked up a lot of debt during her mother's illness, paying out of her own pocket for the treatment when her mother's insurance company refused to cover her. Dix had to make a choice. Quit grieving, move back north and try to find a job at a high-pressure law firm—she's a lawyer, whip-smart and no-nonsense and she still manages to be a genuinely kind person—or declare bankruptcy.

She chose option A. Xavier and Brody had a bidding war for her services, and Xavier won. She's now doing high-powered-lawyer stuff at one of his many companies.

She's also a friend. I shouldn't really allow myself friendships—it's a self-indulgent thing to do, and I'm putting her in danger—but when Dixie Ketcham sets her mind on something, she's impossible to deflect.

"Should you really be complaining about the weather? You're from the South. Aren't you used to this?"

She raises an eyebrow. "Nice try. What are you doing here? You don't work Saturday mornings."

Answering her question would involve explaining Caleb and Nolan and the events of last night. "I had something to do," I say vaguely. "What about you? I thought fancy-ass lawyers don't have to work the weekends, unlike us mere mortals."

I work for Xavier, and Dixie works for Xavier too, but that's where the similarities between us end. Dixie grew up solidly middle-class. Both her parents were teachers. There were always books in their house. The only thing you could find in our trailer were cigarette butts and empty bottles of booze.

Dixie chuckles. "Ah, Kiera. Fancy-ass lawyers, as you so elegantly put it, work all the time. As Xavier's pointed out more than once, he pays me to be at his beck and call."

"What are you working on?"

She grins. "I'd tell you, but I'd have to kill you. Changing the subject, I never did hear back from you. Are you coming to brunch? Avery is in New York for the weekend, but Fiona's coming."

I give her a blank look, and she sighs. "Didn't you check your texts?"

Not since last night. "No."

"Brunch, Kiera. Come on."

I look down at my shorts and t-shirt. "I'm not really dressed for it."

"We're not going anywhere fancy," she replies. "You're fine."

I'm tempted. If I go home right now, I'm going to fret about the split-second pause before Miles Armstrong had assured me nobody was looking for me. I'm going to brood about how badly I failed Bianca. I was the older sibling. It was my responsibility to protect my baby sister, and I'd fucked it up so much that she died.

If I can somehow manage to keep the past at bay, I'm going to think about what might happen tonight. About Caleb and Nolan's hands roaming over my body. About getting naked in front of them in one of Club M's back rooms. I'm going to second-guess myself, and I'm going to want to phone Caleb and call the whole thing off.

Nothing good is going to happen if I go home.

Come on, it'll be fun," Dix wheedles. "Banana chocolate chip pancakes with a mountain of whipped cream on top. Tell me that doesn't sound amazing."

I reach a decision. "Okay, I'm in."

"Good." Her expression turns wicked. "And when we get there, you can tell me why you're still wearing last night's clothes."

My mouth falls open. "How...?"

She winks at me. "I know things, Kiera. See you at the Good Earth."

DIX DRIVES her mother's powder blue Volkswagen Beetle. Built in 1965, the car is in pristine shape. "Salt is the car-killer," Dix had said when I'd asked about it. "It causes rust. They don't need to salt the roads in Biloxi." She'd rolled her eyes. "There was a dusting of snow in 1996, and people are still talking about it."

I follow her car now through winding roads. In thirty minutes, we pull up in front of the Good Earth. It's a small, family-run restaurant that's only open for brunch on Saturdays. Fiona's already got us a table in the back. We exchange greetings, I order coffee and the aforementioned pancakes, and then brace myself for the inevitable cross-examination.

Dix doesn't disappoint. "So, Kiera," she says, her voice innocent. "What'd you do last night?'

Fiona looks confused. "What's going on?"

I groan. "Can we talk about something else for a bit? Give me a chance to drink my coffee before the inquisition starts?"

"Okay." Dix turns to Fiona. "How's DC?"

"Quiet. The city gets so empty during the summer that I can even find parking in front of my office. It's unreal." She takes a sip of her water. "We're going to be at the club next weekend," she tells me. "Adrian and Brody have a surprise planned. You wouldn't know what it is, would you? They're refusing to tell me."

I laugh at Fiona's disgruntled expression. "You love surprises. When they flew you to the Caribbean for your birthday, you were thrilled. So why ruin it?"

"Ruin it? If I'm going to be on the main stage at the club, I'll have to get my lady-bits waxed. A girl likes to know these things in advance."

I giggle. Dix does too, but she's shaking her head. "I still don't get the appeal," she says. "I mean, don't get me wrong. I like Adrian and Brody; I used to work with them. But isn't it enough that guys tell us what to do all day? Yesterday, some jerkwad still in law school tried to mansplain how torts work. *To me.* After that, if a guy told me what to do in bed, I think I'd snap."

I wait for Fiona's reply. I've never been in a BDSM relationship either. I've seen all kinds of dominants at the club. Good ones. Bad ones. None have made me want to try it.

You wanted it last night. Admit it, you want it now. You want to know what it would feel like to submit to Caleb and Nolan.

Fiona chuckles. "Dix, I run my own detective agency. Half the people who walk through my front door turn around and leave because I'm a woman. I get it. But the thing with Adrian and Brody, it's freeing. If either of them tried to tell me what to do outside of the bedroom, I'd knee them in the groin. But that's not who they are. They have no desire to be in charge of someone else."

The waiter arrives with our food, and we fall silent. Once he's out of earshot, Fiona continues. "In a session, I don't worry about clients. I don't worry about my employees. I don't remember my to-do list. There's only room for Adrian and Brody, and it is *amazing*."

Dixie leans forward. There's something about her expression... wistfulness mixed in with curiosity, mixed in with defiance. "Hang on," I say slowly. "This isn't an academic discussion, is it? There's someone you're interested in. Someone who frequents the club? Who is it? Do I know him?"

Her expression shutters. "I don't want to discuss it."

Fiona and I exchange looks. Dix is friendly and chatty. She won't talk about what she does for Xavier—attorney-client privilege—but apart from that, her life is an open book. Or so I thought.

"The club just isn't my thing," Dix continues, picking up her fork and stabbing her pancake with it. "Kiera, you can understand that. You work there, but that doesn't mean you've ever considered being someone's submissive."

I take a big, fortifying gulp of my coffee. The two women here are my friends. I don't want to lie to them any more than I have to. "Actually, I'm going to play there tonight."

Their mouths drop open. Dixie is completely speechless. Fiona recovers quicker. "With who? Caleb Reeves?"

My cheeks flame. "I didn't realize I was that obvious."

"I'm a private detective. It's my job to notice things. So, is it Caleb tonight?"

I'm going to die from embarrassment. "Caleb and Nolan. We made out a little last night." I bend my head over my pancakes, in the futile hope that I can avoid any follow-up questions.

No such luck. "Nolan Wolanski?" Dixie squeaks. "Big broad guy, built like a tree, shoulder-length hair?"

"That's him," I confirm. "Do you know him?"

"He used to drop by at Lockhart & Payne from time to time. I think they collaborated on jobs. Fiona, have you met him?"

"No," she replies. "But I've heard Adrian and Brody talk about him. They went to college together."

I set my coffee cup down. "Hang on. What do you mean, they collaborated on jobs? Farid told me Nolan was a rich billionaire playboy. He dates models, owns castles in Europe, and drives fast cars. Right?"

Dixie's eyes narrow. "You don't know anything about him but yet you're going to scene with him?" She levels a glare at me. "You don't do casual sex. You don't do hook-ups. What's going on, Kiera?"

Fuck. I walked into that one.

In eight years, I've never told anyone about my past. The most obvious reason for my silence is safety. If I tell someone the truth, and it gets out, then Vladimir Sirkovich's men might come calling.

But there's another powerful reason for my silence. I don't want to endanger anyone else. I gave testimony and got the mob boss locked up for life, and because of that, I will always be in danger. I don't want to draw people into my world.

"Kiera?" Fiona's expression is concerned. "Are you

alright?"

"Does Nolan work for the Russian mafia?" I blurt out. *Oh, nicely done, Kiera. Real subtle.*

"What?" Dixie blinks in confusion. "Tell me what's going on."

"Please, Dix. I really need to know."

Fiona and Dix exchange a long look. "No, he doesn't," Dix says. "Not unless his personality has undergone a very dramatic shift."

"I very much doubt it," Fiona says. "Nolan went to undergrad with Brody and Adrian, as did Caleb and Xavier. They've all known each other for a very long time. There was a group of them that had a common interest in BDSM. They were young, experimenting sexually for the first time in their lives. And then a woman died."

They'd told me this story. "Lina. Caleb and Nolan told me about her last night."

Fiona's eyes go round. "They did? Oh wow. That's interesting."

"Fiona, I hate when you go mysterious and cryptic."

"They made a promise at Lina's grave," she says. "They would do everything in their power to see that it didn't happen again. That's why I can tell you with confidence that Nolan would never work for the mob. It goes against everything he stands for."

The oppressive weight pressing down on my shoulders disappears. Relief shudders through me, the intensity of it taking me by surprise. I didn't want to be afraid of Nolan. If I close my eyes, images fly into my mind. The way he'd held my gaze as he stroked himself. The growl in his voice as he ordered me to ask for permission to come.

Our desire last night had been real. *Not a lie.*

"I'm really surprised they told you about Lina," Fiona

continues, holding my gaze. "None of them talk about what happened. If they told you, they really like you, enough to take you into their confidence. You're not walking into a hook-up tonight. It's something more serious than that. And if you're hiding something from them... well, it's not a good idea."

Goosebumps rise on my skin.

"Kiera?" Dix asks gently. "Is everything okay?"

I take a deep breath and make a decision that feels momentous. Fiona is with Brody and Adrian; the two men own one of the best private security firms in the world. Dixie is protected by Xavier Leforte. It's time to tell my friends the truth about my past.

"You wanted to know why I'm going to scene with Caleb and Nolan." My fingers crumple the end of a paper napkin and then straighten it out. "My last name isn't O'Leary. It's Thompson. I changed it when I entered the witness protection program."

I don't look at their faces. "Eight years ago, I saw a Russian mafia boss shoot two of his people in the head. They'd tried to steal from him." Crumple and straighten. Less messy than tearing the paper napkin to shreds. "Later that night, there was a huge fire in the same bar. My fifteen-year-old sister Bianca was burned to death, as was her deadbeat boyfriend, Greg Dratch. Greg was Sirkovich's IT guy."

Bianca's body was so badly burned in the fire that the charred figure looked nothing like my sister. The facial features had been burned off. All was left was a human-shaped lump.

Dixie's face betrays her horror.

"I testified against Sirkovich." The edge of the napkin, weakened by my repeated fiddling, starts to tear. "I did it for Bianca. It was my responsibility to keep her safe, and I failed. I had to make amends." I wipe my sweaty palms on my thighs. "The rest of the story is simple enough. Sirkovich got life in prison, and I entered witness protection. I moved around a lot at the start. This is the longest I've ever been in one place."

"Three years?"

"Three years, five months and seventeen days, if we're being precise." I fall silent once again as the waiter refills our coffee. I ignore my full cup. I feel jittery. My body is filled with a nervous energy that's making the corner of my eye twitch. I've never told anyone this story.

"That's the reason you don't date," Fiona breathes. "You don't think it's right for you to be happy." Her voice fills with sadness. "Oh, Kiera."

The sadness will overwhelm me if I let it. "I don't date because it isn't fair to draw someone into this mess."

Fiona doesn't correct me, though I can tell from the expression on her face that she wants to. Dixie leans forward. "Why did you ask if Nolan worked for the Russians?"

With each word I speak, I make them a part of my problems. It's not fair to them. I should shut up.

"Kiera," Dixie prompts, her eyes narrowing. "Fiona runs a private detective agency. I know I don't look like a badass, but trust me, I'm capable of taking care of myself. If you're beating yourself up about involving us, stop it. We're your friends. *We're already involved.*"

"I saw a photo of Greg Dratch on one of their laptops." My fingers tremble as I reach for the cup of coffee I don't need. "Why? Why now, after all these years?"

Fiona frowns. "Why don't you ask them?"

It's an obvious question, but I don't have a good answer. I know I need to find out how Caleb and Nolan are connected to Dratch, but there's a small, secret part of me that would prefer not to know the truth. Last night had been so magical. If I ask them about Greg and I don't like what I hear... Maybe I want to bury my head in the sand just a little bit longer, and cling to my illusions.

Dixie notices my hesitation. "We've got your back, Fiona. You're not in this alone. Now, let's change the topic." Her smile turns mischievous. "Were you with Caleb and Nolan last night? Tell us everything. Are they hung like horses?"

14

CALEB

Ellie emails us the pictures of Bianca Thompson from the party in Colombia. I look through them. In a couple of the photos, the blonde woman is smiling tightly at the camera. The diamond choker around her neck looks like a collar. I hand Nolan my phone, and he surveys the image expressionlessly. "What do you think? Does she look happy?"

"Let's find her and ask."

"If she's still alive. People associating with the Colombian cartels don't have long life expectancies."

Nolan leans back, propping his legs on the coffee table. "You want to pull Megan Matuki off the search for Dratch and put her on this?"

"No need. I have more than one competent analyst." I dial Derek Haas. Just twenty-three, the kid is smart, talented, and fiercely ambitious. This is the sort of challenge he'd relish.

He picks up on the first ring. "Mr. Reeves."

He sounds like he's standing at attention. "Call me

Caleb, Derek. Everyone does. Question for you. Who's my best analyst?"

"Megan." He sounds sulky.

"Here's your chance to narrow the gap. I just emailed you some pictures."

"One second, Mr. Reeves." I hear the ping of his email, and then he's back on the line. "Yup. Got them."

"Those photos were taken two and a half years ago at a Christmas party in Cali, Colombia. The woman's name is Bianca Thompson." I reel off her social security number.

Derek must be in front of his computer because I can hear the clack of keys. "It says here that she died eight years ago in San Diego when she was fifteen. Cause of death unknown."

"She didn't die when she was fifteen."

"Obviously," he says, sounding distracted. Nolan bites back a grin. "You want me to find her?"

"Yes. Today, please, if you can. Her social media accounts haven't been active for eight years. She'll be using an alias. Look in all the usual places. Instagram, Facebook, you know the drill."

"Yes, sir."

I hang up. Nolan quirks an eyebrow. "Who's my best analyst? Is that meant to be a motivational speech?"

I grin. "It is if you're Derek Haas. The kid's been gunning for Megan's job ever since he joined. One way or another, we'll have an answer tonight."

Please be alive, Bianca Thompson.

ALL DAY, I wait for the phone to ring, for Kiera to call off this whole thing. I want to sleep with her; I'm not going to lie. But I always thought that if we slept together, it'd be because she wanted me. Not because she wanted to pump me for information.

Kiera could have asked me about Dratch's photo. She hasn't. She doesn't trust us enough to ask us a direct question, nor does she trust us enough to share the details of her past. Knowing that, I can't scene with her tonight. There's no way. Dominance and submission, is, above everything else, about trust. About knowing that the person who is tying you up has your safety and well-being at heart.

Last night was amazing. Kiera was incredible. The way she tasted... She gasped softly and called out my name as she came. Her voice rings in my ears, lives in my brain.

Last night was everything I've fantasized about. But unless we can be honest with each other, there will be no repeat. Kiera matters too much for me to pretend otherwise.

15

KIERA

"You're joking." Dixie and Fiona stare at me as if I've grown a second head. "Tell us you're joking."

I swallow my sigh. My girlfriends don't think I should scene with Nolan and Caleb tonight. I've heard their protests for the last twenty minutes. "You know we'll find out what's going on," Dix says. *Again.* "You don't have to sleep with them to learn the truth."

I believe Dixie; she'll get answers. There's no earthly reason to go through with my insane plan. *And yet...* I can't seem to stop myself.

"What if I want to?" I ask my friends mildly. "I mean, I've been flirting with Caleb for months. Nolan's a good-looking guy. I'd be a fool not to be attracted to them."

They open their mouths to argue with me, and I hold up my hand. "I'm not changing my mind."

Fiona frowns at me, clearly unhappy with my plan. "Fine," Dixie says after a long pause. "You're an adult. You have the right to make your own decisions, stupid as they are. I'll be at the club tonight. Just in case."

She tilts her chin up, daring me to challenge her. "Are you going to interfere?" I ask.

"I'll sit in a corner and glower at Caleb and Nolan," she says. "But I won't do anything else."

I picture Dix, who weighs less than a hundred and twenty pounds soaking wet, giving Caleb and Nolan death glares, and the image makes me laugh. "Fair enough." I toss some money on the table and get to my feet. "I've got to go home and change. See you tonight, Dix. Fiona, will you be there too?"

She nods vigorously. "Oh, I wouldn't miss this for the world."

Great. That's what I really need tonight. An audience.

I START my shift at seven. Normally, I am too busy to think, but tonight, I'm incredibly distracted. I keep looking at my phone every five minutes to see if one of the guys has texted me. Adrian and Brody will sometimes give Fiona instructions on what she's to wear to the club. I thought that Caleb might do something similar, but he doesn't call.

Maybe he's changed his mind about tonight.

"You're jumpy." Farid reaches over me to get at the beer taps. "What's going on?"

I dance out of his way to give him room. "I didn't get a lot of sleep last night."

He gives me a sympathetic look. "No air-conditioning?"

Caleb's house was perfectly cool. When I eventually went to sleep, I slept well. But I seize on the offered explanation. It's not like I can tell Farid the truth. "Thank heavens there's rain in the forecast."

Dix comes in at eight. She's wearing a shimmering gray dress with complicated shoulder straps. She draws several admiring looks from the men in the room. Ignoring them all, she makes her way straight to the bar. "Well?" she demands. "Any sign of the dangerous duo?"

"No." I look around to make sure there's no one within earshot. "Maybe they're going to stand me up."

She rolls her eyes. "Don't be ridiculous, Kiera. You're amazing. They're lucky you want them. They're not going to stand you up. If they do, I promise you that I'll personally knee them in the groin." She chuckles. "It won't be a hardship. Really."

I bite back my smile. "Down, Sparky. Want a glass of white wine?"

"Yes, please."

AT HALF-PAST-NINE, Caleb finally walks into the club. I'm busy with customers, but I notice the second he appears at the entrance, and my heart skips a beat.

For an instant, I forget everything that's happened since last night. Xavier's warning. Greg Dratch's photo. The reason I asked to scene with Caleb and Nolan tonight. For an instant, when Caleb Reeves walks into Club Ménage as if he owns it, nothing else matters except that he's here. *For me.*

He's wearing a black suit tonight. His shirt is gray. No tie. He's gorgeous. I can't stop staring at him.

He holds my gaze in his as he walks up to the bar. "Hello, Kiera," he says, sitting down. Dix is scowling at him, but he doesn't notice.

His mouth was on my pussy last night. His talented tongue licked my clit until I came, screaming and flailing. "Mr. Reeves."

His lips curl up. "Is that how we're playing it?"

His voice is a soft growl that sends shivers through me.

"At ten, I'll obey." My hands are trembling. I set the glass I'm holding down on the counter before I break it. "Until then, not so much."

His fingers brush mine, a fleeting touch. He glances at his watch, a smile playing about his lips. "Seems reasonable."

That watch probably costs more than a year's rent. I try not to let that thought bother me. "Would you like a drink?"

"Yes, please." Laughter dances in his eyes. "I'd like a Harvey Wallbanger."

"Wallbanger. Funny." I grin at him. "I thought you would have asked for a Blowjob."

He shakes his head. "Too obvious. Unimaginative."

Will he ask me for a blowjob tonight? Will he order me on my knees, free his erection and slide his thick cock into my mouth? Anticipatory goosebumps rise on my skin. I take a deep, shaky breath. "Your drink," I stutter. "I'll make it."

Thankfully, the Harvey Wallbanger is an easy drink to make. Conscious of his gaze, I fill a glass with ice, pouring the vodka and orange juice, and topping it up with a Galliano float. "Here you go."

"Thank you."

Just as he takes a sip, Nolan walks into the club, also in a suit. He's not alone. He's locked in an animated conversation with two men. I've seen them before, but I don't know their names.

Nolan comes up to the bar. "Kiera." He catches sight of Dix, and his smile brightens. "Dixie Ketcham. It's a small world. I thought you were in Louisiana."

"Mississippi," she corrects. She doesn't look at the two guys that flank Nolan. "I moved. How are you, Wolanski?"

"Can't complain," he says easily. "You still working for Lockhart & Payne?"

"No, Xavier Leforte hired me."

Nolan's lips twitch. "That sounds like Xavier." He indicates the two men on either side of him. "Have you met Eric and Hunter? Eric Kane, Hunter Driesse, Dixie Ketcham."

Dixie's voice is coated with frost. "Unfortunately, yes."

Huh. Interesting reaction. I've never seen Dixie be rude to anyone, ever. Until now.

The guy Nolan introduced as Eric Kane laughs out loud. "Tell us what you really think, Dixie. Don't hold back." He smirks at her. "I'm surprised to see you here. What did you call the club the last time we met? Oh right, a place for men with small dicks to boss around women who are too dumb to know better."

Dixie says something in response that I don't manage to catch. Nolan grins and moves away from the arguing threesome, snagging a seat next to Caleb. I walk up to him. "Can I get you something to drink, Mr. Wolanski?"

Caleb lifts his hand up and glances at his watch. His smile deepens. "You're out of time, sweetheart," he says. "And, if I'm not mistaken, your replacement just arrived." His green-gray eyes rest on me. "There's a private room with your name on it. Are you ready?"

Am I ready for this? *Not in the slightest.*

I feel Dix's worried gaze. Fiona's arrived as well, and she too looks concerned. This is my chance to back down.

I lift my head up. "I'm ready if you are."

I GREW up in San Diego; I loved the beach. Whenever I could, I'd escape there. I'd slather myself with sunscreen and sit on the sand for hours on end, watching the waves crash into the shore. There was a rhythm to it that was almost hypnotic. At low tide, the sea would become peaceful, but it was a deceptive sort of calm. There was a wild current underneath, and if you weren't paying attention, it would pull you under.

I would sit at the edge of the water and watch the quietness of low tide build to a crescendo. Slowly, gradually, the waves would get bigger. They would crash into shore with heart-pounding intensity. Over and over, they would batter the beach, powerful and relentless.

My arousal is like the sea.

All day, ever since I made my phone call to Caleb, my lust has simmered underneath the surface. But now, wave after wave of anticipation pummel me. My knees tremble as I take off my apron. I murmur a greeting to Kellie and a farewell to Farid, and all the while, tides of excitement batter my body.

Caleb and Nolan have already made their way to the back room. I appreciate their discretion and their thoughtfulness. If I were to head there with them, everyone here would know exactly what was going on. I'm nervous enough about tonight; I don't need the stares, the whispers, and the gossip.

I'm wearing my Club Ménage uniform. Black tank top and a short flared black skirt. It's ordinary. Boring. The club floor is busy, filled with suit-clad men and expensively dressed women. They are peacocks, and I'm a blackbird.

I don't belong in the private rooms.

As a bartender, I blend into the background. No one looks at me, no one pays any attention to me, and that's just the way I like it. I thought I was content with the way things were. I thought I was content to look, but not touch. *Until last night.*

Everything changed last night.

My world is shifting around me. Walls are being torn

down. Rules are being rewritten. It's a brave new frontier out there, and I stand at the threshold of it, staring at a closed black door, terrified about the prospect of stepping in.

Before I can raise my hand to knock, the door swings open. Nolan stands there, big and broad and unsmiling. He's taken off his jacket. He was wearing a tie earlier; that's gone as well. He's rolled up the sleeves of his white shirt, baring his forearms. He looks impossibly sexy.

I want to pinch myself. Am I dreaming? Is this real? Is this some sex-soaked fantasy that will end with the cruel blaring of my alarm, right when I'm at the edge of climax?

His dark eyes rake over me. "Come on in," he invites. "If you dare."

I lift my chin and step into the room. *This is it. No turning back.* "One would think you were trying to scare me away."

He doesn't smile back. I take a deep, steadying breath and look around. I've seen the room before; I've worked at Club M for three years and am intimately familiar with the castle. But it's different from this side. Tonight, I'm not cleaning the room. I'm not restocking sex toys and condoms. Tonight, I'm experiencing the club the way the members do.

It's a little terrifying.

Candles are everywhere. Dozens of them, the room illuminated only by their warm glow. They're laid out in concentric rings on the floor, dividing the space into circles.

Caleb stands in the center of one of them, his face hidden in shadow. He holds out his hand to me in a wordless invitation, and my pulse starts to race. Watching where I put my feet, I step over the tapers and enter the ring of fire. "This feels very ominous," I quip. "Should I be worried?"

He doesn't answer my question. "There are five security cameras," he says, pointing them out. "Together, they cover every inch of the room. There are no blind spots."

I try to reconcile the Caleb Reeves I know—smiling, good-natured, and flirtatious—with this grim-faced man. "You need to work on your bedside manner."

He hears the quaver in my voice, and his expression softens. "Let's talk for a bit." He picks me up as if I weigh nothing and sets me down on a padded leather bench.

I take in the room's contents. Apart from the bench I'm sitting on, there's a Saint Andrews Cross in the corner, surrounded by its own semicircle of candles. Whips, cuffs, and other assorted equipment decorate one wall. Chains hang from the ceiling, and iron rings are embedded into the floor.

All the better to tie me up with. A hysterical laugh bubbles its way up to the surface, and Caleb's eyes sharpen with concern. "Are you afraid?"

He looms in front of me. There's something dark about him tonight. Something dark, and dangerous, and unleashed. "A little," I admit. "You seem different today."

He doesn't respond. He trails the tip of his fingers over my forearms. "How much experience do you have, Kiera?"

Fiona had warned me this would come up. *Be honest,* she'd said, her expression serious. *Don't lie to them about this.*

I look up at the two men. "None," I confess. "You'll be my first dominants."

An expression of shock flits across Caleb's face. "You've never done this before?"

I don't know how I thought they'd react. I expected them to be surprised. I do work in a sex club, after all. This isn't the sort of place that attracts novices. But they don't just look surprised. Nolan steps into the circle of light, and I take in his expression. He looks... unhappy.

"No."

"Never?" Nolan presses.

I swallow back my nerves. "Is it a problem?"

Caleb starts to say something and then clamps his mouth shut. "No."

He's lying. They both look like they're having second thoughts. "I know the basics," I hasten to assure them. "I've worked here for three years. I'm not going to run screaming if I see you with a whip in your hands."

Nolan raises an eyebrow. He crosses the room to the Wall of Torture, as I've mentally nicknamed it. Selecting a black flogger, he returns to my side. His expression is, once again, unreadable.

"Never been whipped," he murmurs. He runs the tails of the flogger over my arm, slow and gentle. "Ever been tied up?"

"No."

He purses his lips. "I like the club." The suede brushes my neck. Goosebumps dot my skin. "Xavier has created something important here. A safe place to explore your needs. You step in here, brave and eager, your eyes shining with anticipation, because inside these four walls, you are protected. Somebody's watching everything we do."

The tails of the flogger caress my bare thighs. "Somebody's listening to every word of this conversation," he continues. "If they see or hear anything that seems out of place, the door will open. A club monitor will enter, and they will not leave until they are assured of your safety. You know this, don't you, Kiera?"

My throat is dry. "Yes."

Caleb steps in front of me, a bottle of water in his hands. "Drink."

I take a grateful sip. When I'm finished, he takes the bottle from me and sets it down on a side table. "BDSM is, at its heart, about trust. You trust me enough to be vulnerable, and I trust you to tell the truth. Unfortunately, the club's safety mechanisms allow us to bypass that critical step."

Pinpricks of guilt stab me. He's right. BDSM is all about communication and faith. About letting go of control. About closing your eyes and falling, knowing with absolute certainty that your dominant will catch you.

I grew up in a trailer park. My mother was an alcoholic. I learned to take care of myself at a very young age. Even before Sirkovich, I hadn't let myself be vulnerable. I don't let myself lose control.

Tonight is no exception. I'm hoping to seduce Caleb and Nolan into telling me what I need to know, when I could have, as Dix pointed out, just asked them about Greg Dratch's photo.

But asking would require that I lower my walls to them.

Realization sweeps over me. *They know what I'm trying to do.* I thought I'd hidden my reaction to Dratch's photo this morning, but I thought wrong. That's got to be why Caleb's giving me a speech about trust and telling the truth.

My palms are damp with sweat. I wipe them on my skirt, my mind racing. *They might not know,* I try and reassure myself. *You might just be imagining things.*

Caleb and Nolan are staring at me, waiting for me to respond. "I understand," I stammer. "It's about trust. I trust you."

"Do you?" Caleb's eyes are stormy. "Do you know what a safeword is?"

I nod.

Nolan's voice cracks out of the darkness. "Use your words please, Kiera."

"Yes." I bite my lower lip nervously. "I'm familiar with the concept of safewords."

Caleb hands me the bottle of water again. I take a sip,

my fingers trembling, and I slosh some water down my front.

He notices. "If you don't feel safe with us," he says, his voice hard as steel. "You shouldn't be here."

"I do feel safe with you." It's not a lie. I might not trust them with my secrets, but I trust them with everything else. I don't sleep well in new places. My subconscious is always on edge, wondering if I'm in danger. I slept like a baby last night in Caleb's guest bedroom.

I don't know if he believes me. "Hard and soft limits," he continues implacably. "You're a novice. I don't expect you to have all the answers. Just tell me the things you're absolutely sure you don't want to try."

Over time, some of the memories of that fateful day when I saw Vladimir Sirkovich shoot his two underlings have faded. I don't remember what the victims were wearing. I don't even remember what they look like. But if I close my eyes, I can see the blood-splattered walls of the Rose and Crown. I can breathe in that sharp, coppery tang, mixed in with the smell of gunpowder residue. "No knives," I whisper. "No blood."

Caleb gives me a sharp, concerned glance. "What else?"

I feel myself flush. I've been flirting with him for months, yet, aside from the fact that Caleb's a dominant, I know nothing about his sexual preferences. And Nolan is a perfect stranger. What if I'm too restrictive? Too boring to scene with? "No fluids either."

"Clarify fluids," Nolan says. "Will you swallow my come?"

My cheeks burn at his blunt words. "Yes," I whisper, mortified. I can't look them in the eye. This is the most embarrassing conversation in the world. Forget obeying their orders. This is the truly hard part. "I meant golden showers and stuff."

Caleb's lips twitch. "Very well," he agrees, laughter coating his voice. "We'll avoid golden showers *and stuff.*"

As much as I'd like it to, the floor doesn't open up in front of me. I can either run out of the room like a blushing virgin, or I can plunge forward. "I don't think I'd like a lot of pain. I've seen people being caned on the main floor. It never turned me on."

"Okay," Caleb says agreeably. If he finds my limits restrictive, he gives no sign of it. "Anything else?"

I shake my head. "That's all I've got right now. Everything else, I'll have to try before I know whether I like it or not."

"That's fair," Caleb says. He exchanges a glance with Nolan. The two of them have some kind of wordless communication, and then Caleb turns back to me. "Okay, here are my rules. When we're doing this, you don't lie. I ask you a question, you answer me as honestly as possible. Is that clear?"

Oh boy. "Yes, Sir."

He shakes his head. "As pretty as that sounds coming from your lips, I've had enough of you calling me Sir, or Mr. Reeves. In here, you call me Caleb. Nolan, how do you want to be addressed?"

"Nolan's fine."

"Yes, Sir," I start to say, before correcting myself. "Sorry. Yes, Caleb."

His smile widens. "Very nice," he says approvingly. "Is there anything you want to try today?"

Last night, I'd asked him if he was going to spank me as punishment. He said no. Thinking about it after the fact, I realized why. He had been drinking, as had I. We hadn't discussed limits. It would've been irresponsible to proceed.

Today's a new day. "Will you spank me?"

Dark heat flashes in his eyes. "So eager to be punished," he murmurs. "What do you think, Nolan? Has Kiera earned a punishment?"

Nolan moves behind me. He brushes the hair at my neck aside, and kisses me there, his big hand wrapping around my throat. "I'm not going to choke you," he assures me. "I'm not into breath play."

My heart is slamming against my chest like a caged animal. There's a slick, wet heat between my legs. My breasts ache. Nolan is huge. Caleb is sleek and lean and lethal. Either man could snap me like a twig, but strangely, in this room, that thought doesn't fill me with panic. My fear fractures into shards of need.

Caleb places his hands on my thighs, urging them apart. He stands in the space between my legs, so close that I imagine that I can feel the heat of his body, imagine that I can hear the beat of his heart. "Take off your shirt."

It begins.

Nolan lets go long enough for me to draw my T-shirt over my head. I set it down on the bench.

I spent a solid hour this evening agonizing over my underwear. I'd lingered over black lace, but at the last minute, I change my mind. Black lace implies a sophistication I just don't have. I finally picked a cream satin set with pink roses. It's a recent purchase, an indulgence that I probably shouldn't have given into, but it had been my birthday, and I wanted to treat myself to something pretty.

"Very nice," Nolan rasps. His big, callused hands stroke my shoulders. "Very sexy." His teeth nip my earlobe, and a sharp ache spreads through me.

I squirm in my seat, impatient for more. "Should I take it off?"

Caleb's fingers trace circles on my thighs. "What's the hurry, baby? We have all night."

Nolan draws my hands behind my back. He holds my wrists in one hand, firm enough that I can't wriggle free, not hard enough for it to hurt. "Do you like this?" he growls in my ear.

Yes. Oh God, yes.

Caleb tilts my chin up. "For months," he murmurs, his green-gray eyes locked on mine, "I've been fantasizing about this moment. About you trusting me enough to let me do this." He drags his thumb over my lower lip. "And now that I have you here, the reality of this moment..." His voice trails away.

It's not just him. I've been dreaming about this too. Sexual tension has built between us for months. Every drink I've made for him has been foreplay. Last night, he'd put his mouth between my legs, and he'd dragged an orgasm out of me, the best orgasm I've ever had in my life. *And now that we're here...*

Regret slams into me like a plow truck. *What am I doing?* Am I really going to sleep with them for information? Last night, our desire had been real. Last night, I had wanted them so much that denying myself wasn't an option anymore.

Tonight is different. Tonight is just one big lie.

I can't go through with this.

I open my mouth to call it off, but the quiet is punctured by a sharp ring. Caleb reaches for his phone.

Hang on. How does he have his phone with him? The club has a strict no-electronics rule.

He looks at the screen. Tension fills every line of his body. “Derek came through,” he says to Nolan.

“And?”

“It’s good. I think.”

I stare at them, not quite sure what's going on. “Caleb?”

He looks at me for a long time, and then he hands me the device. I glance down at the screen and freeze.

Bianca's face stares back at me.

Her photo is attached to a text message. *This photo was taken last week.*

My sister is still alive.

Caleb's expression is shuttered. Nolan hands me my shirt. “Get dressed, Kiera. We need to talk.”

16

NOLAN

What a clusterfuck.

Caleb is looking like a kicked puppy. Kiera's on the verge of a breakdown. Things are imploding spectacularly.

I should have never walked into this room. Serves me right for thinking with my dick.

"She can't be alive," Kiera whispers. "How can she be alive? It's not possible."

Keep her talking. "Why not?"

"What do you mean, why not?" she snaps. "I was in the morgue. I saw her body, what was left of it. Vladimir Sirkovich ordered Greg's death because he skimmed off the top. Bianca got in the way." She shakes her head from side to side. "I don't know what this is," she says, gesturing to Caleb's phone. "I don't know what kind of sick and twisted game you're playing. I don't want any part of it."

Her hands are tightly wrapped around her body. She's biting her lip. Her face is pale. We threw one hell of a curve-ball her way.

None of us have handled this well.

"Two years before you met him, Miles Armstrong's wife was arrested in Los Angeles and sentenced to five years in prison for dealing drugs. She was working for one of the cartels. Armstrong worked at the LAPD at the time. His career fell apart as a result of her arrest. He divorced her and moved to San Diego." Caleb and I have spent most of the day gathering information. "Armstrong loathes the mafia. He blames them for what happened. He will stop at nothing to see them all in jail." I stare absently at the flogger in my hands and toss it on the floor. "He needed your testimony to convict Sirkovich. You wouldn't have risked your sister."

Her knees start to tremble. "But they did a DNA test."

I grab her shoulders and guide her into a couch. While I'm about it, I turn on the light switch. This is not a conversation for candlelight.

Caleb still hasn't said a word. Damn it all to hell. "In that case, Armstrong lied about the results. You were a means to an end. He used you."

Her eyes fill with tears, and I feel like a dick. "What happened to Bianca? Why didn't she find me? It's been eight years." They overflow down her cheeks, and she brushes them away with the back of her hand. "I disappeared," she gasps. "I went into witness protection. Oh God, this is my fault."

"It's not your fault." Caleb clenches his eyes shut. "Armstrong deliberately misled you. The rest of the department was too busy celebrating Sirkovich's conviction to dig deeper."

"Where is Bianca now? Where was this photo taken? When can I see her?"

Caleb's phone beeps again. He glances at the screen.

Whatever he reads there isn't good news, because his expression turns grim. "This photo was taken in Belize last week," he says. "Your sister was on vacation. Most of the year, she lives in New York."

Kiera's not stupid. "You didn't answer my last question. When can I see her?"

Caleb runs his hand over his face. My gut tightens. Whatever it is that Derek Haas has found, it isn't good.

"Tell me about your sister," he stalls. "Why was she involved with Greg Dratch? He was much older than her."

Kiera opens her mouth to protest, and Caleb holds out his hand. "Please. Humor me."

"Okay," she sighs. "What do you want to know? Bianca is six years younger than me. My mother was an alcoholic, so it fell on me to raise her." She gives us a small smile. "Even when our mother was alive, we were dirt poor. We didn't have money for clothes or food, let alone presents and pretty things." Her gaze turns wistful. "One day when I was fifteen, one of my mother's boyfriends gave us twenty bucks because he felt sorry for us. It was the most money either of us had ever seen in our lives. We were so excited..." Her voice trails away. "We went straight to the mall."

"What did you buy?"

She shrugs. "I gave Bianca my money. There was a doll she wanted to buy, and it was thirty-five dollars."

I grew up rich. My parents were distant, but I never wanted for material possessions. I always had more toys than I knew what to do with. Not so the woman in front of me. I can picture a much younger Kiera taking her baby sister to the mall, selflessly giving up her money so Bianca can buy the toy she wants. It's heartbreaking.

"What did you want to buy?"

She doesn't meet our eyes. "Nothing important." Her cheeks are pink. "I wanted to shop at the Gap. I'd never bought clothes at a mall." She shakes her head, dispelling the past. "I was used to being poor, but Bianca hated it. She was beautiful. She loved pretty things. Then, when she started high school, she met Greg. He took her shopping. Bought her clothes, gave her jewelry." Her eyes darken. "She was a good kid, she really was. But she'd never had nice things in her life. Greg Dratch was a twenty-two-year-old man grooming a fifteen-year-old child, and there wasn't a damn thing I could do. Bianca wouldn't listen to reason."

One way or the other, Dratch will pay for this, I vow silently. *I will make sure of it.*

"So that's why she was involved with him," Kiera finishes. "Now tell me what's going on."

Caleb doesn't look at either of us. He walks around the room, mechanically blowing out each candle. There's a metaphor here about his dreams going up in flames, but my head aches and I'm too tired to think.

"Your sister isn't with Dratch now," Caleb says. "She's the mistress of an arms dealer."

Ice trickles down my spine.

"His name is Luis Martinez."

No. Tell me this isn't happening. Tell me that life isn't filled with such cruel coincidences.

"Your sister wears designer clothing. She vacations at expensive resorts. She's surrounded, at all times, by half a dozen bodyguards. I don't know if she's with Martinez because she wants to be, or if she's with him because she doesn't have a choice. She might be ignorant of what he does for a living. She might not know what he's capable of. Or she might be fully aware of what he is but is ignoring it because she likes what he can buy her."

Martinez is a ghost. He travels under a half-dozen passports. He communicates with his people electronically. Nobody knows who he is.

Until today, I thought that the only way to get to him was through Gregory Dratch. Now, there's a second way. Bianca Thompson. Except that would put her life in danger.

Kiera looks like her heart is slowly being crushed.

Fuck it all. "I will help you," I say out loud, throwing three years of hard work down the drain. Caleb lifts his head and stares at me, and I ignore him. "I will find a way for you to contact your sister. If she wants out of her relationship, I will make it happen. Okay?"

"Okay." She exhales shakily and looks around the room. "I'm sorry."

"Sorry about what?" Caleb's face could be carved from ice. "Sorry you were prepared to sleep with me to find out what you wanted to know?" He gets to his feet and stalks to the door. "I thought that there was real attraction between us, but you were willing to throw it all away the moment you saw Dratch's photo." He puts his hand on the doorknob. His voice is very quiet. "You just needed to ask, and I would have told you everything."

Then he leaves.

I want to leave too. It feels like a pit is opening up inside me. Women have slept with me for information before. It's never mattered until now.

Kiera's shoulders slump. "He's angry with me."

It's not a question. I don't answer. There's nothing to say.

"Will he come around?"

I look at her for a long time. "I can either tell you the truth, or I can tell you what you want to hear."

Her face falls. "The truth."

"Caleb cares about you. You were going to use him." I

need air. I need to be anywhere but here. I get to my feet. "Caleb will help you because he's a decent guy and that's what he does. But whatever this was..." I gesture to the candles. The leather bench. The flogger that lies discarded on the floor. "It's over."

17

KIERA

Nolan stalks out of the room. I stare at his departing back, but I don't call out to him; I don't ask him to stop. A voice whispers that I owe both him and Caleb an apology, but my head swims and thoughts buzz around my mind like a swarm of angry bees, and I can't process anything.

Bianca is still alive.

For a long time, I sit on the couch. Eventually, there's a knock on the door. "Kiera?" Dixie calls. "Are you okay?"

She's my best friend, but right now, I can't face her. I can't face anyone. I get up, my knees shaky, and crack open the door. "I'm fine," I lie.

Concern is written all over her face. "I saw Caleb stalk out of here an hour ago. Nolan wasn't too far behind. What happened?"

Whatever this was... it's over.

I swallow back the lump in my throat. How can I possibly be thinking of them at a time like this? How can I be looking at tonight with an acute sense of regret, wishing I could rewind time and have a do-over? Everything—my thoughts, my focus, my heartache—should be reserved for Bianca. A sister I unwittingly abandoned when she needed me the most. "I just need to be alone. Go home, Dixie. Please."

THE WEDNESDAY after my disastrous Saturday night, I get a brief text from Caleb. 'Write your sister a note,' it says. 'Leave it with Henri. Bianca is being watched twenty-four-seven, and it'll take time to make contact, but I'll get it to her.'

Leave it with Henri. He doesn't even want to see me.

I do as he says. A week passes. Neither Caleb nor Nolan make an appearance at Club Ménage. I tell myself that it doesn't matter—the only thing that matters is Bianca—but I'm not very convincing. There's a dull, ever-present ache in my chest. Fiona does her promised scene at the club the following Saturday, and when I see the way Brody and Adrian look at her, love shining in their eyes, tenderness in every caress, I can't breathe. Tears prickle in the corners of my eyes, and I have to take an unplanned break. "What's going on with you?" Farid asks when I get back. "You haven't been yourself all week."

"It's nothing," I lie. "It must be PMS."

Like every guy in the world, the topic of PMS makes Farid edge away.

I drown myself in work. I pick up every spare shift. Walmart finally has air-conditioners in stock again, and I install a window unit in my apartment, willing the memories of that first night in Caleb's pool to fade.

I'm working a Thursday afternoon shift in the cafe that's attached to the club when Dixie finds me. "You've been avoiding me," she says. Her voice is matter of fact, not accusing, but from the set of her jaw, I know I can't put her off any longer. "You sent me that bombshell of an email, telling me your sister is still alive. You didn't answer any of my emails; you ignored my texts. That ends today. I'm all caught up with my work. It's a nice, sunny afternoon. I'm going to hang out here until you talk to me."

If I'm being perfectly honest, I'm glad she's here. "My shift ends in fifteen minutes."

Twenty minutes later, I join her on the patio. It's blazingly hot, and the cafe is almost empty. Only two tables are occupied by guests, and they've both chosen the air-conditioned interior. A wise choice. The sun beats down on us, and even though I've slathered myself with sunscreen, I feel myself start to burn.

"You're very persistent. Has anyone ever told you that?"

She grins. "Xavier called me a bulldog today, so yes, I have heard it before."

"He did?" That doesn't sound like Mr. Leforte, who is always unfailingly polite.

"I asked him about some credit card transactions in Thailand, and it clearly touched a nerve. He threw me out of his office." She shrugs, unconcerned. "He'll get over his snit."

"Speaking of snits… what's the deal between you and those two guys at the club? Hunter and…"

"Eric," she bites out. "Nothing's the deal. I don't have any patience with fragile male egos, that's all."

"That's a non-answer, and we both know it."

"You're changing the subject." She takes a sip of her iced tea. "I've been able to piece together most of what happened that evening. Caleb and Nolan told you Bianca was alive?"

I nod.

"And you were in shock."

"Yes."

"And the reason both Caleb and Nolan looked pissed as hell when they left the club that night?"

A dull ache fills my heart. "They thought—correctly—that I was using them for information."

She leans forward. "Here's what I don't understand, Kiera. Why *did* you do it? You were attracted to Caleb and Nolan. You knew that they weren't working with the Russian Mafia. You knew they were trustworthy."

Yes. I had known. On some deep, instinctive level, I had always felt like I could trust them. That's why I'd gone over to Caleb's house that first night. "I guess so."

She gives me a frustrated look. "You wouldn't discuss it with Fiona and me; you shut us down when we tried to talk you out of it. You don't normally make stupid decisions, but this one was monumentally dumb. Why did you scene with them?"

"Does it matter?"

"Of course, it does. You found out your sister's alive, and instead of being happy, you're walking around looking like you found out you have a terminal illness." A shadow passes over her face, and I know she's thinking of her mother. "It clearly matters to you. So, tell me why."

I cast around for an explanation. "It was just supposed to be one night. According to Xavier, Nolan and Caleb don't do relationships. Besides, Caleb flirts with everyone." I shrug, uncomfortable with where my thoughts are leading me. "I guess on some level, I thought it wouldn't matter to them."

Dixie's eyes rest on me. "Caleb might flirt with every woman in the place, but does he scene with any of them?"

I search my memory, but I can't find anything. In the last six months, maybe even longer, Caleb shows up at the club, comes up to the bar, and orders an obscure drink. If someone approaches him, he talks to them, but otherwise, he seems happy enough nursing his drink and talking to me.

Oh.

"Exactly." Dixie interprets my shock correctly. "The man likes you."

"He liked me." Until I ruined everything. "Nothing would have come of it anyway. He's in billionaire-territory, and so is Nolan. I'm a bartender. We're from different worlds."

"Hmm." Dixie's eyes sharpen. "You're right. Let's look at the evidence, shall we? Maddox Wake, who is either a billionaire or pretty darn close, is in a relationship with who? Oh right, Avery. Is Avery wealthy?"

Dix is wasting her time with corporate law. She should have been a litigator.

"Brody and Adrian are wealthy," she continues. "Who are they with? Fiona."

"Fine." I hold up my hands in surrender. "Maybe my theory is a little flawed."

"You think?" She arches an eyebrow. "Try again, Kiera. Why didn't you just ask them outright about your sister? Why did you sabotage what might have been a chance of happiness?"

"I'm not interesting. Fiona and Avery have fancy degrees. I barely graduated from high school."

Dixie gives me her patented 'you-have-got-to-be-kidding-me-how-dumb-are-you' look. "I've never heard something so ridiculous in my life. More than half the people in my graduating class are crushing bores, and some of the most interesting people I know never went to college. My mother didn't. One has nothing to do with the other."

She looks exasperated. “Caleb keeps asking you for obscure cocktails. How do you know how to make them?”

“He has a thing for pre-prohibition cocktails,” I reply. “I bought a recipe book and memorized its contents.”

“Aha.”

“I’m just doing my job.”

She rolls her eyes. “Didn’t you say that Farid is going to Barcelona because he’s an architecture buff? What’s he looking forward to seeing most?”

Where is she going with this? “The Sagrada Familia, Gaudi’s unfinished cathedral.” I’d looked it up when Farid had announced his trip. “He worked on it for forty-three years, and it was only a quarter done when he died.” I take a sip of my water. “He was run over by a tram. Poor guy.”

“Mhm.”

Dix’s smile is smug. I know exactly what she's thinking, and it drives me up the wall. “Stop it,” I tell her. “It's not going to happen, okay? Even if they did like me, I can’t let anything come of it.”

“Why?”

The lawn is blurry. I blink away the tears that obscure my vision. “I failed Bianca. Because of me, she got killed. Or so I thought. And now I find out that she's not dead, and she's the girlfriend of some mobster. I can't even imagine what she's been through in the last eight years. What she’s had to do to survive.” I swallow hard. “I caused that. I could have dug deeper into the truth, but I didn’t. I believed the cops when they told me she was dead. This is all my fault, don’t you understand? I don't deserve to be happy.”

Dixie looks sad. She puts her hand on mine. “I pieced together a few things,” she says, her voice soft. “Your mother died when you were twenty-one. If I’m calculating the timeline correctly, she died right before this happened, didn't she?"

"Five months."

"Your mother died, and you had to take care of your sister."

Dixie's my friend. It's her job to put the best possible interpretation on this situation, but I can't let her. "My mother wasn't much of a parent. I've always had to take care of Bianca."

"Bianca was a minor. Did CPS get involved when your mother died?"

"Yes. I had to prove that I was fit to take care of her, otherwise, they would have put her in foster care. I had to show them I was making enough money, that I was stable enough to provide her a good home... The caseworker they assigned us was very conscientious. She wanted to place Bianca in a two-parent household." I feel the tears well up again. What the hell is wrong with me? I never cry. "Bianca was terrified. So was I. Neither of us knew how to navigate the system."

Dixie's voice is gentle. "You had to deal with all of that. And at the same time, the asshole was grooming Bianca. Kiera, she was targeted. You were just twenty-one. What happened was awful, but it wasn't your fault."

"I don't..."

"It wasn't your fault," she repeats, cutting me off. "Everyone deserves happiness, Kiera, you more than anyone else. It's there within your grasp. I saw the way Nolan looked at you. I saw the expression on his face when he came out. I've never seen him look like that."

"Like what? We just met. None of this makes sense."

"Attraction, connection, it doesn't always make sense," she agrees. "But I'll tell you what I saw. You have the start of something special. What's happening between the three of you, it's like a little seedling. You can decide to crush it to the ground, or you can nurture it."

I'm about to reply when the patio door slides open. Xavier Leforte strides toward us, holding a manila envelope in his hands. He's dressed in navy linen pants, and his white shirt is untucked. I've never seen him look so casual before.

He nods to Dixie. "I owe you an apology. I was rude."

She waves it away. "It happens to the best of us. A bottle of Veuve Clicquot will soothe my feelings."

His lips curve into a smile. "Clicquot? God, no. I'll have Henri fetch up a bottle of Krug Clos du Mesnil from my personal cellar." He turns to me. "I was hoping to run into you, Kiera. You're not working tonight, are you?"

"No."

"Great. Could you do me a favor, please?" He holds out the envelope. "On your way home, could you drop this envelope off with Caleb Reeves? He's expecting it. He'll be at Andrews Park until eight tonight."

"Andrews Park?" Dixie is biting back her smile. "Does Caleb live in that neighborhood?"

"No, I believe he's there because he coaches his niece's soccer team."

My heart hammers in my chest. I stare at the envelope Xavier's holding out to me. See Caleb on my way home? I'm not ready for it.

Except Xavier warned me not to get too involved, and I ignored him and got involved anyway, and if I protest, he'll get to the bottom of what happened at the club, and he'll probably fire me.

"Okay."

18

CALEB

When I get home on Saturday night, I pound back drink after drink. It numbs the pain and deadens my brain cells, but not enough. I fall asleep with Kiera's stricken face swimming in front of my eyes.

Sunday morning, I wake up with the hangover from hell. *Serves me right.* I try to cling onto the sense of betrayal I felt last night, but it doesn't last. Shame fills me instead. What the hell was I thinking yesterday? What the hell was I doing walking into that private room? At the core of every relationship—especially one with BDSM elements—is honesty. And I hadn't been honest with Kiera.

A hundred times that day, I reach for my phone. I need to call her. See her. *Apologize.*

And I freeze every single time. I see Kiera's face after she saw the photo of her sister, and guilt floods my body. What the fuck was I thinking? I should have called her Saturday, right after she propositioned me, and told her everything. Why the fuck did I wait until Derek Haas had something concrete?

Because I didn't want to raise her hopes just to dash them. I'd been trying not to hurt her.

Well, asshole, you did it anyway. I'm pretty sure she's not ecstatic right now. Next time, try honesty from the start.

It's one thing to play games about obscure cocktails. It's another thing entirely to play games with people's emotions, and that's pretty much what I did with Kiera. Sure, I can tell myself that she should have been upfront with me too, but that's a deflection. I'm not in the clear. Not at all.

I fucked up. Not only did I fuck up on Saturday night, but I fucked up a second time by throwing a bombshell in her face, walking out of there and leaving Nolan to pick up the pieces. And now, by not apologizing, but not telling her how sorry I am about what I did, I'm fucking up the third time.

If there's an award for 'Dickwad of the Year,' I'd be the clear front-runner.

Monday morning, the hangover fades, but the guilt intensifies. I spend most of Monday and Tuesday hovering over Derek and Megan, demanding everything they have on Bianca.

On Wednesday, I send Kiera a text asking her to write her sister a note. "Leave it with Henri," I tell her, because I'm too much of a pussy to see Kiera and grovel, the way I should have all week.

A week rolls by, miserable and colorless. I stay away from Club M. I exchange a couple of texts with Nolan, but that's about it. My mother watches me brood and asks me what's going on, and I bite her head off. I'm winning friends and influencing people all over the place.

Thursday afternoon, Hunter Driesse drops by unannounced. "Come on," he says. "This is an intervention. We're going out for lunch."

"Did my mother call you?" Hunter's a psychiatrist who works in the same hospital as my mother did prior to her retirement. He specializes in PTSD, and she's sent several patients his way.

"Yes," he says calmly. "But I'd have looked you up anyway." He waits for me to finish sending the email I was working on. Once we're in his car, he continues. "I was at Club M the Saturday before last, remember? What the fuck happened that night?"

"I screwed up," I mutter. "I don't want to talk about it."

We arrive at our destination, a diner that both Hunter and I frequent regularly. To my surprise, Nolan's already there. "Are you part of this intervention?" I ask him.

He shakes his head. "I think we're both targets."

"You are," Hunter says crisply. We wait until Emma, our regular waitress, pours us coffee and takes our order. Once she's out of earshot, Hunter glares at the two of us. "I find myself in a very odd place," he says. "Dixie Ketcham called the two of you idiots. It's not often that I agree with her about anything, yet here we are. So, what really happened on Saturday with Kiera?"

Nice to know that everyone's discussing my private business.

"We did something stupid," Nolan says, not looking at me.

"Yes, I'm aware," Hunter replies. "Fill me in on the details."

I take a sip of the piping-hot coffee and tell him the whole story. While I'm in the middle of it, our food arrives. When I'm finally done, Hunter glares at me. "Let's try a thought experiment, Caleb. You lost a brother; you should know what losing a sibling feels like. But let's say that instead of getting that call and finding out he died, you got a call that said he was missing. Presumed dead. And Joha's gone too. Both of them vanish without a trace."

Fuck.

"Let's say that for six years, you think they're dead. You mourn. Then, one day, you find a picture of Theo on Nolan's computer." His stare slices through me. "What would you do to find out the truth, Caleb?"

"Anything." I take a deep breath. "I would do anything. Because I would have to know."

"Kiera does exactly what you would do under the situation, and instead of understanding where she's coming from, you get angry? You jump on your high horse and gallop out of the club?"

Ouch. Hunter's right. I'm a complete asshole.

He switches his attention to Nolan. "Remember Inez Cardoso?"

Nolan grimaces. "I slept with her for information," he says to me. "It was a couple of years ago. Her cousin was someone I wanted to find."

Hunter's voice snaps like a whip. "Did you judge yourself as harshly as you judged Kiera?"

Nolan runs a hand over his face. "I screwed up, okay? It was the heat of the moment." He eyes his coffee morosely. "And I've been too ashamed to go back and tell her that."

Hunter doesn't let us off the hook. "Man the fuck up, you two. It's been twelve days. It's appalling that you haven't apologized to her. You're grown men. Act like it."

Damn it. I hate when Hunter's right. I assume he'll be gentler with his clients, but because he's not our therapist, he feels no need to pull his punches.

Then again, this ass-kicking session is exactly what I need.

He drops a twenty on the table and walks out. I drain my

coffee, reach deep, and lay my cards on the table. "I'm afraid that I've broken something that can't be fixed, and I don't want to confront the truth," I admit in a low voice.

"You're not the only one."

"Kiera matters too much." I look at my friend. "Where are you at in this?"

He doesn't answer for a very long time. The silence stretches between us, and then finally, he breaks it. "That Friday night at your house... It felt like I was living someone else's life. I was flirting with a beautiful woman. Nobody was shooting at me. I wasn't rotting in a hospital somewhere, afraid I was going to die alone and un-mourned. And I wanted that life so badly that it shook me." He focuses on his food. "Alexander has settled down with Ellie. He invited me to join them for Christmas in his farmhouse in Provence. You've changed too. Your house is a home. You have a bag of chips on the coffee table, Nala's artwork on the refrigerator door. Family photographs on your bookshelves."

"All the things you don't think you can have." Nolan is doing his level best to sound unconcerned, but I see through it. "But there's no reason it can't be your life. It's all there for the asking."

"Is it?" Nolan meets my gaze squarely. "Here we are at an inflection point. This is your life. This is the woman you've been flirting with for months. Say the word, and I'll walk away."

"It's not just my choice to make," I say levelly.

"Bullshit. Everyone gets to make a choice. This is between you and me, Caleb. This is me trying to do the right thing. You like Kiera; she likes you."

"After Saturday, I very much doubt that that's still true."

He ignores the interruption. "I'm an intruder into your world." He grips his coffee cup so hard that his knuckles whiten. "You tell me you want me to go, and I will leave. But it's a one-time offer. Our friendship matters, but I won't put my heart through a blender, over and over again."

I've never shared a woman with Nolan. Sure, I've participated in casual threesomes, but sharing a woman I care about? I have no illusions; it won't be easy. We'll have to work at making sure there are no misunderstandings or hurt feelings.

But it's possible. Fiona, Brody, and Adrian seem to manage it, as do Kai, Maddox, and Avery.

Nolan is right. This is an inflection point. I lean into it. "Like I said," I say, meeting his gaze squarely. "This can be your life if you reach out and grab it."

We want Kiera, but after Saturday, she might not want anything to do with us. Either way, we need to apologize to her. And then what...?

I don't know what the future is going to hold. The only thing I know is this. I've been frozen all week. That ends today.

My phone beeps. I glance down at it. "I forgot I have to coach Nala's soccer game this afternoon." I'm about to suggest that Nolan meet me at the club tonight when a thought strikes me. "Why don't you join me?"

"To coach after-school soccer?"

I give him a vicious grin. "Welcome to my life, buddy. It's not all fun and games."

19

KIERA

There's a lot of little kids in Andrews Park, running around, screaming their heads off, and having the time of their lives. Normally, scenes like this would make me wistful for the childhood I never had, but today, I'm far too nervous at the idea of seeing Caleb again.

Should have gone home and changed.

I'm still dressed in my uniform. Boring black from head to toe, that's me. I'm not really surprised I haven't seen either Caleb or Nolan in days. No matter how much Dixie might try to convince me otherwise, the real surprise is that they were ever interested in me. The parking lot is filled with BMWs and Land Rovers and Audis, and my beat-up Ford could not be more out of place here.

Then I arrive at the soccer fields and see Nolan and a blonde woman handing out Gatorade to a gaggle of kids. The woman's standing too close to him, her hand on his bicep, smiling up at him, and I want to turn around and disappear.

"Kiera?"

That's Caleb's voice. Too late to run. I take a deep, fortifying breath and paste a polite smile on my face. He's striding toward me, fast and determined, and my traitorous heart starts to beat faster. "Hello, Mr. Reeves." I thrust out the envelope Xavier gave me. "Mr. Leforte asked me to drop this off."

He barely gives it a glance. "How've you been?" he asks, running his hand through his hair. "Listen, can we talk? I want to apologize for Saturday."

Nolan's caught sight of me now, and he's headed over too. Every nerve ending in my body is attuned to them. I feel myself lean toward Caleb before I catch myself and pull back. "There's no need for an apology," I murmur. "I should go."

He puts his hand on my wrist. It's a light touch, and the second he realizes what he did, he draws back. "Please?" he asks quietly. "I'm almost done here. Please have a cup of coffee with me."

We're drawing attention. People are covertly watching us. A couple of women look put-out. *Don't worry,* I want to tell them. *I'm not a threat.*

Nolan joins us. "Kiera," he says, his voice low and deep. A shiver runs through me. "Hello. What brings you here?"

"Mr. Leforte wanted me to deliver something." I turn to Caleb. "Coffee's not a good idea. I crossed a line that I shouldn't have. I don't want to make that mistake again."

"You weren't the one who made a mistake. I was. I had no right to walk out of Club M in a huff."

"Neither of us did," Nolan agrees. "Kiera, there's no way to sugarcoat it. Nothing we did that night was acceptable behavior. We fucked up. Badly. I'm so very sorry."

Do they regret everything about that night? I don't. I had wanted them. *I still want them.* I just wish that it hadn't been under false pretenses. I should have been honest with them. "I shouldn't have..."

My voice trails away as an older woman and a young girl make their way over to us. "Caleb, honey," the woman says. "Nala and I are going to get ice cream. Do you and Nolan want to join us?" She catches sight of me. "I'm sorry, I didn't realize I was interrupting."

"Of course, you did." Caleb gives his mother a look of mingled exasperation and affection. "Nala, you couldn't keep your grandmother away?"

"I tried," Nala says cheerfully. "You know grandma."

"Indeed." His lips tilt up. "Kiera, I'd like you to meet my mother, Dr. Annette Reeves. And this is my niece, Nala. Mom, this is Kiera O'Leary. And no, I can't join you for ice-cream. I'm trying to talk Kiera into coffee."

Annette Reeves shakes my hand, her eyes twinkling. I study her discreetly. She's dressed in white slacks and a striped t-shirt, and there's not a hair out of place. She looks very WASPy, but the smile she gives me is friendly and welcoming. And Nala's biracial, so that'll teach me to make snap judgments about people. "Nice to meet you, Kiera. Any second now, Caleb's going to tell me to go away."

"Damn right," Caleb agrees. "See you later."

"Nice to meet you too," I manage before Nala drags Annette Reeves away.

Caleb watches them go, an amused smile on his face, and then turns back to me. His smile fades. "Sorry about that," he says. "My mother is incurably nosy." He takes a deep breath. "Thank you for dropping this off. Your sister is constantly surrounded by bodyguards. My team hasn't had much luck getting her alone, so we haven't been able to hand her your note, but I promise you, this is my highest priority right now. I'll keep you posted." He runs his hand through his hair again. "I'm deeply sorry about Saturday night."

He's not going to ask me out again. Neither is Nolan. I've turned down the offer of coffee, and they'll respect my decision. I know them well enough to know that.

The ball's firmly in my court.

"I don't regret everything about Saturday night," I whisper.

"You don't?" A spark of hope lights in Nolan's eyes.

"No." Dixie's voice sounds in my ears. *You have the start of something special. What's happening between the three of you, it's like a little seedling. You can decide to crush it to the ground, or you can nurture it.* "Is the offer of coffee still open?"

"Absolutely." Caleb's voice feels like a caress. "Have you eaten dinner? I was going to put burgers on the grill when I got back home."

It's another scorcher of a day. We'll eat in the backyard. Less than two weeks ago, Caleb went down on me in that same backyard while Nolan watched, and I came harder than I've ever come in my life.

Nolan reads my thoughts. His gaze turns heated. "There's the pool too," he murmurs. "And it's a very warm evening."

I wipe my damp palms on my pants. "There is the pool," I agree. "Are you proposing a repeat of Friday night?"

Caleb's eyes rest on mine. "That depends entirely upon you."

I'm attracted to them. They're attracted to me. I really like Caleb and Nolan. Feelings are happening. But trust isn't something that's built instantaneously. Last time, I jumped into the deep end of the pool, and it bit me in the ass. This time, I want to be more careful.

"I'm game for dinner. The rest... Let's give it time."

20

NOLAN

I don't do relationships. I don't do commitments. I don't stick around. I'm in uncharted territory here.

Don't panic, I tell myself as I drive over to Caleb's place. *All you're going to do is have dinner with Kiera and Caleb. It's not a big deal. It's just a meal.*

Telling myself not to freak out doesn't work.

I didn't mean to pour all that stuff out to Caleb earlier. It just... happened. Ever since that ill-fated Saturday night, thoughts of Kiera have infiltrated my brain. Over and over, I relive our time in Club M. The way her eyes had widened when I'd run the flogger over her arm. The way her skin had broken out into goosebumps. The way she'd leaned forward, her lips parted, curiosity and anticipation written large on her face.

The hitch in her voice. Her pretty and pink and cream underwear, the lingerie of a good girl who so desperately wanted to explore her wilder side. My mind puts these images on auto-replay, and I can't think of anything else but Kiera.

My focus should be on Luis Martinez. I've spent more

than three years of my life hunting for the elusive arms dealer, and I've never been closer to finding him. Bianca Thompson is our best and most promising lead.

I shouldn't be driving toward Caleb's house. I should drive to New York and join Caleb's covert surveillance crew. I still don't have a photo of Martinez. Caleb's team is being extremely cautious, and we still haven't made contact with Bianca. I should be chomping at the bit. Instead, I'm letting Caleb's analysts take point on this job.

And me? I handled the refreshment station at Nala's soccer practice. Yeah. I, Nolan Wolanski, was in charge of the Gatorade today. And I'd enjoyed it. Not the overt flirting of some of the mothers—that had been a little awkward—but I'd liked seeing the kids running around and having fun.

Maybe I'm catching something. Maybe I'm coming down with the flu. That would explain this inexplicable sappiness.

I pull into Caleb's driveway. Kiera's not here yet; her car isn't in sight. I grab the bottle of champagne in the passenger seat and head straight to Caleb's backyard.

Caleb's putting burgers on the grill. He sees the champagne and his lips tilt up. "You shouldn't have," he quips. "Oh wait. You didn't do it for me."

"Yeah, yeah, whatever. You have an ice bucket somewhere?"

"In the kitchen."

I head inside and put the champagne to chill. Grabbing a beer from Caleb's refrigerator, I head outside. It was humid as hell earlier, but it's cooled down. A welcome breeze runs through the yard. "Looks like it might rain."

Kiera arrives in time to save us from a full-fledged discussion about the weather. She's changed. She's wearing a sky-blue sundress that stops two inches above her knees and shows off her glorious legs. The fabric is thin cotton, printed with large red poppies. When she nears us, her scent wafts over me. She smells like roses and jasmine, and I want to close my eyes and breathe her in.

If this is the flu, I have it bad.

Caleb gives her a smile of welcome. "Hey, Kiera. Can I get you something to drink? Nolan brought champagne."

Her eyebrow rises. "What's the occasion?"

"I told Xavier something he wanted to hear, and he was in a generous mood."

"That's very mysterious."

I get up to pour her a glass of champagne, and then elaborate. "Have you met Rafael Garcia?"

"Xavier's friend, the hot Spanish guy? Yeah, he was in the club a few months ago."

A flash of jealousy runs through me at her description of Rafe. I push it back. "Back in college, Rafe and Xavier were in love with Layla Shleifer. Lina, the woman who died in the breath-play scene gone wrong was Layla's twin. Lina's death tore them apart, but I don't think any of them really moved on."

Caleb lifts his head from the grill, where he's tending to his burgers. "You haven't heard the gossip? The three of them scened together one evening at the club. Not too long ago."

"Really?" My beer freezes halfway to my mouth. "Are they back together?"

"I asked Xavier. He nearly bit my head off, and then he told me it was a one-time thing."

I snort. "One-time thing. As if." I turn back to Kiera. "Sorry. Old college gossip. The long and the short of it is that Layla throws herself recklessly into danger, and Xavier and Rafe secretly try and arrange security teams to watch her. I was in Bangkok not too long ago, and I had lunch with

Layla. I might have yelled at her about how reckless she was being. Anyway, she's come around to the idea of bodyguards, and Xavier expressed his gratitude with a case of champagne."

Lightning flashes, followed almost instantly by a roll of thunder. Caleb hastily slides the cooked burgers on a platter. "Looks like it's about to rain. Let's eat inside."

We move indoors and settle around Caleb's kitchen island. "Soledad made potato salad and coleslaw," he announces, taking them out of the refrigerator. "There are brownies for dessert, and also ice-cream, unless Naya's been over this week when I'm at work, in which case I promise nothing."

We start eating. Our conversation stays light. Intentionally or not, we stay away from land mines. We don't discuss Bianca, Greg Dratch, or Luis Fernando Martinez. We don't talk about Saturday night either. We talk about books and TV shows, and we discover a shared love of science fiction and fantasy. "Is that why you have a dragon tattooed on your hip?"

Her cheeks turn pink. "I used to have an imaginary dragon best friend when I was a little kid."

"That's adorable." The story about her imaginary friend, but also the way she's blushing as she tells us about it. "I never had a dragon, but I had a favorite blanket. Until I was thirteen, I never went anywhere without it."

"You did?"

"I was sent away to boarding school when I was seven. I didn't want to go; I was scared. The blanket was a coping strategy."

Her expression turns sympathetic. "What color was it?"

"Red. It's faded and tattered, but it's in my apartment."

"Where do you live?"

Caleb snorts a laugh. "Nolan lives in hotel rooms," he says. "But he owns a very expensive condo in Manhattan. Upper East Side, Central Park adjacent. How many days did you spend in your bed last year, do you think, buddy?"

"I don't know. Less than twenty." I shrug. "My accountants tell me it's a good investment." The words leave my mouth before I realize how tone-deaf I sound. Ouch. *Don't be a dick, Nolan.*

Kiera fixes me with a searching look. "Why do you travel so much?" she asks. "It's not for fun, is it? Dixie said you used to collaborate with Adrian and Brody. Why did you have a picture of Greg Dratch on your laptop?"

I don't talk about what I do. I don't let people in. I don't involve anyone in my life, because knowing too much might put them at risk. And yet, when Kiera looks at me with her amber eyes, my resolve turns to dust. I take a deep breath and prepare to tell her everything.

21

KIERA

Sometime during dinner, a storm has moved in. The skies have opened up, and it's pouring outside.

The weather is a perfect metaphor for my emotions.

I'm being nosy; I know I am. Nolan has no obligation to answer my questions.

They've already done far more for me than is fair to expect. They've told me Bianca is alive. They've tracked down her location, and they're going to deliver my sister a message from me.

I'm friends with Fiona; I know how expensive it is to hire private detectives. They've done thousands of dollars of work without expecting anything in return. I should be expressing my gratitude, not interrogating them.

"No," Nolan agrees in response to my question. "It's not for fun." He stares at the bottle of beer in his hand.

Belatedly, my conscience decides to awaken. "You don't have to answer my questions."

He gives me a faint smile. "It really started in college," he says. "It was a heady time. I'd been in boarding school for years, and I was used to being on my own, but college was different. My parents gave me an allowance, and they expected me to attend classes, but that was it. I was unsupervised for the first time in my life, and I loved it."

"I met Caleb in college," he continues. "Xavier too. Eric and Hunter, who you met the other day. Kai, Maddox, Brody, Adrian—we all hung out. We discovered we liked control. That's what brought us together."

"You formed a college sex club?"

He chuckles. "Nothing quite so tabloid-worthy." His fingers worry at the beer label. "I liked the rush that I got when a woman trusted me enough to place herself in my hands. It was heady, powerful, and exhilarating."

Caleb nods. "Not just Nolan, and not just BDSM. College was the first time it occurred to me that a relationship didn't have to be between two people. Xavier and Rafael were both dating Layla, and it was a real relationship; it wasn't just about kinky sex."

Nolan chuckles. "There was a lot of kinky sex though." He sweeps the shreds of paper into a neat pile and drains the rest of the bottle. "Long story short, college was a time of discovery. I was young and rich. Women were plentiful, even women that would let me tie them up." He takes a deep breath. "And then there was Lina."

"The girl who died," I whisper.

"Yeah." His expression stays dark. "Lina was smart and funny, empathetic and kind. Xavier and Rafe always thought they had the better sister, but I wasn't sure about that." He gets up to get himself another beer. "I was a little in love with her. Not that it mattered. She was dating Stephan, and I never would've made a move."

Oh wow. Poor Nolan.

"Lina was adventurous," he continues. "Most of us were content with a little impact play, a little bondage. But Stephan and Lina seemed to be determined to try everything. Electricity, fire, knives. Stephan would talk about it from time to time, but I tried to stay away from them as much as possible."

Because he was in love with her. My heart clenches in sympathy.

"If I had listened to Stephan, I would have realized that they were hurtling out of control." He doesn't look at me. "You already know what happens next. Because I wasn't paying enough attention, two people I cared about deeply died."

Fiona's told me part of this story. They had all made a promise at Lina's grave, that they would do everything in their power to see that it didn't happen again.

At the time Fiona told me about Lina's death, I'd been more worried about whether Nolan was part of the Russian Mafia, sent by Sirkovich to kill me for snitching on the mob. I'd been desperate to find out why Nolan had Greg Dratch's photo on his laptop.

I hadn't been listening. I hadn't realized how deeply Nolan had felt the woman's death. And above all, I hadn't realized how much trust Nolan and Caleb were placing in me when they told me about Lina.

Neither of them has any obligation to answer my questions, but they're answering them anyway. They're letting me into a deep, intimate part of their lives.

I'd been too stupid, too caught up in my own shit to see it before.

"We made a pact that day, a promise to Lina that she

didn't die in vain. That's why Xavier runs a sex club, even though he is a billionaire, many times over. It's his way of making sure people play safely. Adrian and Brody founded a private security company. Kai is a doctor. Maddox financially supports hundreds of women's shelters all over the world." He finally looks up at me. "I became... I guess you could call it private security. The world is a dark place, and there is a handful of us that patrol the shadows and do what we can to make things better."

"What does that mean?" I ask, staring into Nolan's brown eyes.

"It varies. Sometimes, it involves putting my money to good use. Sometimes I play a more active role."

"He gets shot at," Caleb elaborates bluntly. "He goes undercover, and he infiltrates cartels and mobs, and he puts himself in the line of fire."

Nolan gives Caleb a sidelong look. "We both did. But that brings us back to Dratch." He leans forward. "Dratch used to work for a man called Luis Fernando Martinez."

That name prickles at me until I remember where I heard it. "That's Bianca's boyfriend."

"Yes," he says soberly. "I didn't know that at the start. Martinez is hard to track down. He doesn't meet anyone in person. Only a small handful of people have seen his face, and Greg Dratch is one of them. I thought that if we found Dratch, we'd find Martinez. That's what Caleb was helping me with." He exhales. "Until you reacted to that photo the way you did, we didn't know anything about your sister."

I realize something. "You said Bianca was with Martinez. You don't need Greg anymore to get to him, do you? You could use my sister."

Nolan shakes his head at once. "I would be lying if I told

you that the thought hadn't crossed my mind. But as much as I want Martinez, I won't put your sister in danger. There's a chance that she's up to in her eyeballs in his stuff, but there's an even better chance that she's caught up in something and can't get out."

His eyes rest on mine. "There's another reason."

My palms are damp with sweat. I wipe them on my thighs. "Which is?" I whisper.

Nolan makes an impatient noise in his throat. "Isn't it obvious? She's your sister, Kiera. How can I put her in harm's way?"

I stare at them, my emotions a jumbled mess. Nolan's simple answer has taken my breath away. He's offering me something I've never had in my life.

Unflinching, unwavering support.

They both are.

I don't know if I deserve it. I don't know what to do with it. But I believe them. They're on my side, and the sheer relief of it takes my breath away.

It's all out in the open now. All our cards are finally on the table. There are so many words on the tip of my tongue, but none of them form into sentences.

Except one.

One thought is dominant. "Dixie said something to me earlier today. She made me realize I'd never forgiven myself for what happened to Bianca."

I address Nolan. In some ways, we're kindred spirits. We don't feel entitled to happiness because we let down the people we loved.

"You were how old, twenty-one, twenty-two? Nolan, you didn't kill Lina; you can't hold yourself responsible for what happened for the rest of your life." I pour myself a glass of wine, more from a desire to do something with my hands than from any real need for alcohol. "Dixie told me it wasn't my fault, and she's right. I'm going to pass on her advice to you. What happened to Lina and to Stephan was awful. But it wasn't your fault. You should forgive yourself."

"I agree with Kiera," Caleb says quietly. "You've been throwing yourself into riskier and riskier situations because of guilt. Let it go. I've already lost too many people I care about. Lina. Stephan. Theo. Joha. I don't want to add your name to that list."

There's a long moment of silence. Finally, Nolan breaks it. "So, there we go," he says lightly. "You know how fucked up I am, yet you're not running away, screaming."

He thought I'd recoil because he was damaged? Has he not been paying attention? I'm the queen of fucked-up. "I'm not planning on it."

Caleb clears his throat. "Nolan and I were planning on going to New York tomorrow. Would you like to join us?"

I look up. "To see Bianca? I thought it wasn't safe to approach her."

He shakes his head. "No, not to see Bianca. I just got word from my team. Your sister is flying out to Cancun tonight."

I blink in confusion. "Then why New York?"

Caleb looks at me, intense and focused. In this light, his eyes are more green than gray, and the weight of his attention holds me captive. "I thought we could go out for dinner," he says. His lips curve into a smile. "Catch a show maybe. Go to a club, if that's your thing."

My heart beats faster. "Are you asking me out on a date?"

"Yes."

There are thousand warning voices in my head, but I've

listened to them all my life, and I don't think they've made my life better. Always second-guessing somebody's motive. Always wondering if somebody's going to hurt me. Never allowing myself to trust. I'm tired of living that way.

I take a deep breath and step off the ledge, trusting that I won't fall and shatter into a million pieces. "I'd love to."

22

KIERA

There's a knock on my door Friday morning. It's a man carrying a garment bag. "Delivery for Kiera O'Leary," he says.

"That's me." I sign for the package, and, as soon as I shut my front door, I unzip the bag, excitement coursing through my body.

Everything about today is unbelievable. I keep pinching myself. I'm going on a date with Caleb and Nolan tonight. It feels like I've entered bizarro world, where up is down and down is up, and two handsome, successful men are interested in me.

And they've sent me a dress.

It's a whisper of fabric, the softest sliver of a garment, in a shade of purple so deep that it could be black. I try it on, and it fits perfectly. The fabric skims my curves in a way that makes me look subtly sexy. The neckline is a simple vee, and the skirt falls to my ankles in delicate, dreamlike tiers.

It's so pretty. I feel like a princess. All I need is a tiara.

There's no tiara, but the dress comes with a pair of strappy silver sandals. They fit, of course. I shake my head—

when did Caleb and Nolan learn my shoe size?—and put them on.

When I was growing up, we shopped at the Salvation Army. I've never owned such a beautiful dress. I've never bought myself something this nice.

Club M pays decently. Xavier Leforte does not stint on benefits, and the members tip well. But I've still never indulged myself. Every spare cent I earn I set aside in case I need to run at a moment's notice.

Last night, Nolan and Caleb told me that I had nothing to be afraid of anymore. Sirkovich wasn't getting out of jail anytime soon, and he wasn't in a position to send people after me.

I've spent so many years in hiding. It still hasn't sunk in that I don't have to look over my shoulder for a threat. I can finally relax. I can do things that I didn't think were possible.

I spend an embarrassing amount of time staring at my reflection in the mirror. *I am safe.* My sister is alive. I'm going out on a date with Nolan and Caleb.

If this is a dream, I don't want to wake up.

AT THREE-THIRTY, there's a knock on my door.

My pulse starts to race. I grab my bag. A Christmas gift from Fiona last year, it's silver in color and beaded, and just large enough to fit ID, a credit card, and a tube of lipstick. I take one final look in the mirror—this would be an awful time to find spinach stuck in my teeth—and open the front door.

Caleb and Nolan are standing there, both wearing charcoal gray suits. Their eyes go hot when they take me in. "You look amazing," Caleb says.

I drink them in. It's rare to see Nolan in a suit. "You look pretty good yourselves. Thank you for the dress." I smile up at them. "Should I be scared that you guessed my size so accurately?"

Nolan grins. "I'd love to pretend to be some kind of dress whisperer," he says. "But we called Dixie for help."

Oh, I am never going to hear the end of this. "You did?"

"Is that okay?" Caleb runs his hand through his hair. "I wanted to make sure we got you something that you'd like, not just something we wanted to see you in."

That's really thoughtful. "I'm surprised Dix agreed to help you."

"We had to do some groveling," Nolan admits. "And she promised to cut off our balls if we screwed with you again."

My mouth falls open. "Dix didn't say that."

Caleb laughs. "Not in those words," he says. "We read between the lines." He hands me his arm. "Shall we?"

We head to a waiting limo. Whoa. Pretty dress. Sexy shoes. Luxury car. Broadway tickets. Looks like Cinderella's going to the ball tonight.

Caleb shuts the partition between the driver and the back as soon as we get underway. "Drink?" he asks me, quirking an eyebrow. "Champagne?"

Why not? It's a long drive to New York. "Yes, please."

The limo is well-stocked. Apart from the champagne, the cooler holds bottles of water, beer, as well as a tray of fruit. Fancy. Nolan pours me a glass of champagne. The three of us chat as the car eats up the miles. For a while, we continue the animated conversation we had last night about our favorite books, movies, and television shows. I discover that Nolan loves watching cooking programs. "It's weird, I know," he says, shrugging disarmingly. "But I find it relaxing."

I picture him on a couch, drinking beer and watching

Gordon Ramsey throw a tantrum, and I giggle. "What about you?" I ask Caleb. "What's your guilty pleasure?"

"I have an inexplicable love for cheesy eighties movies," he admits. "My dad had quite the collection. Other kids would read their fathers' Playboys. Not me."

"What's your favorite movie?"

He winces. "I watched 'My Stepmother is an Alien' eight times."

I burst out laughing. "You're joking."

He shakes his head, a smile playing about his lips. "Sadly, no." His fingers brush against mine. "Do you want a refill?"

It's a light touch, but it's left me breathless. Their thighs bracket mine. My skin feels tingly. My breasts ache. My insides coil and twist with need.

I'm a lightweight, but this isn't the effects of one glass of champagne. This is me responding to them. This is desire, pure and simple. This is the culmination of days and weeks of wanting them.

"I probably shouldn't," I whisper.

Nolan puts his hand on my thigh. "You don't want champagne," he says. "Do you want something else?"

You.

Caleb takes my hand in his. His fingers trace soft circles on my palm. My skin breaks out into goosebumps. We're in the back seat of a limo, and we're just seconds away from making out. One word from me. One whispered 'yes.' That's all it'll take.

Anticipation claws through me, heady and intoxicating.

"Open your mouth, Kiera."

Nolan removes a chocolate-covered strawberry from the cooler and dangles it at my lips. He teases the seam of my mouth with the sweet fruit and coats my lower lip with chocolate. I gasp, and he dips his head toward me. "Here's something you don't know about me," he murmurs. "I find chocolate irresistible."

Then he sucks my lip into his mouth.

I feel his kiss everywhere. My toes curl, my core tightens, and my body ignites with desire. There is an ache between my legs that won't be kept at bay, not any longer.

With a muffled growl, Nolan pulls me onto his lap. I feel his thick erection straining to break free, and I grind against it, too needy to be embarrassed by how wanton I'm acting.

One glass of champagne and I've gone from zero to sixty in the space of five seconds.

"That's it," Caleb encourages, his voice low, deep, and dark. He exchanges a glance with Nolan, who shifts me so I'm sideways on his lap. "You want this, don't you, Kiera? Tell us. *Show us.*"

His big hand glides up my bare calves. Slowly, deliberately, he inches higher. I shift against Nolan and part my legs to give him easier access. His low chuckle causes heat to flush through my cheeks.

Nolan offers me the strawberry. I hold his gaze in mine and bite into the juicy fruit. He growls, deep in his throat. Wrapping his fingers in my hair, he pulls me closer. "Are you wet, Kiera?" he demands, velvet-steel in his voice. "If Caleb spreads your legs and pushes his face in your sweet little pussy, is he going to find you soaked?"

Oh God. My face blazes. I thought that the first night in the pool was hot, when Caleb had eaten me out while Nolan jerked himself off. I thought that my brief flirtation with BDSM was wicked and tempting. Nolan trailing the tails of a suede flogger over my body... Caleb promising to tie me up and spank me...

But as deeply, intensely, sexy as all of that was, it's

nothing compared to now. I had no idea how much of themselves they'd been holding back until I see the raw heat blaze from their eyes.

"He asked you a question, Kiera." Caleb's hand stops at my knee. The dress is bunched around my thighs. "Don't you think you should answer?"

I shake my head, a wicked thrill shooting through me. A grin curves over Caleb's lips. "That's how we're playing it, are we? Someone really wants to get punished."

He spanks the inside of my thighs, and I gasp at the sharp contact. "Keep your voice down, sweetness," he warns. "Unless you want the driver to hear you moan."

I shiver again, every nerve in my body ablaze.

Nolan licks the seam of my lips. "So fucking sweet," he rasps. His grip on my hair tightens. His mouth meets mine, demanding entrance, demanding surrender, demanding *everything I have to give and more.*

I cling to Nolan, wrapping my arms around his neck, kissing him back, even as Caleb's hands inch higher. Inch closer and closer to my wet heat.

"Soaked." Masculine satisfaction drenches Caleb's voice. He skims his fingers over my damp panties, and I whimper into Nolan's mouth. "Absolutely fucking soaked."

His thumb presses my throbbing clit through the silky fabric, and I almost arch off Nolan's lap. Nolan's grip on me tightens, and Caleb chuckles darkly. "Do you want to come, Kiera?" he growls.

So much that I'm ready to beg for it. Caleb and Nolan are like a drug, and I'm addicted, and I don't care. I want more.

"Please," I moan, grinding my ass against Nolan's thick, fat cock. "Please make me come."

"Such a pretty little plea," Caleb murmurs, his fingers

once again grazing the gusset of my panties. "I'm almost tempted to give you exactly what you need. But..."

Damn. "But what?"

His smile widens. "There is the matter of your punishment. Pick a number between one and five, Kiera."

A brief pulse of disappointment flickers through me. Just five? I don't know how hard Caleb will spank me, but I'm pretty sure I want more than five strokes on my bottom.

Nolan pulls his mouth off mine. His hands cup my breasts. He squeezes them, hard, and I groan and arch into him, wordlessly asking for more. "Five," I gasp, realizing I haven't answered Caleb's question.

He laughs, low and soft. "You want to edge five times? That's a much higher number than I thought you'd pick."

Wait, what? I bolt up. "I thought you meant to spank me." Belatedly, I realize he'd never specified why he wanted me to pick a number.

Argh. I've totally screwed myself.

Caleb grins wickedly. "Here are the rules, Kiera. You warn me when you get close, and I'll back off until you're ready." His eyes narrow. "You don't have permission to come. Is that clear?"

Nolan pinches my nipple through my dress, and I yelp, more from surprise than pain. Shivers wrack my body. I meet Caleb's hard, dominant, gaze. "Yes, Sir."

"Very nice." He pushes the edge of my panties aside, and his fingers shove into me, hard and fast and deep.

Nolan's mouth swallows my gasp. He unzips my top and undoes my bra, and he groans at the sight of my bared breasts. "So fucking gorgeous."

His powerful hands squeeze my breasts, and he rolls my throbbing, aching nipples between his thumbs and forefingers. Caleb thrusts his fingers in and out of my pussy, his thumb pressing unerringly on my clit, and I squirm, intense need surging through me.

"That's right," Nolan whispers, his hot breath tickling my ear. "I want to hear you moan against my lips, Kiera. I want to feel you writhe on my lap. You want to come so badly, don't you? Draped over our laps, your dress bunched up at the waist, uncaring whether the driver can see you or not."

A flush stains my cheeks. I glance up at the partition and realize Nolan's just teasing me. The glass is tinted. Even if the driver were paying attention to us instead of to the road, he wouldn't be able to see anything.

Caleb spanks my thigh. "Should you be paying attention to the driver?"

"No, Sir."

"Very good. What should you be paying attention to, Kiera?"

"To you, Sir."

"That's right," he growls. He adds another finger to my pussy, and I feel my muscles stretch around him, and I can't get enough. My need grows, flares into an inferno. "I'm going to come," I gasp. "Please..."

He stops immediately. I want to weep. "Good girl," he murmurs. "Take a deep breath. You're doing really well, sweetness." His voice is soothing. Gentle. He traces small circles over my skin with his fingertips.

Nolan's touch gentles too, and his lips meet mine in a soft kiss. "Exhale," he says. "Breathe. Relax. You've got this, Kiera. You can do this." He kisses my cheek, the side of my jaw, the nape of my neck, and then sucks my earlobe between my teeth. "You know your safe word," he murmurs. "Use it if you need."

I take a deep, shuddering breath as the intensity recedes.

One down, four to go. I wrap my arms around Nolan, shamelessly clinging to his big, broad chest. "Okay," I tell Caleb. "I'm good to go again, you sadist."

He chuckles. "You think this is sadistic?" He shakes his head. "Ah, Kiera. You have so much to learn about me." He swipes his finger through my aching slit. "Let's do this."

Over and over, Caleb brings me to the edge. Over and over, Nolan teases my nipples, squeezes my breasts, kisses me senseless. By the time I've backed away from the edge of my orgasm five times, I'm a sobbing, sweat-soaked, quivering mess.

"Good girl." Caleb kisses my naked thighs. "Do you want to come?"

"Yes."

His fingers stroke me, sure and steady. This time, when the intensity builds, I don't hold back. I surrender to the ratcheting pressure. I explode for them, shaking, writhing, moaning as I come apart.

When I finally collect my thoughts, I sit up, refasten my bra, and adjust my dress. "Wow," I say softly. I glance at Caleb and Nolan, and they're both sporting massive erections. "I should take care of that."

Nolan winks at me. "No time. We're almost at the Lincoln Tunnel." His eyes rest on me. "After the show, we can either head back home, or we can spend the night in Manhattan."

I swapped shifts with Kellie; I don't have to be back home until Wednesday. "Would spending the night in Manhattan involve sex?"

"You better believe it."

"Then yes," I say promptly. "Let's do that."

23

CALEB

If I had any doubt that Kiera wants us as much as we want her, they vanish during the show. As soon as the lights dim, the little minx puts her hand on my thigh, and she inches up toward my cock. She strokes me through my trousers, and it takes all the restraint I possess to keep from exploding.

Blue balls. I have them.

From the sound of Nolan's choked off breath, she strokes him too. I wait for jealousy to wash over me at the idea of her touching him the way she's touching me.

It doesn't come.

I've been in a ménage before, but I've never shared someone I was serious about.

Thursday afternoon, I'd told Nolan I was fine with it, but I'd bent the truth. When it came down to it, I hadn't known how I'd react.

Intellectually, I don't have a problem with it. I recognize that the connections between Fiona, Brody, and Adrian are just as deep as those between a more traditional couple. Hell, they're probably deeper. Adrian,

Brody, and Fiona face judgment every day from ignorant people who feel entitled to comment on their lifestyle. It's not an easy choice to make, but their bond is rock-solid, and as far as I know, they've never once regretted their decision.

Same thing with Avery, Kai, and Maddox. When Avery had first joined Club M, Xavier had asked me to show her around the club, but one look at the expressions on Kai and Maddox's faces, and I'd known. I don't believe in destiny, but as ridiculous as it sounds, those three were destined to be together.

And of course, if there's ever a trio that's drawn together like magnets inexorably tugging toward each other, it's Xavier, Rafael, and Layla. No matter what happens, no matter how many obstacles life throws in their way, those three will always be there for each other. Will they figure out how to heal their fractured relationship? I'm not sure. But I know that even if they can't make things work, they'll walk through fire for each other.

In the limo, when Nolan pinched Kiera's nipple, I'd braced myself for a hot rush of jealousy. If it had come, I would have dealt with it.

Shockingly, watching her writhe with pleasure had just ramped up my arousal. Listening to the sounds of her moans, my cock had hardened. Nolan rolled her pert, pretty nipples between his fingers, and her pussy had clamped hard around my fingers. She'd gushed, hot and wet, and it was fucking amazing.

When the show is done, we get back into the waiting limo. "You're a bad girl," I whisper into Kiera's ear.

Her look is pure innocence. "So, it's okay for you to take me to the edge, over and over again..."

"Five times," Nolan interjects. "He took you to the edge

five times." His smile widens. "I seem to remember you enjoying it."

She flushes. "It's okay for you to take me to the edge over and over again," she repeats, "but when I stroke your cocks, ever so lightly, I'm a bad girl."

"Exactly." I wink at her. "I see you already understand how this works." I put my hand on her lap, and inch it upward, tormenting her the way she'd tormented me. "What do you want to do now? We can either get a drink, or we can head to Nolan's condo."

"Can we grab a drink first?" she asks, her voice uncertain. "I might need some liquid courage."

I exchange a look with Nolan. "Of course." I get on the intercom and ask Andrei to take us to the Jump Club. The jazz bar isn't the most exciting place in the city, but it has one thing in its favor. It's in the same building as Nolan's condo. "You always have the right to change your mind. If you don't want to sleep with us..."

Sex has always been a pleasurable game. I'm in my thirties. Over the course of my life, I've invited many women to share my bed. I can't remember the last time I was nervous about their answer.

"I definitely want to sleep with you," she says instantly.

"You want to sleep with us, but you need a drink first," Nolan says, his expression confused. "You look nervous. I'm missing something."

Her face goes red, and she doesn't look at either of us. "It's been a while. And I've never done anything particularly adventurous. I've never had anal sex. I've never been tied up. I'm not an experienced submissive, and that's what you're used to." She takes a deep breath. "Now that this is actually happening, I'm afraid I'm going to be boring."

Relief floods through me. That's what she's concerned about? "I don't think that's going to be a problem."

Her face sets in stubborn lines. "You don't know that."

The limo pulls up at the club before I can answer. Andrei opens the door. I get out and help Kiera out. "We're done for the night, Andrei," I tell my driver. "We'll probably head back tomorrow afternoon. I'll text you."

"Of course, Mr. Reeves."

He pulls away, and the three of us head inside. A singer is belting out a cover of Nina Simone's Sinnerman, and she's quite good. Most of the crowd is in the front, listening to her sing. Nolan has a low-voiced conversation with the hostess, and she finds us a secluded table on the back patio.

It's late. Strings of lights illuminate the space. Candles flicker on the tables, reminding me of the candles I'd lit in the private room in Club M. That night had ended disastrously. I really don't want to make the same mistake again.

A waitress takes our drink order. Once we're alone, I pick up the abandoned thread of conversation. "Can I tell you why I don't think it's going to be a problem?"

She nods.

"The difference between bad sex and good sex is chemistry," I murmur, keeping my voice low. I brush my fingers on Kiera's forearm and watch goosebumps rise on her skin. "There's no shortage of chemistry here."

She inclines her head, conceding my point.

"The difference between good sex and great sex is passion." I wrap my fingers in her hair and pull her in, close, so close. Her light, floral scent washes over me, drugging me. Her amber eyes are liquid pools of desire. "I saw the way your pretty pink tongue licked the chocolate off the strawberry Nolan fed you," I whisper. "I heard your breathy little moans. Felt your muscles tighten around my fingers. Somehow, I don't think passion is a problem either."

Her nipples are rock hard under her dress. I can see the clear outline of those tightly beaded buds. I want her so badly that it is a physical pain, but more than that, I want her to walk into this with no reservations. I won't be holding anything back; I don't want her to be either.

"What about my lack of experience?" Her eyes are wide and luminous. "You scene with experienced submissives. I don't fit the bill."

"Dominance and submission have a way of messing with people's emotions. I scene with experienced submissives not because they've been tied up before, but because they already know how to manage those complex feelings that churn up to the surface in an intense scene." My lips twist. "Not to mention that I haven't scened with someone for over a year." It's been even longer than that. Six months after Kiera started working at the club, I'd scened with Maeve, a casual play partner, but my mind hadn't been on the scene or on the woman tied up in front of me. My thoughts had kept returning to the pink-haired bartender.

I'd ended the session early, and that had been it.

I've had a thing for Kiera for a very long time. I've tried to fight it. I've tried to stay away from the club and from her. She thinks there's a scenario in which I find her boring? It doesn't exist.

The waiter brings us our drinks. Once he's gone, I take a sip of my beer. "Of course, sexual compatibility matters. I'd be lying if I said it didn't. If you only wanted to have missionary-style sex in the bedroom with the lights turned off, chances are, this wouldn't go very far. If you thought oral sex was disgusting, or if you called me a pervert because I broached the topic of bondage, that would absolutely be a problem."

She laughs softly. "God, no. I love oral sex, giving *and* receiving."

I picture her on her knees, her pretty pink lips wrapped around my cock, and I almost explode right there. Kiera's going to be the death of me. "Do you?" I murmur, holding her gaze in mine. "Finish your drink. We're going upstairs, and then, you can show me exactly how much you love giving oral."

24

KIERA

I should be nervous. There's two of them, after all. Two powerful, *dominant* men, used to getting their own way.

Two hard bodies, pressed into me.

Two callused sets of hands, running over every inch of my body.

Two thick, fat cocks, splitting me open.

My throat is dry. My skin is covered with goosebumps as we ride the elevator all the way to the penthouse. But strangely, I'm not nervous.

Maybe it's because this moment has been so long coming.

I've wanted both Caleb and Nolan from the first moment I saw them.

I resisted Caleb for months. I lied to myself, pretending the reason I couldn't get involved with him was because he was a member of Club M.

Then Nolan came along.

I might have been able to say no to one of them.

But together?

Together, they're irresistible.

The first night I swam in Caleb's pool, he'd made me come while Nolan had watched. I would have slept with them then, but Caleb had been called away.

Then I saw Dratch's photo. I invited them to scene with me. I wanted them to tie me up. Spank me. Possess me. Control me.

Had Caleb not put an end to it, I would have slept with them then.

Had they said the word, I would have stayed over last night.

This isn't because they're helping me find Bianca. This isn't because of how irresistibly gorgeous they are—and they're really, *really,* good-looking. This isn't because of the sense of competence and power they exude, though that's sexy as hell too. This isn't even because of the need that burns through me like an inferno, leaving me shaken, panting, desperate for them.

This is... *more.*

I've never believed in love at first sight. I still don't believe in it. But there's no denying that there's something here. Something deeper than raw, carnal desire.

A connection.

Nolan opens the door and punches a code into the alarm system. "I'll give you the tour in the morning," he says, his voice rough with need. "Right now..."

I'm with Nolan; screw the tour.

Right now, I want them too much.

I gasp as Caleb's mouth crashes onto mine, his hand tangling in my hair. I melt into him, desperate for more. At the same time, Nolan presses into me from behind, his large hands on my waist. He buries his face in my neck and nips at my throat.

"Bedroom," Nolan orders, his voice hungry. "Now."

Heat radiates all through my body. I whimper into Caleb's mouth. I'm sandwiched between the two men. I'm about to sleep with both of them. Caleb *and* Nolan.

He pushes me backward, down a corridor, and then I'm in Nolan's bedroom.

There's a package on the bed, an unmarked box the size of a brick. Nolan puts it on the nightstand with a smirk.

That smirk is trouble. "Should I be curious about what's in the box?" I ask.

He chuckles darkly. "You'll find out soon enough."

I don't have time to solve the mystery. Caleb shrugs off his suit jacket and tosses it on a brown leather chair. He loosens his tie, takes it off. His eyes gleam with anticipation. "You look fantastic, Kiera," he says, a growl in his voice. "Take off your clothes."

Our gazes collide. I stare into his gorgeous green-gray eyes. My fingers tremble. I reach behind my neck and start to unzip the dress.

Nolan moves behind me again. His hands encircle my hips, and he pulls me closer to him. I feel heat radiate from his body.

Need zaps through me, an electric current shocking every nerve ending in my body.

Nolan's fingers brush my skin. He bends his head and kisses my neck again, and then he takes over the task of pulling down the zipper.

Slowly.

Oh-so-slowly.

Time stops. I forget to breathe.

Nolan's breath tickles my back. I shiver. Goosebumps rise on my skin. My nipples are tight, swollen, and aching. My panties are soaked.

The dress falls to the floor in a soft whisper of fabric.

Caleb inhales sharply.

"You take my breath away," he murmurs. His eyes lock on me, drinking me in, *feasting* on me. "Every single time."

He closes the distance between us. He picks me up and tosses me on the bed. I land on Nolan's soft mattress, naked except for my bra and panties.

A full-body shudder runs through me. I've spent weeks fantasizing about this moment. I've spent night after night dreaming about Caleb and Nolan, touching myself, imagining that it's their hands on me. Spreading my legs. Sucking my nipples between their teeth. Plunging their cocks into my wet, willing heat.

Now, it's actually happening.

Oh. My. God.

Nolan climbs on the bed. "I've watched Caleb taste that sweet pussy," he growls. His big hands rest on my knees. "I've been very patient."

"You have," I agree. My voice comes out breathy and needy.

His teeth flash in a grin. He pushes my thighs apart. "I'm going to claim my reward now, Kiera."

I bite my lower lip. Shiver as he breathes on the wet spot on my panties Whimper as his beard tickles the insides of my thighs.

"What's that, Kiera?" He lifts his head up. His lips curl into a sexy smile. "Did you say something, baby?"

"Keep going," I gasp. Need blazes through my core. "Please..."

Caleb chuckles as he climbs on the bed. *He's naked and he's huge.* "I love hearing you beg for us," he says darkly, "Open your pretty little mouth, Kiera. You like oral, giving *and* receiving? Show me."

He moves to the head of the bed. He straddles me. His thick cock dangles in my face. There's a drop of precum on the tip.

My mouth waters. The tip of my tongue darts out and licks it up. Mmm.

"Fuck," Caleb groans. "Fuck, yes. Keep doing that, baby."

A sense of heady power blazes through me at the ragged edge in his voice. *The raw hunger.* Caleb's always calm. Always in control. To see his iron self-control unravel, because of me...

It's the hottest thing in the world.

Nolan's breath teases my pussy. "So wet," he murmurs. "You like this, Kiera?" He swats my panty-covered mound, and I gasp and arch off the bed. "Your legs spread wide, a man licking your juices while another man shoves his cock down your throat. Does this turn you on?"

I'm so aroused I think I'm going to combust. I'm just going to explode out of sheer need. Nolan's cleaning crew will be scraping pieces of Kiera from the expensive woolen drapes, the one-thousand-thread-count Egyptian cotton sheets, and the plush, thick-piled carpet.

Before it comes to that, Nolan's fingers push my panties aside, and he plunges two fingers into my wet heat. Blood leaves my brain. The room blurs around me. My toes curl. My fingers grip the sheets; my back arches. He strokes in and out of my pussy, twisting his fingers to find my g-spot and pressing down, making me shudder with desire.

My pulse races. "Please..." I beg, not knowing what I'm pleading for. Maybe an orgasm. Earlier this evening, Caleb took me to the edge five times. Five. Over and over, I got to the precipice before he yanked me back. Maybe I'm begging for my release, or maybe I'm begging for a repeat of that pleasurable torture.

Nolan pulls his mouth off my pussy. "You know what Caleb wants you to do?"

I nod, heat flushing through me.

Nolan's not going to let me off the hook. "Tell me what he wants you to do," he orders.

"He wants me to..." Oh God, my cheeks are on fire. "He wants me to suck his cock."

"And how can you tell that?"

"Umm..." I can't meet Nolan's darkly amused gaze. "He's naked and..." My voice trails away, and my entire face blazes. Caleb's erection is in my face. I don't need to be a rocket scientist to figure this out.

He spanks my ass, hard enough to sting. "Then what are you waiting for? Wrap those pretty little lips wrapped around Caleb's cock." He gives me another sharp spank for punctuation, and I arch my back and whimper.

"You like that, you bad girl." Nolan laughs, soft and low. "Next time, I'm going to put a vibrator between your legs when I spank you."

I almost come at his suggestion.

This is naughty and wicked. This is better than my wildest fantasies.

Caleb's eyes turn speculative, and I know he's taking mental notes. *Lucky me.* "Open your mouth, baby."

I suck his erect cock between my lips. He throws his head back and hisses with pleasure. "Yes," he groans. "Take it all the way, Kiera."

I suck him deeper, taking as much of his length as I can, shivers wracking my body. His grunt of approval sends a thrill of delight through me.

He leans forward and his big hands wrap around my breasts. He pushes them together, squeezing the heavy, aching globes. He's not tentative, and he's not gentle.

It's perfect.

Caleb's fingers tease my nipples, tugging and pinching the tender nubs. They stand up under his attention, pert, erect, and swollen. I whimper around his cock, and my tongue licks his rock-hard shaft, all the way from his swollen head to the base.

Nolan's clever tongue joins his thrusting fingers. He yanks my panties away, and he spreads me open. I feel cool air on my pussy, and then his hot mouth takes its place.

Wow.

I moan helplessly around Caleb's cock as Nolan's tongue circles my clit. He sucks it between his lips, and it drives me wild. I writhe on the bed, lost. Caleb's huge cock in my mouth. Nolan's wicked tongue and fingers, teasing my clit and thrusting into my core. Caleb's big, powerful hands, crushing my breasts and tweaking my nipples. Every nerve ending in my body is firing on max.

Nolan growls and swipes my slick, wet heat with his tongue. A shudder of desire runs through me, and my legs fall open for him. He teases each inner lip between his lips and teeth and wetness gushes from my pussy.

His fingers penetrate me. His tongue dances over my clit, harder, faster. I whimper and flail, and suck Caleb's cock deeper. I feel light-headed, dizzy as wave after wave of pleasure repeatedly batters my body.

Nolan's thumb teases my asshole. "You want to know what's in the package?" he asks, his sexy, smoky growl sending a fresh shiver of lust through me. "It's a butt plug, Kiera. I'm going to push it into this tight little hole."

Oh fuck.

Those words push me over the edge. My muscles clench. I start to tremble. The dam bursts and the orgasm tears out of me, searing and scorching. An inferno of pleasure ravages my body. My entire body shivers in ecstasy as I hurtle over the edge.

They let me float back to earth. Their warm bodies blanket me. For a few minutes, there's perfect silence in the room. Then Nolan props himself up on an elbow.

"Ready for the butt plug?"

Caleb's phone rings, shattering the moment. He looks at the display with a frown. "What?" he barks.

A voice says something on the other end.

His expression turns tense. "Why didn't you call me?" he demands, and then runs his hands through his hair. "Yeah, sorry. I know what I said. Okay. Keep me posted."

He hangs up and turns to me. "My team found out earlier this evening that your sister never made it to Cancun. She's still in New York." He hesitates. "We made contact."

A shiver of apprehension runs through me. "And?"

He laces my fingers in his. His expression is somber. "It's not good, Kiera."

25

CALEB

Cockblocked again, this time by Mandy.

Not going lie, my dick is extremely frustrated. I have a case of blue balls like you would not believe. *Everything hurts.*

But when I saw Mandy's number on the display, I had to answer. I knew she wouldn't call unless it were important. And when I heard what she had to say...

Not telling Kiera was never an option. I'm done playing games. Relationships can't be built on lies and half-truths.

My mind spins. I take a second to digest everything Mandy told me, and then I turn to Kiera. "My team found out earlier this evening that your sister never made it to Cancun. She's still in New York." I take a deep breath. "We made contact."

Kiera's not a fool; she can tell from my voice that something's wrong. "And?" she asks hesitantly.

I hold her hand. "It's not good, Kiera." I ignore my aching cock and gather my thoughts into coherence. "Most of my people work in IT. They sit behind desks, and they find information on people. That is my company's expertise.

Fieldwork isn't really our specialty. Brody and Adrian's people are much better at it." I'm aware I'm stalling. "I have a very small set of operatives that do surveillance work in the field."

She nods wordlessly.

"Four people have been taking turns to watch Bianca. It's been a challenging assignment. They can't get into her building, not without arousing suspicion. Conveniently for Martinez, a US Senator lives on the fortieth floor. The security is very rigorous. Anyone who enters that building needs to be signed in and out. There are Secret Service agents everywhere, trained to detect anything suspicious."

We should have had this conversation on Thursday. We hadn't. Instead, we'd talked about the ghosts of our pasts, about Stephan and Lina, and how their deaths had influenced our lives. I'd told her—truthfully—that I was doing everything in my power to contact her sister, and we'd left it at that.

I guess that I'd been hoping for a happy ending.

From what Mandy told me, there are going to be no joyous family reunions in the near future.

"Bianca does not go out very much. She works out in her building's gym. She doesn't appear to have many friends. No lunches with girlfriends, no happy hour cocktails. The only social gatherings she attends are with Martinez."

Martinez keeps a constant watch on Bianca. She doesn't have any friends. Two red flags.

Kiera hears what I'm not saying. "He's abusing her?"

"We don't know for sure. *Yet.*" I exchange a look with Nolan. Once we found Bianca, identifying Martinez was easy. Getting him is now a matter of time—we're just waiting until we find him alone. We won't endanger Kiera's sister.

He's not going to be able to melt back into the shadows. Not this time.

"Tonight was one of those gatherings. A birthday party for one of Martinez's associates, held in some nightclub in Hell's Kitchen. Mandy, one of my operatives, was able to follow Bianca into the ladies' room. Your sister was alone. Mandy handed over your note."

Kiera's eyes are very wide in her face.

"What did your note to your sister say?" Nolan asks, sensing that I'm avoiding what comes next.

"You don't know?" She sounds surprised. "You didn't read it?"

I shake my head.

"Caleb wouldn't invade your privacy," Nolan says wryly. "He didn't even run a background check on you, even though he's been interested in you for months. You have no idea how rare that is."

I give my friend a quelling look. "It was between you and your sister. I didn't see any reason to read it."

"It wasn't anything personal," she says. "All I said was that I thought she was dead—Miles Armstrong had been pretty persuasive—and that once I testified, I went into hiding." She swallows. "I told her I had no idea that she was alive and that I was very sorry. I should have searched harder for her. And I gave her my phone number." She looks up. "That was okay, wasn't it?"

"It was fine." There's no putting it off any longer. There's no getting around it. As much as Bianca's words are going to break Kiera's heart, I have to tell her. "Your sister took out her cigarette lighter, and she burnt your note. And..."

Kiera holds up her hand, outrage on her face. "She smokes now?"

“Really?” Nolan interjects in exasperation. “That's what you're going to focus on?”

Kiera gives me an abashed look. “Sorry. It’s just that she...” She shakes her head. “Never mind. This isn’t about Bianca’s smoking habit. She burned the note, and then what?”

“She told Mandy to tell you that she knows where you are, and she doesn’t care. As far as she’s concerned, she doesn’t have a sister. She doesn’t want to hear from you.”

Nolan stiffens imperceptibly. Shock flashes across Kiera's face. “She knows where I am?” Her voice is thin and shaky. “For how long? She knew I only live a few hours away from her, and she never once wanted to contact me?” My words fully sink in. Pain fills Kiera’s eyes and saturates her voice. “As far as she’s concerned, she doesn’t have a sister? That’s what she said?”

Fuck.

Tears well in Kiera's eyes. I put my arm around Kiera’s shoulders, holding her as she cries. Nolan looks helpless, and then he pushes himself off the bed and pulls on his pants. He opens a dresser drawer and throws Kiera a T-shirt. “Come on,” he says. “Let’s go outside for a bit and get some air.”

Good idea. There are conversations that one can have when naked, but this isn't one of them. Kiera is justifiably upset, and as hard as I am trying to be a decent human being, I'm still sporting a semi. I get dressed too, and we head to the rooftop.

It's late. From this vantage point, the park is mostly dark, but the rest of the city is brightly lit. Manhattan never sleeps.

Kiera walks to the edge of the balcony and takes in the view. “This is incredible,” she says faintly.

"It really is," Nolan agrees. "I don't appreciate it enough."

She doesn't respond. She stares into the distance. I want to jump in and offer words of comfort, but really, what could I say? This is a shitty, *shitty* situation.

"I don't know what I did wrong," she says finally. "Yes, I told Bianca what to do. Someone had to. My mother was a terrible parent. I had to step up more often than I wanted to. Then Bianca got caught in Greg Dratch's web. She started hanging out with him and his friends. The wrong crowd. I tried to keep her from him. She resented me for it. I thought she'd eventually realize I did it out of love." Her voice trails off. "Instead, she hates me."

She sounds desperately sad.

Nolan joins her at the balcony edge. "We don't know that," he says softly. "Martinez is dangerous. We still don't know if Bianca is with him voluntarily, or if she's being pressured into a relationship. I don't want you to get your hopes up to have them dashed again. But it is possible that your sister has never tried to contact you because she's protecting you against him."

She doesn't appear to hear him.

"We know who Martinez is now," Nolan continues. "When we found your sister, that was the break we needed. When the time is right, we will make a move against him. It's just a few more weeks, Kiera. And then, I promise you, you'll be able to talk to your sister. We will get to the root of this."

She's still staring into space, still lost in her own private grief. "It's so ironic," she says softly. "My sister is in Manhattan, and so am I. She is less than half an hour away, and yet the distance between us seems as vast as it was when I thought she was dead." She smiles ruefully, but her eyes are bleak. "For eight years, I felt all alone in the world. When I found out Bianca was alive, that changed. But now, it's just me again."

I walk up to her and rest my hand in the small of her back. "You're only alone if you want to be. We're here for you."

She doesn't say anything for a long time, and then she nods her head. "You're right," she says. "I'm not alone. Thank you for everything you've done. That you've both done."

"I don't see how we've made things better."

She smiles at me. "You helped me when you didn't need to. It happens less often than you think."

She puts her arms around both of us. "I could spend what's left of the night fretting about Bianca, or I could spend it doing something else. I know what I'd rather do." She gives us a hopeful look. "Want to go back to bed and finish what we started?"

26

KIERA

It's beautiful here on Nolan's rooftop. Below us, Manhattan is a tapestry of light, but up here, the noise is muted, and it's oddly peaceful. There's room here to think.

For so many years, I've lived my life in the past. A thousand times, I've replayed the events of that fateful evening when I went looking for my sister. I've obsessively examined and re-examined every decision I've made. Every action I've undertaken. Every mistake. Every flaw. Over and over, I've poured over them. I've lacerated myself with my failures. I've rubbed salt into the wounds of my heart, and I've refused to allow them to heal.

Moving on, when Bianca was dead, would have been wrong. Disloyal.

Then I found out that my sister was alive, and I'd been yanked back into the past again.

Three weeks ago, if someone had asked me why I avoided relationships and entanglements, I would have blamed Vladimir Sirkovich and the witness protection program. There was always a chance that the mafia would come after me for putting one of their own in jail. If they found me, I would be at risk. Under the circumstances, I couldn't justify dragging someone into my life.

I would also have been lying.

It's not Sirkovich that's the problem.

It's me.

I've never been able to forgive myself for what happened to Bianca. I've never been able to forget how badly I failed my baby sister.

Dixie has told me repeatedly that what happened to Bianca wasn't my fault. Nolan's said that to me. Caleb has too. I've heard their words. My head knows they're right. *But my heart has stayed frozen.*

Then Nolan promises me that I will get a chance to talk to my sister, and Caleb steps in with words of reassurance that I'm not alone, and something unexpected and magical happens.

It all clicks into place. Peace descends over me.

I finally forgive myself.

If Bianca's trapped with Martinez, Nolan and Caleb will get her out. They've said they will, and I believe them. But if she's with him out of her own free will, then there's nothing I can do. My sister is an adult now. I am not responsible for her decisions; she is. And as much as it kills me to watch from the sidelines, it's her life. She's allowed to screw it up.

I let go of the weight I've carried around all my life.

What the future holds, I don't know. Only one thing is certain.

It's time to make room in my heart for Caleb and Nolan.

WE HEAD BACK to the bedroom. "We can have sex in the morning," Caleb says. "You don't have to do this now."

I've been stuck for eight years. I finally feel free. I appreciate Caleb's consideration, but I don't want to wait. "I want to."

"Are you sure?" Nolan asks. He gives me a wicked smile that sends the butterflies in my stomach into a rampaging frenzy. He holds up the package. "You know what's in this."

I nod.

His smile grows. "Tell me what I'm holding, Kiera."

Heat creeps up my cheeks. "A butt plug." I swallow back my nerves. "I'm ready."

Caleb laughs. "Are you now?" He moves right next to me. His fingers close on the hem of my t-shirt, and then he lifts it over my head. He crushes me into his warm chest. His fingers tangle in my hair, and his lips meet mine.

I stand on tiptoe and return his kiss. I can feel the hard, thick length of his erection against my stomach. Pleasure spirals inside me as his hand trails down my side. He wedges his knee between my thighs. "Spread them," he orders, his voice thick and hoarse. "Spread them for me."

"It's your turn," I protest. "I came already."

He raises an eyebrow. "Are you in charge, Kiera?"

Oh fuck. There's an edge to his tone that sends a shiver of pure lust through me. In real life, Caleb is the soul of consideration, and would never dream of barking orders at me.

But in the bedroom?

Things are different here. He might not wander around with a T-shirt that says, 'Obey Me or Else,' but Caleb Reeves has a dominant side to him.

A side that so far, I've only caught glimpses of.

A side that I very much want to see.

"No, Sir. I am not."

His teeth flash in a predatory grin. "You're right about

that," he agrees. "And because you're not in charge, if I tell you to spread your legs, what do you do?"

I'm so turned on that my breath is coming in shallow pants. "I spread my legs."

"And if I push my fingers into your slick, wet, heat, what do you say?"

I almost sob out loud; my need is that overwhelming. "I say, 'thank you, Sir.'"

"Good girl." He tilts my face up and brushes a kiss over my lips. I melt into his body, wrapping my arms around his neck. My boobs are crushed against his chest. My swollen, sensitive nipples ache and throb.

Damn that phone call. They'd been seconds away from fucking me. Now, we're back to 'Tease Kiera until she's a whimpering mess.' I'm not grumbling about foreplay—okay, I'm grumbling a little bit—but I want more. I want to feel their cocks inside me.

There's a sound of a package being opened. Nolan moves behind me. He moves my hair out of the way and kisses the back of my neck and the curve of my shoulder. His beard rasps against my sensitized skin, and goosebumps break out all over my body. He moves to my earlobe, sucking the tender flesh between his teeth. "Do you know what I have in my hand?" he growls.

I can guess. "The butt plug?"

"Mm-hmm." He kisses my neck again, and every nerve ending in my body tingles with heat.

Caleb's lips turn up in a dark smile. "I think you should help Nolan. Spread your cheeks for him, baby."

My cheeks blaze with heat. I bite my lower lip. I can't do that. *I just can't.* It's too lewd, too wicked. I'd die from sheer embarrassment. "I..."

Caleb raises an eyebrow. "Consider your next words

carefully," he advises. "Is this a real limit, or do you just not want to obey because you're embarrassed?"

Damn it. No, it's not an actual limit. "It's just... awkward," I whine, giving Caleb a death glare.

His lips tilt up, but he shows no sign of relenting. "You have another ten seconds to make up your mind, Kiera. And then, there will be punishment."

Damn it again. Blushing furiously, I remove my hands from around his neck. I can't meet Caleb's eyes. I grab my cheeks and spread them open for Nolan.

Nolan exhales in appreciation. "Fuck me, that's hot," he groans. Pleasure spreads through me at the raw need in his voice, at the undisguised desire in Caleb's expression.

I'm sandwiched between two men. One of them has ordered me to spread my ass cheeks apart so that the other can stick a butt plug inside me.

I can't believe I'm doing this. I can't believe how turned on I am.

Caleb eases two fingers into my dripping pussy. "You like this, don't you, Kiera?" he growls. "You might blush, and you might protest, but your body doesn't lie. You're soaked. Absolutely drenched."

I cry out as his thumb grazes my swollen clit.

Nolan's fingers move to the cleft between my globes. He teases the sensitive skin around my tight hole, and I inhale sharply as a fresh flood of heat fills me. "Relax," he murmurs. He squirts some lube onto his fingers, and then he circles my ring before gently pushing a slick finger inside.

It feels... different. Not unpleasant. Sort of naughty, if I'm being honest. As if I'm doing something forbidden. It's sending all kinds of tingles through my body. Caleb plunges his fingers into my pussy, Nolan plays with my ass, and I'm absolutely overflowing with sensation. The room blurs around me. The world narrows to the feel of their hands on my body.

Nolan adds another finger. My muscles stretch to accommodate him. I whimper in slight discomfort. "Relax your muscles," he orders. "Don't fight me, Kiera."

I take a deep breath and make myself calm down. There's no pain; Nolan's using plenty of lube, and he's going slow. I'm expecting it to hurt, but it really doesn't.

I don't have much experience trusting anyone, but I can trust Nolan and Caleb.

Feeling me relax, Nolan slides his fingers in deeper. Another shiver runs through me. Caleb's thumb circles my clit, applying the perfect amount of pressure.

Desire coils tight in my core. Surely, I can't be at the edge again, already? Except I am. I'm so close. "I'm going to come," I moan.

"No." Caleb's voice is very firm. "Not yet."

I whimper out loud. Caleb arches an eyebrow. "Is that protest I hear?" he asks politely.

The first night, in his backyard, I'd asked him if he was going to spank me as punishment. I still remember his reply. *If you don't behave, I'll take you to the edge, over and over, and I won't let you come. No matter how much you beg.*

"No, Sir," I murmur meekly. Fuck me, I can't hold this feeling back. I grit my teeth and try to hold on. Try to ignore the shiver that runs through my body each time his thumb grazes my clit. Try to ignore the heat that blazes over my nerve endings when Nolan removes his fingers from my ass and then eases them back, stretching me, readying me for the plug.

"Please," I beg, my voice breaking. "Please... I need... I can't..."

Nolan removes his fingers. I feel a cold, blunt object at

my back entrance. "They make butt plugs out of plastic, and they make them out of steel," he says conversationally, as if he weren't at the point of pushing a plug into my ass. "Personally, I'm partial to glass."

He pushes it steadily, and my muscles yield. There's a brief second of discomfort as my tight ring stretches around the widest part, and then it's in.

"Such a good girl," Nolan says, his breath tickling my ear. "Would you like your reward now, Kiera?"

My throat is dry with desire. My body is burning up with need. "Yes, please."

I can't wait. I'm so ready. I've never wanted anything more in my life than I want them to sink into me. To take me.

To make me come.

27

KIERA

I've been waiting all night for this moment.

Caleb pushes me back, his arms around my waist. He kisses me, deep and possessive. The back of my knees collides with the bed. I sink onto the mattress, my back hitting the headboard. Nolan moves closer, his thick, erect, cock inches from my lips.

Need shivers through my blood, setting every nerve ending aflame. I'm so keyed up I could cry. They've teased me relentlessly all night, but the time for foreplay is finally over.

I open my mouth and take him in deep.

He hisses in pleasure. "Fuck, yes," he says, his voice so deep it's practically a growl. "That's so good."

Arousal thrums through me like an insistent drumbeat. My need is a tidal wave, powerful and relentless. Caleb's hands run all over my body, squeezing my aching breasts, teasing my throbbing nipples, ghosting between my legs, caressing every sensitive inch of me. "Please," I whisper.

My mouth stretches around Nolan's cock. Every groan,

every growl sends fresh heat through me. I haven't had a drink in hours, but I feel drunk, heady with exhilaration. Every time I move, the plug shifts within me. I'm incredibly aware of it. It's made me soaking wet. It's made me desperate. Feverish.

Caleb stretches out on the mattress next to me. He reaches over, grabs a condom from a drawer, and rolls it over his length. He grabs my hips, his callused fingers digging into my flesh, and he drags me over to him, and pulls me down onto his length, plunging deep inside me.

Oh. My. God.

This is so good. Stars flash in front of my eyes. Fireworks explode all over my skin. I suck Nolan's fat cock between my lips again, almost sobbing in pleasure as Caleb lifts me up, and then slams into me.

My muscles stretch to accommodate his thickness. I dig my nails into Nolan's hips—oops—and whimper as pleasure spirals through me. I'm filled so *completely*. Caleb's thick length, the feel of the butt plug, Nolan's cock in my mouth—it's overwhelming, and it's perfect.

Is this what it will feel like with both of them taking me at the same time? A shiver rolls through me, part nerves, part anticipation.

I can't stop moaning. It's just too intense. It feels like I've been starved for years, and I've somehow turned a corner and stumbled upon a buffet of male perfection. After months, no, years of self-imposed abstinence, I'm overloaded in the best possible way.

Before Caleb and Nolan exploded into my life, my world was in shadows. No more. Everything is awash with color and intense, shimmering sensation.

Caleb's hands grip the cheeks of my butt as I ride him. Each thrust jolts the butt plug deeper inside me. Each thrust sends a shockwave of desire through my core. As many times as I've come tonight, my muscles clench as I once again, inexorably climb the peak toward my climax.

Nolan's fingers tangle in my hair, and he tugs me closer. I open my mouth wider and take more of his length down my throat. "Fuck, yes," he groans. "Oh, fuck yes."

I glance up at his face, and it's clenched with raw need.

I'm doing this. I'm causing this reaction.

I don't know what sensation to focus on. Should it be the feeling of Caleb's cock stretching me and slamming into me until I see stars? Or the pinpricks of pleasure-pain in my scalp as Nolan's grip tightens on my hair, urging me to take him deeper down my throat?

I wrap my fingers around the base of Nolan's erection as I swallow his thick length, but he's having none of it. "No hands," he says, his voice stern. "Use your mouth."

A full-body shudder runs through me. I didn't think I'd be turned on by dominant men growling orders at me. *Until I met Caleb and Nolan.*

"Hands behind your back, Kiera," Caleb orders. He holds my wrists in place with one hand. His other hand moves between my legs to find my clit. I'm overstimulated, and my nub is swollen and sensitive, but when Caleb's fingers graze me, my body comes to life.

Pleasure tears through me. This is so good. *This is unreal.*

The sounds of sex fill the air. Caleb's cock slapping into me. Nolan's harsh breathing. My breathless whimpers. I lock my fingers behind my back, and my body jerks between the two men. I feel frantic and out-of-control, and I love it. There's no room for thought. There is no room for anxieties or self-consciousness or insecurities. Everything is driven out. Only pleasure—raw, intense, and primal—remains.

Caleb lifts me off his length and positions me so I'm

lying on my side. He parts my legs and slides into me, his fingers finding my clit and stroking it with a feather-light touch.

Nolan kneels in front of me, and I once again take him in my mouth. "The next time we do this," Nolan growls. "Caleb will be in your ass, and I'll be in your sweet pussy."

I groan around his erection. I picture the scene he's describing, and a shiver runs through my body. My muscles clench involuntarily at the sheer eroticism of the thought.

Caleb chuckles. He teases my clit with his fingertip. "You like that idea, don't you, Kiera? You want both of us to take you at the same time."

His voice turns deeper, hoarser. "Under that good girl exterior, there's a passionate woman straining to break free." He thrusts into me, hard and deep. "Whatever you want, we're here for you." His thumb circles my swollen, throbbing clit. "Whatever your fantasies are, we're going to make them come true. Anything you want. Everything you didn't know you wanted. Everything you've craved, but been too afraid to ask for, I'm going to give it to you."

"We're going to give it to you," Nolan corrects. He pulls free of my mouth and rolls a condom over his length. Caleb pulls out of me, and before I can complain about it, I'm on my side, and Nolan's thick shaft thrusts into me from behind.

Oh God yes.

Nolan's fingers play with the butt plug as he sinks into me. He pulls it out, so the widest part stretches my ass, and then pushes it back in.

Uncontrolled shivers wrack my body. Caleb loses the condom, and then he places the crown of his erection at my lips. I open my mouth and swallow his length, greedy for him. "Good girl," he says, his voice hoarse. His iron control is finally showing signs of wear. "Take me deep."

Nolan drives into me. I can't hold on. "Please," I beg, the words coming out garbled around Caleb's cock. "I can't hold on."

"Don't," Nolan growls. "Come for us, Kiera."

Fuck. I don't know if it's because the intensity of Nolan's thrusts picks up. I don't know if it's because I needed their permission to orgasm. All I know is that I hear Nolan tell me to come, and, as if on cue, I fall apart.

Dimly, I'm aware of Caleb cutting off a shout as he erupts in my mouth. I'm conscious of Nolan's fingers gripping my hips as he finds his release. But I'm not paying attention. My orgasm hurtles toward me, and then I can't contain it any longer. My muscles clench, my control shatters. My climax rips through me with the force of a hurricane.

Sometime later—I've lost track of time—I go to the bathroom and remove the butt plug. I clean it and set it on the counter, giggling to myself as I do so.

Then I wander back into the bedroom.

Both Caleb and Nolan are sprawled there, big and male and perfectly unselfconscious about their nakedness. Nolan pats the space between them. "Come here."

For a fraction of a second, I hesitate. It's probably weird, given that I just had sex with them, but spending the entire night with someone is far more daunting than the physical act of sex. Sleeping with someone, waking up with them in the morning... these things are intimate. They make me vulnerable.

You're not going to live in fear anymore, Kiera. You're done with that.

"Okay," I reply. I wedge myself between them. Nolan

turns out the light. For a few minutes, I lie awake, acutely conscious of the two male bodies on either side of me. The cadence of their breathing. The steady beat of their hearts.

It feels *right.*

Sandwiched between Nolan and Caleb, I fall asleep.

28

NOLAN

When I asked for Caleb's help finding Greg Dratch, I hoped that the hacker would lead me to Luis Fernando Martinez.

Then the situation had got incredibly complicated. We don't need Dratch's help to locate Martinez anymore. Thanks to Bianca, we've found him.

But Dratch isn't totally useless.

Kiera's sister fell off the grid eight years ago. She was presumed dead; she disappeared with Greg Dratch when she was fifteen. Then, two and a half years ago, she showed up in Cali, wearing designer clothing and expensive jewelry.

There's a gap. Dratch is going to fill in the missing pieces for us, and when he's done, we'll know if Bianca needs rescuing from the arms dealer. Or, if, as Kiera fears, her baby sister genuinely wants nothing to do with her.

Megan Matuki, Caleb's best analyst, comes through. On Tuesday, she emails us. "Found him," she writes. "Sorry about the delay."

Caleb and I read her email in silence. Dratch is going by Greg Denton now. Somehow, the guy's managed to obtain forged id documents. He moved to Atlantic City three months ago and is working as a blackjack dealer in a casino there.

"He never stays in one place long," Megan writes. "It's almost as if he's hiding from someone."

Caleb looks up at me when he's done reading the email. "Sounds like someone's put a price on his head," he comments.

"That doesn't surprise me." Dratch has stolen money from a lot of very bad people. I'm shocked he's still alive. Then again, cockroaches will survive a nuclear holocaust. People like Dratch always seem to manage to evade consequences.

"Want to drive to Atlantic City tomorrow?"

I glance at my phone. It's six in the evening. "I don't want to wait. Let's borrow Xavier's helicopter."

Caleb raises an eyebrow. "Champagne last week, and now the chopper. Xavier's that grateful, is he?"

Layla had been in real danger. Xavier and Rafe are worried sick about her, as they should be. But some wounds are too deep to heal. Layla's still torn up about her sister's death. It pushes her to be reckless, to jump heedlessly into danger.

In a very real way, I understand Layla. We've found similar ways of dealing with our pain.

I shrug in response to Caleb's question. "It's not really my story to tell."

He laughs. "Curiosity is an occupational hazard. Fair enough. Let's go talk to Xavier."

We reach the cheap motel Dratch is holed up in at eight. Caleb goes to talk to the manager, and, after the exchange of some cash, the manager agrees to both rent us the room right next to Dratch as well as disappear for the evening. It's that kind of place.

We enter the room. The furniture is particle board. The air is saturated with the smell of stale cigarette smoke. The armchair is stained, and the TV remote is chained to the unit. "The guy's broke."

"Moving every three months will do that," Caleb comments. He strips the coverlet off the bed, then sits down on the edge of the mattress. "I saw a special on TV," he says in response to my questioning look. "The bedspreads are never cleaned, just the sheets, even in really expensive hotels."

I shake my head. Caleb is full of weird pieces of trivia.

We sit down to wait. At ten, we hear Dratch enter the room next door. Five minutes later, he picks up his phone and orders pizza, a conversation we hear easily through the paper-thin walls.

Excellent.

He starts to take a shower; I can hear the water running. We leave our room. Stay out in the parking lot for a few minutes, just in case he can hear us as well as we can hear him.

Then, we knock at his door. "Pizza," I yell out.

Dratch opens the door. The instant he yanks it ajar, I kick it in and slam the man against the wall.

This scumbag targeted a fifteen-year-old. "Hello, Greg," I tell him, keeping the fury out of my voice with an effort. "I have some questions for you."

29

NOLAN

Greg Dratch looks like hell. I frisk him, and as I pat him down, odors of booze and cigarette smoke waft off him and nearly make me choke. Caleb's right—the guy's living rough.

"Who sent you?" he stammers.

I backhand him. "Let me clarify the rules of engagement," I say as he picks himself off the floor, eyes Caleb's gun, and straightens himself carefully. "You don't ask the questions. We do."

"Or what? You're going to shoot me?" He sneers at me. "Go ahead then."

"Shoot you? Oh no." I gesture to the bed. Dratch gingerly takes a seat at the edge. "That would be too quick and too easy for a piece of shit like you. No, Gregory. You don't talk, and I'm going to load you on a plane to Norilsk." I bare my teeth in a smile. "Anton Nekrasov's private plane."

His face turns the color of curdled milk. Mention of Nekrasov tends to have that effect.

"Or you talk. In return for your cooperation, I'll call the

cops. They'll run your prints. You have a half-dozen open warrants. You'll serve time. A decent lawyer will be able to limit it to five years, maybe ten."

The barrel of Caleb's gun doesn't waver. "You'll probably walk out of prison alive," he says. "Unfortunately. If you go to Siberia, on the other hand..." His voice trails off.

Caleb doesn't need to complete his sentence. I could shoot Dratch in the balls and let him bleed slowly and painfully to death, and it would be a kindness compared to sending him to Anton's fortress on the outskirts of Norilsk.

Dratch swallows visibly. "What do you want to know?"

"Let's start with the Kitai Bratva. Why'd you disappear from San Diego?"

"I stole money from Vladimir Sirkovich." His voice is barely audible. "Almost half a million dollars. I had to run before he found out."

"And the girl?"

Shock flits across his face. *Didn't expect us to know about Bianca, did you?*

"Tell us about the girl, Greg," Caleb says. His voice is quiet and calm, and it sets the hair at the back of my neck on end. Make no mistake. Caleb hides it well, but I know my friend, and he is furious.

"Bianca Thompson." He doesn't meet our eyes. "She was nothing. Trailer trash. No mother, no father. Only a pain in the ass sister."

This fucking asshole. "Where did you run?"

"Vegas."

"Why take the girl with you?"

Dratch shrugs his shoulders. "She was a hot piece of ass," he says. "She was young. I thought she'd earn her keep in Vegas." His expression turns disgusted. "But she wouldn't spread her legs, the fucking bitch. She kept crying. The clients got nervous."

Bianca was *fifteen*. He raped a child. He took her from the only home she knew, groomed her, and used her. *Then he decided to prostitute her for extra money.*

Hitting Dratch once wasn't enough. Beating him bloody won't be sufficient. This guy deserves everything Anton Nekrasov would do to him, and more.

Caleb moves in a blur and sinks his fist in Dratch's gut. I ignore the criminal's hoarse grunt of pain. "Why'd she stay with you?" I ask, relentless. "Why didn't she go back home?"

"To what?" Dratch gasps out. "Her sister was dead, killed by the Bratva. She had nothing to return to."

He doesn't know that Kiera is alive. That's a blessing, at any rate.

"That's not the whole truth, is it?" Caleb's mind is a steel trap. "Bianca didn't have to stay with you. Whatever illusions she'd had about you, she must have lost when you tried to whore her out. So, why'd she stay?"

"I don't know," he mumbles.

I exchange a look with Caleb. "Fine," I say dismissively, reaching in my back pocket for my phone. "We'll do it the hard way. Nekrasov it is." I scroll through my contacts and dial Anton's number. Twice in the same month. The Russian will be thrilled.

He answers on the first ring. "*Da?*"

"I've got a present for you, Anton," I tell the other man cheerfully. Truth is, if Nekrasov truly wanted Dratch dead, he'd be dead, and there's not a damn thing in the world to prevent that. Nekrasov has an ungodly long reach. It's best not to get on his bad side. "A two-bit thug who stole from the Kitai Bratva."

Exactly on schedule, Dratch shakes his head frantically.

"Hang on a second," I tell Nekrasov before turning to the defeated man slumped at the edge of the cheap motel bed. "Yes?"

"I lied to Bianca," he says. "I told her she'd been implicated in the theft of the money, and that the Bratva was hunting her."

"Anton, I'll call you back." I hang up on him. Caleb shakes his head wryly. We'll be owing the Russian a favor for this, but that's a different problem for a different day. She thought you were protecting her."

He nods.

I wish we hadn't promised him safety, because this guy deserves Siberia. Resisting the urge to beat his face into a pulp, I go back to the questioning. I have eight missing years and a lot of gaps. "Then what?"

"She was a liability," he says, avoiding our gazes. "I was running out of money." His jaw tightens. "I sold her after a year."

Ice drenches my spine. "To whom?"

"Some billionaire with a secluded ranch in the middle of the Utah desert," he says. "She had it good, all things considered, but she ran away after six months. I had to refund the guy his money. It took me another five months to find her."

That's two of the eight years filled in.

We wait for him to continue. "She was sixteen," he says sullenly. "Pretty. I had too much invested in her to let her go, so I paid for fake ID and took her to Bangkok. The Sicilians were interested. Alessandro Messina bought her for his son, Luca." He shakes his head. "Two years later, she ran away again. Luca fancied himself in love with her. The kid was idealistic. He wouldn't search for her. So, I did."

"Why?"

He keeps his gaze fixed on the floor. "Half a million dollars doesn't last forever. Especially in Vegas. Alessandro Messina wanted his money back, but I didn't have it."

In other words, the piece of shit gambled away his stolen fortune.

"This time, it took me longer to find her. Eventually, I did. She didn't want to come with me. I had beat sense into her. I called in some favors and took her to Colombia." He frowns. "I was running out of options. The Sicilians were looking for me. The Bratva was looking for me. I needed money, fast, and Bianca was my meal ticket. But then Luis Martinez took an interest in the girl."

Bianca had been young. She'd never led a stable life. She'd been raped by the men in her world. Sold, used. She could have given up, but she'd fought back as best as she could.

She'd tried so desperately to escape her past. I can relate to that.

I clench my hands into fists. "You sold a teenager to a fifty-year-old criminal."

"I didn't want to. I didn't want Martinez after me when she ran away. I worked for him; I know the guy. He's crazy; he'll slice me up."

Not a thought for Bianca. Greg Dratch's only capable of thinking about himself. Kiera, who is a pretty astute judge of character, had seen it right from the start, but Bianca, who had been young and impressionable, hadn't.

Her only crime was to trust the wrong person. Poor child.

"I tried to reason to Martinez," Dratch continues. "I warned him about her. Told him she'd run away from her previous two owners. He said he could control her."

"How?"

He shrugs. "You know how I stay alive? I don't ask too many questions. He had something on her, that's all I know. Whatever it was, it's worked. She's been with him more than two years."

I can guess what that is. Dratch thinks Kiera is dead, but Bianca knows her sister is alive. Intuition tells me this is the lever. I'm willing to bet that Martinez told her that Kiera was still alive, and if she tried to leave, he'd hunt Kiera down and hurt her. That's why she pushed Caleb's operative away. That's why she's never tried to contact her sister. *She's trying to protect her.*

It's a theory, nothing more. But it's enough for us to act.

Caleb and I exchange a glance. He nods slightly and pulls out his phone. He dials a number. "It's done," he says into the receiver.

Less than three minutes later, we hear sirens in the distance, growing closer. The cops are here. "You should be profoundly thankful I don't renege on a deal," Caleb says grimly. "Rot in prison, Dratch."

I give the thug one last look, and then follow Caleb out of there. Once we're underway, I turn to Caleb. "We need to get Bianca out before we go after Martinez."

"Agreed. Let's put together a team."

First Bianca. Then Martinez.

And then what?

Retirement, I think.

Caleb got out of fieldwork. Alexander fell in love and retired. They're both still making a difference. They're just not putting their lives on the line anymore.

Once, I would have equated retirement with a death sentence. But the wound that has propelled me forward my entire life has healed. I see something to live for. Nights with Kiera. Lazy summer barbecues.

Laughter. Love. Happiness.

After so many years of feeling unworthy, I'm finally ready.

But before that, we need to get Kiera's sister to safety.

30

CALEB

We wanted information. We certainly got it.

I puzzle over everything we learned as we head back. "Dratch didn't know Kiera was alive," I muse. "But Martinez does."

Nolan's lips thin. "How did he find out?"

I frown. "It's got to be Miles Armstrong. He told Xavier's people that Kiera was in witness protection. It's not a stretch to imagine he also told Martinez."

Bianca has been through hell for the last eight years. Raped repeatedly by Dratch. Sold by him to the highest bidder. And it all started with Armstrong. He wanted his conviction. His lies ruined Bianca's life.

So much suffering.

Greg Dratch will pay for his sins. So far, Armstrong has gotten away scot-free. I make a silent promise to myself. Whatever happens, I will ensure that the corrupt detective pays for the harm he's caused.

But that's further down the line. We have a more immediate concern, one that sends fear shooting down my spine.

"If Martinez knows about Kiera, he'll come looking for her when Bianca disappears."

Nolan looks grim. "We can protect her."

Kiera might not realize it, but she's surrounded by people that care for her. Not just Nolan and me. Her friends Dixie, Fiona, and Avery have her back. Xavier will do whatever it takes to make sure his employees stay safe. Club M is practically a fortress, and there's more security there than Fort Knox.

Luis Fernando Martinez is powerful, but he's not invincible. If we go to war, Martinez will lose. He hasn't survived and thrived in the cutthroat world of arms-dealing by being a fool. He'll calculate the odds, realize what he's up against, and most likely, walk away.

Even if he doesn't, we can't turn our back on Bianca. If she's with Martinez against her will, we need to help her, and not only because she's Kiera's sister. We all stood at Lina's grave. We all made a vow. *Never again.*

"We should pull in Adrian and Brody," I tell Nolan. "My team isn't set up for this kind of operation. This is Lockhart & Payne's bread and butter."

"Good idea. We need to warn Xavier too. Tell him to be ready." He shifts in his seat. "Are we going to tell Kiera what we found out tonight?"

I grimace. "She'll blame herself for everything that has happened to Bianca."

"She'll have to meet her sister eventually, Caleb."

"I know." I just don't want her to get hurt.

I dial Brody's number. Even though it's late, he picks up on the first ring. "What's up?"

"I need a favor." I explain the entire situation to him. "Can you get Bianca Thompson out?"

"Absolutely," he says without hesitation. "I'll talk to your surveillance team in the morning. We'll get the lay of the land, find out how many people are guarding the girl, and figure out the best extraction point."

"Thank you."

He hears the tension in my voice. "This is fairly routine for us, Caleb," he assures me. "We'll move quickly. Unless something unexpected comes up, this time next week, the girl should be in a safe house."

"Thank you," I repeat.

Brody's misinterpreted my worry. Adrian and Brody are the best at what they do; I'm not concerned that they will screw this up.

But my stomach clenches at the idea of Kiera in danger, and bile fills my mouth. Theo died. Joha killed herself. I like to think that the wounds have healed, but they're still there. I will always be scarred.

Joha couldn't bear the idea of life without Theo. She tried. God knows she tried for Nala's sake. In the end, she just *couldn't.*

I finally understand. If anything were to happen to Kiera, every wound would rip open once again, and this time, I'm not sure I will be able to heal.

31

KIERA

As much as I try not to think of Bianca, and her refusal to see me, it swirls about in my thoughts, as relentless as a powerful whirlpool sucking me down.

Count your blessings, Kiera. You're alive. Nobody's chasing you. The two guys you're crazy about seem to like you back. You're embarking on an exciting new relationship, the first actual relationship of your life.

Bianca's alive too. Though, from Caleb and Nolan's description of her life, I don't think she's doing well. *What if Luis Martinez hits her? What if he hurts her?*

To keep myself from brooding, I pack my schedule with work. I call Henri and ask him to book me on every available shift. He's only too happy to oblige. I work an eight-hour shift on Monday and a twelve-hour shift on Tuesday.

Nolan calls me Wednesday morning. "Are you busy tonight?"

A smile breaks out on my face. We've texted back and forth a few times in the last couple of days, but I haven't seen either Caleb or Nolan since the weekend. I know it's ridiculous, but I've missed them. "I'm working during the day, but I should be done by five."

"Want to grab dinner?"

"Sure. Can it be somewhere low-key? There's a great pizza place in my neighborhood."

I hold my breath. I don't want to be in a relationship where the guys make all the decisions. I've been on my own for too long; I've grown used to being independent and taking care of myself.

Caleb assured me that their dominance was bedroom-only. I'm going to hold them to it.

"Pizza sounds great," Nolan replies. "What time?"

I release the breath I didn't know I was holding. "How about seven?"

"Sure. Do you want us to pick you up, or will you meet us there?"

They've never been to my apartment. It's nowhere near as nice as Caleb's house or Nolan's Central Park-adjacent condo, but it's mine, the air-conditioner is working again, and I refuse to be ashamed of it. "Pick me up, please."

"See you at seven."

EXACTLY AT SEVEN, there's a knock on the door. I open it to find Caleb and Nolan there. "Want to come in for a drink?"

Caleb smiles at me. "I'd love to."

The two of them enter and give me a hug. Nolan brushes a kiss over my lips and then flops onto the couch. Caleb kisses me too. He looks around curiously before sitting down. "I see that you and Nolan have the same decorator," he quips.

Whatever I thought he was going to say, it isn't this. I look around my apartment, seeing it with Caleb's eyes. It's clean and furnished, but that's about it. No pictures on the walls, no photos on the side tables.

I've been running for so long that it still hasn't sunk in that I don't have to run anymore. It still hasn't sunk in that I'm safe.

"It's a work in progress," I tell Caleb loftily. "I'm getting a plant this weekend."

He laughs. "Good idea," he agrees. "What are you making?"

It takes me a second to realize he's talking about the drink I promised him. I move to my tiny home bar. "Rum and coke for you, Nolan?"

Nolan grins up at me. "You remembered."

"It is my job." I flutter my eyelashes at Caleb. "What are you in the mood for, Mr. Reeves?"

His eyes darken. "If you keep taking that tone with me, Kiera," he murmurs. "We're not going to make it to pizza."

My insides clench. Desire flares to life. "How about a martini?"

He grins. "Only if you make it dirty."

There is a jar of olives in the refrigerator. I wink at Caleb. "For you, I'll make it extra dirty."

32

KIERA

I thought for sure that Caleb or Nolan would have a quip in response. It's not like them to shy away from the sexual jokes.

Caleb cracks a grin, but his smile quickly fades. "There's something I want to talk to you about."

My heartbeat speeds up. "What's wrong?" Is it sad that I automatically think something's wrong? But everything in my life has taught me to always be braced for bad news, to always anticipate the worst-case scenario.

"Nothing's wrong," Nolan says. He fiddles with his shirt cuff. "It's just complicated." He grimaces. "That sounds like something out of a dating profile. Let's go get pizza, and we'll explain."

"Okay," I agree. I'm still convinced that whatever they have to say to me, it's not good. But, if I'm going to have to listen to bad news, it might as well be over a slice of pizza. Ideally, with extra black olives.

By tacit agreement, for the first few minutes after ordering, we talk about everything and nothing. We squabble amiably about pizza toppings. Nolan insisted on loading our pizza up with spinach and broccoli, and Caleb ribs him about it. "What's next?" he asks, rolling his eyes. "Kale smoothies for breakfast?"

Nolan is unfazed. "I like spinach, asshole."

I don't mind the vegetables. We get extra olives, and that's all I really care about.

Debbie, the woman who runs the tiny pizzeria, takes twenty minutes to make our food. I'm starving by the time it arrives, and when it shows up, I dig right in, completely shameless. "Sorry," I apologize, my mouth filled with pizza, because I'm classy like that. "I didn't have time to eat lunch."

Caleb takes a bite of his slice, and his eyes widen. "This is really good." Sauce dribbles down his chin, and he shakes his head ruefully. Laughing a little, I hand him a napkin. I'm used to Nolan being dressed casually, but Caleb is almost always in a suit. Not today. He's wearing khakis and a Baltimore Ravens t-shirt. He's eating pizza, and he's even spilling food on himself. It's all very normal. "Why didn't you have time to eat lunch?"

"There was an all-day corporate retreat," I reply. "The restaurant was short-staffed, so I pitched in."

"Xavier's lucky to have you," Nolan says.

It's a nice sentiment, but I'm the lucky one. I worked in a handful of bars before landing at Club M. You want to know how many of them offer benefits to a bartender? *None.* "I have healthcare, dental, paid vacation days, and a 401K," I tell Nolan. "It's a good job. I'm grateful to have it."

"Do you like bartending?" he asks. He leans forward, his eyes on me, entirely focused on my answer. *It's nice.* A pair of women get up to leave from the neighboring table. As they pass me, the women give me sidelong glances. It doesn't take an expert in body language to interpret their meaning. They look at Nolan and Caleb, who both exude that aura that rich people have, and then they look at me, in my department-store dress and drugstore makeup, and I can tell they're wondering what's so special about me.

I've never been the object of envy before. Call me petty, but I like it.

Nolan's still waiting for an answer. "I like talking to people," I reply, helping myself to my second slice of pizza. "At the start, listening to other people's problems took me away from mine. Then I realized I really liked helping people out. I don't even have to do much. Most people just want to feel listened to."

Caleb puts his hand on mine. "You're very good at it."

"Listening? Or bartending?"

"Both."

My cheeks heat with his praise. I contemplate a third slice but tell myself it's just greedy. I've almost succeeded in talking myself out of it, and then Nolan puts it on my plate. "So," he says. "The elephant in the room. Should we talk about it?'

Caleb looks around to make sure there's no-one within earshot. "Nolan and I have wrestled with this all day," he begins. "Finally, we both realized something. Any relationship we have has to be built on the truth, or it will fail."

Relationship. They want to be in a relationship *with me.* This thing between us is actually real. I still can't believe it.

"Yesterday," Caleb continues, his face serious, "Nolan and I went to Atlantic City to have a little chat with Greg Dratch."

My exhilaration evaporates. "Oh."

"I wanted to find out more about your sister," Caleb says. "I wanted to find out everything that happened to her from the moment she left San Diego to the present day. I wanted to learn how she met Luis Martinez."

Nolan cuts in. "Most of all," he says, an edge in his voice, "We wanted to know if she was with him of her own free will."

"And?"

Nolan takes a deep breath. "What we heard isn't good, Kiera," he says soberly. "Dratch repeatedly sold your sister to the highest bidder. He sold her to Martinez."

"He sold her?" The pizza turns to ash in my mouth. "Like a sex slave?"

Caleb nods, his expression grim. "Yes. Bianca thought you were dead. Dratch had stolen money from Sirkovich. He convinced Bianca she would be implicated in the theft. She didn't have any choices."

I feel nauseous.

Nolan leans forward. "She's not with Martinez by choice, Kiera. She's there because..."

The pieces click into place. "Because of me. She's trying to protect me from Martinez, isn't she?" Yesterday, I would have given anything to learn that Bianca wanted to meet me. Today, I just want to hurl. My baby sister was sold to this man, and she endures her gilded cage, because she's trying to keep me safe.

My guilt presses down on me, thick as a shroud.

"That's our best guess, yes." There's one solitary slice of pizza. Nolan gives me a questioning look, and I shake my head immediately. Caleb waves the slice away as well, so Nolan deposits it on his plate. "We have a plan to get her out."

I look up. "You do?"

"Of course. I called Adrian and Brody and asked for a

favor. Their company, Lockhart & Payne, provides security services all over the world. This is right up their street."

A lump forms in my throat. They don't know Bianca at all. She's a complete stranger to them. And yet here they are, steadfast and supportive, and they're rescuing her.

"There's one more thing," Nolan says. "When you joined Club M, Xavier did a background check on you. His intermediaries were able to bribe Detective Armstrong into disclosing the details of your real identity. I'm reasonably confident that the reason Luis Martinez knows that you are alive is because Armstrong talked. Once Bianca disappears, Martinez is going to come looking for her. He'll start with you."

"It would kill me if anything were to happen to you," Caleb says quietly. "I want you to move in with me until Martinez is behind bars. Nolan will be around too. Adrian is putting a security detail on my house, and on everyone involved."

He's looking at me as if he's expecting me to make a fuss. But why would I? They're freeing Bianca. They're protecting me. They're amazing. "Of course. Whatever you want."

My reply takes them by surprise. "Well, that was easy," Nolan says, blinking in confusion. He puts an arm around my shoulder, and I lean into his comforting presence. "Matters are coming to a head, Kiera. Brody and Adrian will move quickly. Most likely, they'll act later this week or early next week."

That soon? My palms are damp. I wipe them on my dress. "How soon should I move into your place?" I ask Caleb. "I have plans with Dix, Fiona, and Avery tomorrow. Should I cancel?"

He shakes his head, giving me a familiar smile. "I know better not to intrude on Girls' Night. If it's okay with you,

Andrei will pick you up at the end of the night and drive you back to my place."

"It's actually breakfast. Six-thirty in the morning."

"That sounds dreadful," Nolan says, shuddering in horror.

I laugh at his expression. "I'm not thrilled about the early start either. I'll have to set three alarms to wake up." I bite my lip. "I don't know if you wanted me to come over to your home tonight, but..."

"But it's really far away and you have an early start tomorrow." Caleb tilts his head to one side. "You could invite us to stay in your apartment."

He wants to crash at my place? "It's not fancy," I warn him. "No Egyptian cotton sheets. And my bed is a double. It'll be a tight squeeze."

"Remind me to tell you about the camp my parents insisted on sending me to as a kid every summer," Caleb replies. "The mattress was an inch thick. The cabin was filled with spiders. Without fail, it managed to rain for at least a week. Trust me, Kiera. I can sleep anywhere."

Nolan's eyes linger on my lips. "I'm looking forward to tight squeezes," he murmurs. "If you're in the mood for it."

I shouldn't be in the mood for sex. I'm still devastated about what Bianca has gone through in the last eight years. I thought I had it hard, being in witness protection, living with the constant fear of being discovered, ready to run at a moment's notice. But it turns out that compared to my sister, I've been living in the equivalent of a five-star resort.

But though my emotions are in a turmoil, I want them. No, not want. *I need them.* "In that case, let's get out of here."

33

NOLAN

We get up to leave, and Kiera reaches for her purse. Caleb shakes his head immediately, a mutinous look on his face. "You're not paying," he says. "Nolan is. It's the least he can do after making us eat spinach and broccoli."

I roll my eyes—Caleb likes spinach just fine—but grab my wallet and turn toward the counter. "Seems reasonable."

"No," Kiera protests. There's a strained edge in her voice, one that gives me pause. "I invited you. I picked the place. I should pay for dinner."

She works as a bartender. Her car doesn't look like it'll survive another year. Her clothing is practical and serviceable. She doesn't wear jewelry. In the meanwhile, I own a condo overlooking Central Park that lies vacant fifty weeks a year. I hire people to manage my money for me. Last year, thanks to a competent fund manager and a red-hot NASDAQ, my portfolio appreciated thirty million dollars. It's not anything I *earned.* I started out with wealth, and through the magic of the stock market, it multiplied. I didn't work for it, not the way Kiera does for her paycheck.

I really don't want Kiera to pay for our pizza. I want to spoil her senseless. I want to buy her everything her heart desires—fast cars, pretty baubles, everything.

I give her a searching look. "Really?"

Her shoulders straighten. She lifts her chin in the air. "I thought Bianca was dead; you discovered she was alive. I thought she didn't want to see me; you figured out the truth. You've spent so much of your time, your energy, and your money on this, and what do you get in return? Nothing." She lifts her shoulders in a helpless shrug. "There's nothing I can do to repay the debt I owe you. Please let me pay for dinner."

Is she nuts? The past few weeks have been the best weeks of my life. I take her hands in mine. "There is no debt."

"I know you're rich and money doesn't matter..."

I cut her off. "There's no debt," I repeat. "I don't keep score with the people I love."

The second I say those words, the truth of them resonate in me. I came here to find Martinez. I found Kiera instead. Sometimes, the universe kicks your balls, and sometimes, when you least expect it, it gives you a gift.

I love Kiera.

She's been taking care of herself since she was a child. Her mother was an addict. They were poor. Nothing's come easy for her. Everything's been a struggle. Everything she has is hard-fought.

I love her independence.

When she's alone, Kiera will grieve about what happened to her sister. Whether the emotions are logical or not, guilt over her inability to shelter Bianca will lacerate her.

I love her empathy.

But she's too much of a survivor to let it tear her apart. Kiera won't crumble into pieces. She'll hold it together and she'll march forward, because that's what she's had to do her entire life.

I love her strength.

I haven't known her for very long. A few weeks, really. But sometimes, you don't need weeks or even months to realize the truth. I'm thirty-five. I've crammed a lot of living into those years. There's been a lot of women.

I've never wanted to upend my life for any of them.

I love everything about her. The shades of pink in her hair. The curved, sweeping line of the dragon on her hip. The twinkle in her eyes. The smile on her lips. Her willingness to do what's right. Her boundless enthusiasm. Her curiosity.

Kiera's face is a mask of shock. "What did you say?" she whispers.

I'm still holding her hand. "I love you," I tell her. "I'd do anything for you. It's that simple. If it's important to you to pay for pizza, then have at it. Thank you for dinner. It was delicious. Despite what Caleb might think, spinach and broccoli are excellent toppings."

My friend finally decides to join the conversation. "Repay the debt you owe us?" He sounds outraged. "Ever since Theo and Joha died, I've existed in a fog, going through the motions. You saved me from that. If it weren't for you, I'd have drifted forever. Is there a price I can put on that? Nolan placed himself in increasingly dangerous situations because he never stopped feeling responsible for what happened to Stephan and Lina. Last year, he got shot in Somalia. He was lucky; he didn't die. But his luck would have run out soon enough."

The table next to us is occupied. There's a TV in the

background, showing the baseball game. The Yankees are playing the Red Sox, and the announcer is very excited. His commentary fills the small restaurant, and I have to strain to hear Caleb.

"Then he met you. Now, instead of heading back to Somalia or to the Congo or wherever else he was planning, he's finally using his head. He's giving up on recklessness. I owe you a debt for saving my friend's life. How much do you think that would be worth?"

Kiera draws a deep, shuddering breath. "You love me?" she whispers.

Caleb gives Kiera an exasperated look. "Of course I love you. Now, can someone pay for the pizza, so we can go home?"

She gives us a peculiar look. "I love you too."

I didn't realize how much I needed her to say it back until intense relief sweeps through my body. "Good." I wait until my heart stops racing. "Now, let's go test that bed of yours."

THE SEX WAS AMAZING over the weekend. It's even better this time around. Some of it is just knowing Kiera's body better, but mostly, it's the intimacy. We have something special, the three of us, and we know it.

I lose my clothes. Pull her t-shirt over her head. Her expression is etched with need, her eyes glazed with desire.

She's so beautiful. She steps out of her pants, and her tattoo comes into view, the lines of the dragon vivid against her skin. Her tiny pale pink panties follow, and my throat goes dry.

My cock is hard, achingly so. Her eyes rest on my erection, and she licks her lips, and the gesture sends a shockwave of lust through me. A growl tears free from my throat, and I close the distance between us, wrapping my arms around her hips and tugging her closer. My lips crash down on hers. Our tongues tangle. I feast on her sweetness, and it's addictive. I can't get enough of her.

This feels so damn right.

I love her. She loves me. I'm the luckiest guy in the world.

Caleb gets naked too. He kisses the back of her neck, and she moans as his stubble grazes her sensitive skin. I feel her shiver in response, and God, it's hot. She's so keyed up, so responsive.

I tease her pert nipples, squeeze her lush breasts. Her quiet gasps, her whimpers, her sighs of pleasure, they inflame me. I trail my fingers between her legs, and she's slick. She's ready, so ready. She's quivering with anticipation, and fuck me, she's so hot, I almost lose my load right there.

"Bed," I grind out.

Any other day, we'd make her wait. Tonight, I can't. I'm just too impatient. I want to sink into her softness. I want to feel her muscles grip my cock, and I want to hear her moan out my name, her eyes hazy with lust.

"Excellent idea," Caleb agrees.

We half-walk, half-stumble to her bed. It is a tight squeeze, but it doesn't matter. I lie back on the mattress and roll a condom over my cock. Kiera straddles my hips and sinks onto my length, and I groan out loud, the harsh guttural sound tearing from my throat.

She's so hot, so slick, so fucking perfect.

"I want to suck your cock," she whispers to Caleb. Her fingers close over the base of his shaft, and she opens those perfect lips and takes him in. I grab her hips and thrust up into her.

I've been controlled before. I've taken her to the edge of orgasm, over and over again, until she's a quivering mess, desperate to find her own pleasure.

But today, my self-control is in tatters. Pure hunger is all that is left. Our lovemaking is raw and real. It's fevered and almost desperate. And when her muscles tighten around my cock, and I explode, her name is on my lips.

I never expected to fall in love. Love was for people that were whole, and for most of my adult life, I've felt broken.

I don't feel broken now. I feel sated and at peace.

But the peace is a fragile illusion. We're going to take Bianca away from Luis Martinez. Martinez is a dangerous, vicious killer, a predator who knows about Kiera's existence.

The moment Bianca goes missing, he'll home in on Kiera like a deep-water shark sensing a drop of blood in the ocean. A cold chill runs down my back. As long as Martinez remains free, Kiera is in danger.

I stare up at the ceiling. It's up to Caleb and me to keep her safe.

I failed Stephan and Lina. In the quiet of Kiera's bedroom, I make a silent promise. This time, I won't screw up.

34

KIERA

The morning comes far too early. I'm in the middle of a very pleasant dream when my alarm goes off.

I roll over, tug the cotton sheet over my face, and bury my head under the pillow. I don't want to wake up. Nolan, Caleb, and I are driving on a winding mountain road in a red convertible. On one side of us are cliffs that reach for the cloudless sky, and on the other, a sheer drop to the ocean.

The sun shines down on us. Music is playing on the car radio. Nolan's driving, a daredevil gleam in his eyes. There are no guardrails, and if we fall, we will plunge to our deaths. I'm not the slightest bit afraid.

The alarm shrieks again, rudely intruding into my fantasy. Grr.

Slapping the button, I sit up. Neither Nolan nor Caleb are in bed, but I hear sounds of voices in the kitchen. I pull a long t-shirt over my head and follow the smell of freshly brewed coffee.

Caleb looks up when I walk in. "Rise and shine," he says cheerfully.

“Oh God, you’re a morning person,” I groan. I can barely keep my eyes open, and he looks like he’s ready to run a marathon. Kill me now. “I’m rethinking our relationship.”

Relationship. Shit. *Should I have said that?* I mean, we said we loved each other last night, and yes, Caleb asked me to move into his place as long as Luis Martinez was a threat, but we haven’t really discussed things. What if I’m jumping to conclusions?

Fuck. I’ve never been in a real relationship. I don’t know how any of this is supposed to work.

“He’s not,” Nolan says blearily. He looks the way I feel. Half-asleep, and ready to go back to bed and stay there for a few more hours. “He’s good at faking it. He’s had three cups of coffee.”

“You’re giving away all my secrets. Last year, Nala decided she wanted to be a figure skater. Practice was at six. Then the women’s soccer team won the World Cup, and she now wants to be a forward. Thank heavens, no more early morning starts.” Caleb hands me a cup of coffee with a grin. “I hope you don’t mind me ransacking your cupboards.”

I take the mug from Caleb and sit down. “Not at all.”

There are so many dating ‘rules.’ Guys are afraid of commitment. Women can’t chase. Yet I said ‘relationship,’ and neither of them even registered it, much less freak out.

Is this what scening with them would be like? Clear communication, no games, no drama? If so, *I can’t wait.*

“What are you thinking about?” Nolan asks interestedly.

My cheeks heat. “Scening with you in the club,” I admit. “I want to do it.”

A smile blooms on Caleb’s face. “That can be arranged,” he says. “I’m coaching Nala’s team again tonight, and I have a work dinner Friday. How about Saturday night?”

I'm working, but I can trade shifts with Kellie and get off early. "I can be done at nine."

"Excellent. It's a date."

Caleb's voice is drenched with male satisfaction. Nolan's gaze heats. Electricity crackles between us. If I didn't have to be at the diner in forty-five minutes, I'd be tempted to jump them.

Oh, who am I kidding? I'm still tempted. I set my mug down on the table. "I need to shower. Join me?"

No surprise, I'm the last one to arrive at Jenny's Diner. Fiona, Avery, and Dixie are already there, inhaling cups of coffee. I take my place at the table with a murmur of apology. As soon as I sit down, Dixie turns to me with a wide smile.

"So, Kiera." She sounds gleeful. "How come you blew us off last Sunday?"

She knows perfectly well why. I'd been at Nolan's Manhattan condo, having crazy threesome sex with two of the hottest guys I've ever seen in my life.

I give her a death glare; it bounces right off her. *That's the way it's going to be?*

I'm saved by Jenny's son. He fills my cup of coffee. "Are you ready to order?"

Early as it is, we're not the only ones here. Jenny's is popular, and even though it's six-thirty, well over a quarter of the tables are occupied. That explains the harried expression on Matt's face.

We order. Once Matt walks away, I turn to Avery. "I never did ask you how your weekend was."

"It was great," she says. "Until a client called me in the middle of dinner, threatening to kill himself."

"What?" Avery's a psychologist. "Seriously? What did you do?"

"I took the call." She grimaces. "He's not the least bit suicidal; he's just manipulative. His wife is trying to leave him; he doesn't want her to."

Ouch. "It takes all sorts."

"I guess." She sounds tired. "I'm really grumpy; I'm running low on empathy. I need a proper vacation. No phone, no email, no way to get in touch with me."

Fiona raises her eyebrow. "Do it. Take Kai and Maddox and disappear somewhere for a week."

"I'm working on it. Maddox has an exhibit coming up in October, and Kai can't take any time off this month. Maybe November." She shrugs. "Ah well. First world problems. What's going on with you? I hear you're dating Caleb Reeves and some other guy?"

In any other group of friends, the idea that I'm sleeping with two guys *at the same time* would be the topic of intense gossip and scrutiny. Not with these women though.

"Nolan Wolanski," I say. A grin spreads over my face, and I can't hold it back. I'd spill the dirt—these women are my friends, and after so many years of being guarded, it's such a relief not to hold back—but first, I've got to give Dix a hard time. "Speaking of which, Dix, what's the deal between you and those two guys you met at the club? Eric and Hunter, right?"

Fiona's eyes go round. "Hunter Driesse and Eric Kane?"

"You know them?"

"Sure. They're friends with Adrian and Brody. We've had dinner with them plenty of times. You met them at the club? Tell me *everything*."

I bite back my grin. My work here is almost done. "Even better, she was terribly rude to them."

Dixie is from the South. She had a cotillion. She says please and thank you. She's unfailingly polite. She looks around every time she swears, as if she's convinced her mother is going to overhear her and give her a stern talking-to.

"No way," Avery replies at once.

My friend looks like she wants to strangle me. "Mmm," I say solemnly. "I heard she told Eric Kane that Club M was a place for men with small cocks to boss around women."

"You said cock?" Fiona stares at Dix, her expression fascinated. "That actual word?"

Dix sighs. "Thank you, Kiera," she says. My innocent look doesn't fool her in the slightest, not that I thought it would. "Yeah. I said that."

Food arrives, interrupting our conversation. Once Matt sets down the plates and leaves, our heads snap back to Dix. I'm not the only one dying to know what's going on with my friend.

"Fine," she says, resigned. "Here's what happened. A few months ago, Xavier needed to sign something in a hurry, and I had to go to the castle." Her cheeks are red. "It was my first time there. I got lost on my way out and ended up on the club floor. It was a Wednesday, so I thought it was safe to look around."

I exchange a glance with Fiona and Avery. Dixie won't admit it, but she's at least a little curious about BDSM. If she's interested in exploring, Xavier Leforte's club is the perfect place to test the waters. Every room has cameras. The floor crawls with monitors, and they're not at all shy about interfering if they think something is unsafe. Xavier is fanatical about safe, sane, and consensual play.

"And?" Fiona prompts.

"I walked in the middle of a scene, except I didn't realize it." She winces. "The woman was tied to a chair, and these two big guys were *interrogating* her." Her hands make air quotes around the word 'interrogating.' The club was deserted. Dimly lit. There were no monitors to be seen. I jumped to conclusions, thought she was being assaulted, and intervened." She runs a hand over her face. "Hunter and Eric were the doms. I yelled at them, told them they had small cocks for beating up this poor woman."

Avery looks like she's trying not to laugh. "I'm assuming it was a planned scene."

"Of course." Dix groans at the memory. "The woman was a member of Congress. She needed privacy for obvious reasons. I'd just started chewing Hunter and Eric up about what they were doing, when a monitor arrived to clear things up."

Poor Dix. That must have been mortifying. "It was a natural reaction," I tell her.

She shakes her head. "No, I was stupid. Had I stopped for five seconds to think, I would have realized the truth. Why on Earth would intruders wander into a sex club to interrogate their suspect? I ruined a carefully crafted scene." She winces. "The worst thing is, Eric Kane is a financial wizard who's now managing Xavier's portfolio. I see him almost every week. Every time I see him, I relive our hellish meeting."

Avery tilts her head to a side and surveys Dix. "You don't tend to care what other people think of you," she comments. "You like them, don't you? That's why it's so embarrassing."

"I do not like them," Dix says flatly. "Kiera, tell us what's going on with you."

Dix is usually an open book, but she really doesn't want

to discuss Eric and Hunter. I feel bad for bringing up the topic. "I think Caleb, Nolan, and I are in an actual relationship."

"Stop sounding surprised," Fiona chides. "You're amazing."

"Yeah, well." I fill them in on everything that's been going on. Bianca being alive, being trapped with Martinez, everything. Dixie knows most of what's been going on, but Fiona only knows some of it, and I haven't seen Avery for weeks. "Lockhart & Payne are now in charge of whisking my sister to safety."

"I didn't know," Fiona says. "But that's not surprising. Brody and Adrian are very discreet. I rarely know the details about what they're up to." She gives me a confident smile. "I'm biased, of course, but your sister is in very good hands. They'll get her out."

"I hope so." I cross my fingers in my lap as I utter those words. I desperately want everything to work out. My sister has been through hell and back. She deserves a break. More than that, she deserves a lifetime of happiness.

35

KIERA

You know how time seems to slow to a crawl when you're eagerly anticipating something?

Yeah. It takes forever for Saturday evening to roll around. I cast furtive glances at the clock all through my shift. Farid notices my restlessness. "Something the matter?"

"Umm, I guess?" I don't know how Farid's going to react, but as much as I'm a private person, I'm not going to hide what I'm doing with Caleb and Nolan either. "I'm scening with Caleb Reeves and Nolan Wolanski tonight."

I brace myself for judgment, but Farid doesn't look shocked. In fact, he's got a wide grin on his face. "What?" I ask him.

"It's about time," he says, moving past me to reach for a bottle of mescal.

My mouth falls open. "It's about time? That's your reaction? I thought you don't believe in fraternizing with the members."

"I don't," he replies. "I've only seen it lead to one conclusion. Heartbreak and hurt feelings. Club M's members are the one-percenters, Kiera. It isn't their hearts that get broken, and even if that were the case, money can soothe a lot of pain."

His face is serious. "We, on the other hand, still have to show up to work. Still have to face the person that broke our hearts and pretend like nothing's wrong. Pour them drinks with a smile on our faces, while they move on to the next person that catches their eye."

Is he speaking from experience? What I know about Farid is what he chooses to reveal. He likes architecture. He likes to travel. But those are surface things. What lies underneath?

"However," he continues, his tone lightening. "There are always exceptions to every rule. Caleb Reeves hasn't been able to take his eyes off you since you started working here. I don't know very much about Nolan Wolanski, but according to Henri, he rarely scenes at the club."

"I think it's the real thing." It feels surreal to say that out loud. Even more surreal to really believe it. To finally let it sink in.

He pours the mezcal into a cocktail shaker, along with grapefruit juice, simple syrup, and a dash of cardamom-bitters. "I'm happy for you," he says, shaking the drink before pouring it into an iced coupe glass and garnishing it with a wedge of grapefruit and a sprig of mint. The orange-hued cocktail looks delicious, but the woman who's waiting for it isn't looking at the drink. She can't take her eyes off Farid.

"Your guys are here, by the way."

"What?" My heartbeat accelerates. "It's already nine?"

Farid laughs, not unkindly. "Go have fun," he says. "Kelli's not here yet, but it isn't busy. I can handle things until she gets here."

Thanking him, I take off my apron with shaking fingers, hang it up, and then finally turn to Nolan and Caleb. "Hi."

Nolan winks at me. Caleb pushes a key card across the bar. "We've booked Room 203 for the night. Join us?"

It's a different room than the one we were in the last time we tried this. Thank heavens. Back then, I didn't trust Caleb and Nolan, and the night had turned into a disaster.

Things are so very different now.

I pocket the card. "Okay. Give me five minutes to freshen up, and I'll meet you there?"

I KNOCK on the door of the private playroom and wait for it to open. My blood races with anticipation. I'm nervous, but it's a good, excited kind of nervous, the way you feel at the start of a roller-coaster ride.

Nolan opens it. He's taken off his jacket and tie, and his white shirt is open at the neck. His sleeves are rolled up to the elbows. "Come on in."

I take a step into the room, and my eyes widen. The walls are mirrored. Bathed in spotlights, a Y-frame dominates the middle of the room, the Y of the frame horizontal, parallel to the floor. A narrow dresser is tucked away in an alcove, and there's a refrigerator next to it. To my right is a black leather couch. Caleb's seated on it, his legs propped on a highly polished ebony coffee table. When he sees me, he gets to his feet, a smile on his face. "I've missed you," he says, pulling me into his arms.

"I saw you Thursday morning."

"Mmm."

He kisses me, deep and passionate. My knees almost buckle when he's done. "Umm, I'm flattered?"

Nolan chuckles at my expression. "Caleb is a little bit on

edge," he says in explanation. "As am I. Neither of us enjoys waiting."

"Waiting for this?" I point to the Y-frame. "Or waiting for Mr. Lockhart and Mr. Payne to make their move?"

"Both." Nolan's lips twitch at my formality, and then his voice deepens. His stare pins me in place. "Are you going to call me Mr. Wolanski when I'm fucking you tonight, Kiera?"

Arousal prickles through me. "What would you like me to call you, Sir?"

He likes that. His eyes flare in appreciation. "Very nice," he purrs.

Caleb pats the seat next to him. "Come sit," he invites. "Let's talk before we get going. I screwed up the last time we tried this. I don't want to get it wrong this time around."

"You won't," I say confidently, sitting down on the couch. There are no more secrets between us, not anymore.

Nolan sits next to me. "Your confidence is flattering," he says, taking my hand in his. "Let's go over expectations anyway."

"Okay." A sudden thought strikes me. "Should I be kneeling?"

"No," Caleb replies. "Not yet, anyway." His lips lift in a sexy smile, and heat coils through my insides. I can't wait to get started.

"You're a novice," Caleb continues. "We're going to take things very slow. Tonight is about exploring your desires. About finding out what turns you on. The only thing I expect from you is communication. If we do something you don't like, tell us. If we do something that makes you uneasy, please let us know. We're not mind readers."

"I don't know what I like or don't like."

Nolan flashes me a reassuring smile. "Then we'll learn together. Caleb and I have come up with a plan, but if you hate it, we can improvise. Don't feel like you have to love everything we do, okay? I'm not going to push your boundaries in today's scene, no more than I'd throw someone who just started learning to swim into the deep end of the pool."

I nod.

"Now, limits," Caleb says. "Here are mine."

I'm momentarily startled, and then I realize that of course dominants would have limits too. They're human, at the end of the day.

"Like you, I don't like blood. Needle play is out for me. If you ever want to try that, you'll have to explore with someone else."

That's a hard pass. "No blood for me," I say promptly. "I've seen needle play, and it's definitely outside my comfort zone."

"I don't do name-calling," Nolan adds. "I'm not big on humiliation. If you want someone to call you a stupid bitch in session, that's not me."

"You call me a stupid bitch, and I'll knee you in the groin."

Nolan quirks a pointed eyebrow, and I wince. I've been here for less than five minutes, and I'm already breaking the rules. "I'll knee you in the groin, Sir."

"I'll keep that in mind," he says, his lips twitching. "Since it's your first time, I'll give you a choice. Do you want to know what we've got planned, or do you want to be surprised?"

I think about his question. "I want to be surprised."

"Do you have any questions for us?" Caleb asks.

I don't have a question as much as a concern. Part of me wants to swallow my insecurities, but then Caleb's words echo in my ears. *The only thing I expect from you is communication.*

"I'm a complete novice," I murmur, my face flaming. I can't look at them. "You're both experienced dominants. Is tonight going to be boring for you?"

Caleb gives me a stupefied look. "Boring? Kiera, I'm crazy about you. The fact that you trust us with your first time... it's special."

"I'm not very submissive," I persist. I know I'm asking a lot of questions, but I don't want to screw up either. Caleb and Nolan are too important to me.

"What does that even mean?" Nolan asks. "Neither of us are looking for a full-time submissive, is that what you're talking about?"

"What if I hate... everything?" I guess I'm more nervous than I think I am. Not because of what the session might hold—no, when I think of that, all I feel is heady anticipation. I just don't want to disappoint Caleb and Nolan. "You obviously like and enjoy BDSM. You spend a lot of time in the club. If I hate it, what happens?"

Caleb wraps his arm around my shoulder. "I've spent a lot of time in the club since you started working here," he corrects. "Okay, the BDSM thing. Let's see if I can explain it." His forehead furrows, and then his expression clears. "Let's try this. Do you like Coke or Pepsi?"

Why are we talking about pop? "I don't really care. I know most people have a preference, but I don't. Either gives me the sugar fix I need."

Caleb bites back a smile. "You already knew that, didn't you?" I accuse him. "Sir," I add as an afterthought.

"I did know, yes. You've just described my attitude toward BDSM. I enjoy it. I also enjoy vanilla sex. Some people need one and not the other, but that's not me. There is nothing that could happen here tonight that's going to change the way I feel about you." His eyes rest on me. "Any other questions?"

Stop stalling, Kiera. "No," I reply. "No more questions. I'm ready."

"Good." The cadence of Caleb's voice changes. It becomes smoother. Crisper. More self-assured. Dom voice. We're in session now. When he says jump, I don't stop to ask how high. I just jump. "Stand up."

I get to my feet.

Caleb and Nolan rise as well. "Move over there," Nolan says, pointing to a spot to the right of the Y-frame.

I teeter over on shaky feet.

"Tonight," Nolan says, low and intent. "We own you, Kiera. When you moan, it's for us. When your muscles clench with desire, it's for us. Your orgasms belong to Caleb and me. Is that understood?"

I nod, my throat dry with anticipation. "Yes, Sir."

Nolan walks to the dresser and returns with a pair of scissors in his hand. "Do you have a spare set of clothes in your locker?"

Oh. My. God. He's going to cut off my uniform. A dizzy rush sweeps through my body. "Yes, Sir." I clear my throat as a prosaic thought intrudes. "It's hard to find a bra that fits that doesn't also cost an arm and a leg."

Nolan grins. "Don't cut off the bra. Duly noted."

The blade is cool. My skin breaks out into goosebumps as Nolan snips my skirt. The fabric falls in a pool by my feet. Two more snips, and my panties follow. He cuts my t-shirt too, but as promised, he unhooks my bra and tosses it on the couch.

Caleb's been watching me, his expression smoldering. When I'm naked, his eyes widen. "You shaved?"

My cheeks heat. "I got waxed, actually." I went to the

salon Thursday night. The woman said it wouldn't hurt, but she's a liar; it hurt like the devil. Never doing that again. "I thought I'd mix it up. What do you think?"

His mouth finds mine. His tongue swipes over my lower lip. "You're always hot to me," he murmurs. His hand trails down my stomach and his fingers find my folds. "Mmm. Very nice."

I start to lean into him, but he straightens and gives me an inscrutable half-smile. "The first night you came over to my house, you asked me if I was going to spank you."

I remember. The events of that night are seared into my memory. Caleb had positioned me on his coffee table, and he'd gone down on me, and watching us, Nolan had jerked himself off.

"I've been thinking about your request." He circles me slowly, his eyes staying on mine. "I think I'll fulfill it tonight, Kiera."

My breath skips. "You've spanked me a few times since then."

Nolan chuckles, low and amused. "Ah, sweetheart," he says. "You think those were spankings." He nears me, threads his fingers through my hair, and presses a hard kiss on the back of my neck. My scalp prickles. His grip is dominant, and the pain is delicious. He's not pulling hard enough to seriously hurt, but there's just enough edge in his grip to paint another layer of arousal over me.

I shudder with my need, shudder to hold still. "You remember your safewords?"

"Yes, Sir. Green if I'm okay, Yellow if I'm not sure, Red to stop."

"Good." Without warning, he swings me into his arms and sets me down on the Y-frame, stomach down, ass in the air. "Get comfortable," he advises, dark amusement threaded through his voice. "You're going to be here for some time."

The frame is padded, the trunk of the Y wide enough to comfortably support my body but narrow enough that my breasts hang down on either side. My legs are spread wide. I can see myself in the mirrored walls, completely naked, completely open to them.

Another shiver wracks my body as Nolan moves around me, spreading my legs even wider apart and strapping them in place on the frame.

I don't know how to describe the feeling that comes over me as he carefully buckles each strap into place.

Xavier Leforte owns several boutique hotels all around the world. As employees of his organization, we're offered discounts on hotel stays, but it's still far too expensive to afford. However, one Christmas, two years ago, a few of us did a staff trip to a spa in Vermont that Mr. Leforte owns.

There was an underground salt pool there. Amy couldn't do it. "It's too claustrophobic," she'd shuddered. "It's too dark, too gloomy. The room's closing in around me."

Not me. I'd savored every minute in that salt pool. I'd closed my eyes and floated in perfect, meditative silence, and it was freeing. Almost trance-like.

With each strap Nolan buckles around my body, I feel myself fall deeper into that same trance. He ties me up at the ankles. Just above my knees. Another set of bindings sit at my thighs, just below my butt. The leather doesn't cut into my skin, but it's tight enough that I can't wriggle.

My movement's cut off. I should be nervous. I just feel free.

Nolan watches me test my bonds, a small smile playing about his lips. "I don't want you falling off."

"I'm so green," I whisper.

"Yes, you are." He can see my arousal in my eyes; I'm making no effort to hide the way I feel. My nipples are swollen. My pussy clenches with need.

He moves between my legs. In the mirror, I watch him bend down. His tongue swipes through my folds, tasting me, feasting on me. "Wet already," he growls. "Who is this arousal for, Kiera?"

"For you, Sir."

It's all for them. I'm not anti-BDSM, not the way Dix claims she is, but though I've worked at Club M for years, I've never been interested in trying it. Then again, I've never met someone that I dropped my guard around.

BDSM is about trust. I trust Caleb and Nolan completely. That's why I'm here, tied to a Y-frame, entirely at their mercy. That's why my bindings are erotic, not terrifying. That's why I'm turned on. That's why I ache. That's why my entire body vibrates with desire.

It's because I'm doing this with Nolan and Caleb.

I'm restrained for them.

I'm wet for them.

It's all for them. Every shiver. Every moan. Every orgasm.

Caleb moves into my vision. "I'm going to blindfold you, Kiera."

Another shiver runs through me. "Yes, Sir," I whisper. "Thank you, Sir."

The blindfold is a long narrow black scarf. Caleb loops it around my head several times, cutting off my vision. "How's that?" he asks, resting his fingertips on my shoulder.

I can't see anything. "Still green, Sir."

I feel myself sink even deeper into my blissful, floaty feeling. Nolan's hands are at my waist, strapping me in place. He takes my hands in his, extends my arms out to the front, and ties my wrists together, and then to the frame.

Hands touch my breasts. They squeeze them. Sometimes the touch is casual and fleeting, and sometimes, it's more intent. My nipples are swollen, aroused. I whimper, my body ablaze.

A tongue swipes over my right nipple.

Another tongue licks the left.

Oh fuck. A jolt of arousal shocks through me. If my legs weren't tied apart, I'd squeeze them. I want to squirm, to wriggle, to do something to alleviate the ache in my pussy...

Nolan and Caleb suck my erect nipples into their mouths, scraping the tender flesh between their teeth. They suck and they nibble until my thoughts are scrambled, my breath comes faster, and I'm so wet that I'm positive my juices are dripping on the polished wooden floor.

They stop.

Cool air brushes over my over-sensitized nipples, and then something bites down on an engorged nub.

Nipple clamp.

"This is a tweezer-style clamp," Nolan says. "I'm going to tighten it. Tell me when it gets too much."

My nipple throbs. The tension grows as Nolan slides the ring tighter, his breath warm against my ear. My core clenches. My nipple hurts, but in a good way. Caleb's hand rests on the base of my spine, touching me, anchoring me. I can't see him, but I can feel him. He's letting me know he's there.

The ache in my nipple tips from good-pain to bad. "Ouch," I yelp.

Nolan eases the pressure fractionally. His fingers skim the side of my breast. His tongue laves attention on my swollen nipple. I whimper in pleasure, and he pulls his mouth off. "Okay?"

"Yes Sir." Every time I say Sir, it makes me feel a little lighter. A little freer. It's an addictive rush. "I'm green again."

He moves around the other side and clamps my other nipple.

Caleb, in the meanwhile, has moved away. I strain to listen to his movements, trying to hear what he's doing, and yelp like a startled puppy when he says "No," his voice at my ear. Damn it, Caleb can move like a cat if he wants.

"Don't," he says sternly. "You'll find out what we're doing soon enough. Just be."

"Sorry," I whisper, abashed. I take a deep breath. Exhale. Another deep breath. Exhale. *Let yourself sink back into the pool.*

A dozen strings trail down my spine, and then a flogger snaps down on my ass.

I bite my lips to keep myself from crying out. Heat sears my skin. Every muscle of my body clenches in response. Oh God. Why have I never done this before? I've stood on the sidelines and watched submissives get flogged, whipped, even caned, and I've never quite understood the need that drives them. I get it now. Yes, the flogger hurts, but in such a good way. Such a perfect, *necessary* way.

A hard cock brushes against my fingertips. Nolan's voice sounds in front of me. "You know what to do, sweetness."

Yes, I do know what to do.

The wrist bindings don't give me a lot of movement, but I do my best. I stroke Nolan's length, focusing on him, focusing on the way he feels. Velvety smooth, hard as steel. I drag my thumb over the tip, spreading precum around his head, and I shiver as he groans, raw need in his voice.

Caleb cracks the flogger against my ass, quick and forceful. I yelp, more from surprise than pain. "Green," I say quickly before he stops. "Don't hold back. I promise I'll remember my safewords."

Nolan's fingers twist my hair, and I realize I stopped stroking him. *Oops.*

Caleb trails the flogger over my back. "I'm glad you said that," he says, his voice smooth, controlled. He swings, and the tails connect with my skin. I clench, but the pain fades, leaving warmth in its wake. I relax, and the whip comes down again, a sharp bolt of fire. "Because we're just getting started."

We are? *Oh boy.* Fresh anticipation snakes through my blood.

I wait for the next stroke of the flogger, but it doesn't come. Nolan's still in front of me, but where is Caleb? I can't hear him.

"Did I not tell you to relax, Kiera?"

Damn it. You try relaxing when someone's flogging you, I want to snark, but I hold my tongue. Caleb wouldn't ask me to do anything that is impossible. He won't set me up to fail.

I don't want to disappoint him.

Salt pool, I whisper to myself. *Remember the warmth in the room. The absolute peace. Fall into it.*

The room is silent, the quiet broken only by the sound of Nolan's harsh breathing. His massive cock is in my fist, and I pump him, the movement rhythmic, almost meditative. I sink back into my trance.

Something hot splashes the back of my thigh, hardening almost immediately.

Candle wax.

Oh.

Oh.

I've seen wax play at the club. It's always fascinated me. Watching the dom holding the candle over his or her sub, drops of colored wax falling on bare skin... I find it strangely hypnotic. It's one of the few things I've always been curious about. How would it feel?

Has Caleb noticed my interest? I wouldn't put it past him. Or is this just a happy coincidence?

Another hot drop, this time on my shoulder. It cools on my skin almost immediately. I stroke Nolan's thick cock, whimpering as hot claws of need rake through my core.

The blindfold around my eyes comes loose. Nolan's untied it. "I want you to watch," he says, his voice hoarse. "Look how beautiful you are." There's a screen on the wall. Was that always here? It must have been. The screen is showing the security feed from one of the ceiling cameras. I see Caleb's arm in the frame, and then hot ribbons of blue and red pool on my skin.

Drops of wax rain down on me, kissing my skin with fire.

On the back of my thighs.

Down my spine. My lower back. My shoulder blades.

The curve of my ass.

And then, on my newly waxed pussy.

I whimper out loud when the wax drips down my folds. "Please," I beg. My skin is so sensitive. The wax has brought every nerve to the surface. I feel on fire. "Please touch me, Sir. Please let me come."

Caleb laughs, low and deep. "So quickly?" he asks, trailing his skin down my spine. I arch into his touch like a cat. "I don't think so, baby."

He picks up a candle again. I take another deep breath and surrender to the tangle of feelings. It's hot and achy. Pure pleasure and torture, all rolled in one. So good.

I don't know how long I float. I stroke Nolan's cock. I watch my image on the screen, watch my back get decorated with wax. It's happening to me, but it also feels like it's happening to someone else, as if I'm disassociated from it.

The heat builds on my skin, and in my core. Underneath the floaty peace, my arousal roils, an underwater swell that builds higher and higher, until I'm squirming in my bindings, desperate for one of them to touch my clit, my pussy. "Please," I beg again.

"I think she wants to come." Caleb's hot, dark gaze holds mine. "What do you think, Nolan? Should I let her?"

I hold my breath.

"Not yet," Nolan replies casually. My heart sinks. "But soon."

Soon. That's good, right? I cling to hope.

"First," Nolan says, "We've got to do something about that wax."

Caleb chuckles. "Fair enough. Trade places with me."

Nolan pulls away. Before I can whimper about the loss of his cock, Caleb is at my side, his cock inches from my lips. "Open up, baby."

I thought he'd never ask.

I take Caleb's cock in my mouth, moaning in my throat. I suck him and bob on him, my movements almost desperate. Need claws through me, and I know that if either of them just so much as brushes against my clit, I'm going to explode.

Caleb's hips are blocking my vision. I can't see the TV anymore. Can't see what Nolan's up to.

Not until he thrusts into me, his full length sliding deep into my wetness.

Oh. My. God.

Caleb fucks my throat. Nolan pounds my pussy. I'm caught between the two of them, tied up, immobilized, more painfully aroused than I've ever been in my life. The way they feel... it's pure pleasure. They're powerful. All male. I moan into Caleb's cock as Nolan takes me, his strokes deep, fast, raw.

The flogger slaps down on my back. Oh God, oh God. Nolan's whipping bits of wax off my skin. I didn't think my arousal could wind tighter, but it does. My back feels tender. My skin is hot. Blazing. Nolan's strokes sting, but I can take it. I welcome it. I feel myself arch up to meet the tails of the flogger.

Overwhelming. Sensation. Everywhere.

Nolan groans out loud and pulls free from me. His hands undo the straps. Caleb lifts me off the Y-frame and carries me to the couch. "We're going to take you now," he growls. "Both of us. You're going to take my cock in your ass, and Nolan's cock in your pussy."

I almost come from just those words. Nolan lies on the couch and positions me over him. My legs straddle his hips, and I sink onto his hard cock. Caleb's fingers tease my asshole, and I whimper in anticipation. I want this. I want this so much.

"So wet," Nolan growls. His hands dig into my hips, and he fucks me deep and hard. At the same time, Caleb pushes harder on my tight hole, his fingers slick with lube. He spreads me open, two fingers sliding into my ass, and I whimper as another layer of sensation paints my body. This is so naughty, so wickedly good. "You want to be filled up by us?"

"Please," I pant.

Nolan pulls me forward. My breasts mash into his chest, and my clamped nipples ache in the best possible way. Caleb looms behind me. The head of his cock nudges at my tight hole, and then, he pushes, slow and steady.

My muscles stretch as his length invades my ass. An

inferno of pleasure blazes through me. I thought the butt plug was hot, but the plug is nothing compared to the feeling of Caleb's cock sliding into me. I whimper as the head of his erection penetrates my tight ring, and Nolan's mouth covers mine.

"Do you want me to stop?" Caleb sounds strained.

I shake my head immediately. Caleb continues to ease into me, filling me completely. When his full length is in my ass, he threads his fingers through my hair. "Beg us," he orders, his voice hoarse. "Beg us to fuck you."

"Oh God, yes." I'm dizzy with desire. I'm completely filled by their cocks. If they move, even just a little, I'm going to explode. "Please fuck me."

Nolan growls under his breath. "Anything for you, Kiera."

And then they fuck me.

Two thick cocks drive into me, making me mindless with lust. I writhe between them, whimpering, moaning, burning with pleasure. They claim me, and it feels momentous. Nolan's fingers toy with my swollen nipples, and his mouth swallows my moans. Caleb's length plunges in and out of my ass, stretching my tight muscles.

I scream in pleasure. They're so deep, and it's so good. "Please," I beg. "Please let me come."

Nolan grins wickedly. I hear whirring. A vibrator hums against my clit. *Where did that come from?* I whimper, alarmed. "I can't hold back." The words pour from my mouth. "I can't."

Nolan's fingers thread through my hair. He tilts my head up so I can stare into his eyes. "I love you," he says. "Come for us, Kiera."

More than anything else, it's the words and the accompanying tenderness in his voice that pushes me over the edge. Caleb's fingers dig into my hips. The vibrator attacks my clit, and I start to shake. My skin beads with sweat. It's there, so close. It's there, just within reach.

And then I'm hurtling. Lost in an explosion of sensation, drowning in wave after wave of pleasure. I hear their muffled shouts of release. I float in an endless ocean of satiated bliss.

I don't notice them remove the nipple clamps, though I definitely feel it when blood comes rushing back into my nipples. Caleb winces in sympathy, and his mouth closes over my nipples, soothing them until the pain fades. Nolan hands me a bottle of water, and crouches down in front of me. "Drink," he orders.

I do as he says. When I'm done with the water, Caleb smooths cooling lotion over my skin, and then wraps me in a soft robe. I sit between my two guys, contentment filling my heart. "That was amazing. Can we do it again?

Caleb laughs and kisses my cheek. "Yes. But not today."

What about tomorrow, I'm about to ask, when there's a series of knocks on the door. Nolan mutters a curse under his breath. "Go away," he says, lifting his voice.

Another knock. "It's me," Xavier Leforte calls from the other side of the door. "Get dressed. I'm coming in."

Caleb raises an eyebrow, but gets up and pulls on his pants, as does Nolan. I draw the robe tightly around me, a lump in my throat. Caleb notices my anxiety and wraps an arm around me. "Don't worry," he says. "This isn't about you. Xavier wouldn't interrupt aftercare to yell at us."

I hope so.

Nolan opens the door. My boss sticks his head into the room, his expression unreadable.

"Am I fired?" I blurt out.

"What?" Xavier's expression is confused. "No, of course

not." He looks at Caleb and Nolan. "You don't have your phones switched on," he says accusingly.

Caleb raises an eyebrow, keeping his arm around me. "Club rules, remember? Section one-point-whatever? Xavier, this is dreadful timing. Go away."

Xavier exhales slowly. He looks like he's counting to ten. "I need to talk to one of you," he says curtly. "It's urgent."

Nolan puts on his shirt and rises to his feet. "I'll go."

I watch the door swing shut behind them. What's going on? What could be so important that Xavier had to talk with Nolan right away?

36

NOLAN

"We have a situation," Xavier says as the two of us walk out of the club floor in the direction of the elevators. "Lockhart and Payne's team saw an opportunity tonight, and they grabbed it."

I stop dead in my tracks. "They have Bianca?"

"Yes." We walk through a staff-only door. No cameras in this part of the castle. "She's here."

"Here?"

"Our security is good," he replies. "The team hadn't planned on extracting Bianca Thompson tonight. Aydin was in charge, and they were being pursued."

"Ah." In a previous life, Omer Aydin was a commander in the Turkish Army. Maroon Berets, Turkish Special Forces. He's scarily competent. Adrian and Brody put one of their best people in charge of this operation. "Is she hurt?"

"No. She's fine. Henri put her in a bedroom upstairs. I thought you'd want to talk to her before Kiera did. Omer didn't debrief her; that wasn't part of his instructions."

That was thoughtful of Xavier. Kiera's just finished her first scene. If Bianca doesn't want to see her, or if she's going to rage at her sister for abandoning her, I want to protect the woman I love. I have no right to keep Kiera and her sister apart, but I won't expose her to Bianca's anger tonight. "Thank you, Xavier."

"Not a problem." We take the staff elevator to the top floor. "She's in the Orange Room. The access code is nine-seven-three-eight-four-five."

"You locked her in?"

"Would you prefer that she accidentally wanders into the club floor and stumbles on you flogging her sister?" he asks caustically.

Yeah, that might not have been the best setting for a family reunion. "Valid point. Does she know why she's here?"

Xavier shakes his head.

"She doesn't know she's been rescued? She thinks she's been kidnapped?"

The elevator arrives and the doors slide open. Xavier punches in an override code and takes it out of service. "Omer's team took gunfire. Rachel was hit."

Anxiety stabs me. Omer and Rachel Abara have worked together for a long time. "Is she okay?"

"She's stable. Adrian and Brody are at the hospital now, as is Omer." He grimaces. "Martinez's security team fired their guns in the middle of Manhattan. NYPD swarmed the scene."

"Martinez will be on high alert." Fuck. If he goes underground now, it'll be years before he surfaces again. The man has a dozen passports, money hidden all over the world, and powerful connections that will protect him. We've freed Bianca, but at what cost?

Xavier sees the expression on my face. "You put Kiera first," he reminds me quietly. "You made the right call."

I take a deep breath. Xavier's right. Yes, I'd have liked to take Martinez down. But if it comes down to a choice, I will pick Kiera every single day. "Time to talk to Bianca."

THE ORANGE ROOM is at the end of the corridor. I punch in the access code, and the lock disengages. I knock.

"Come on in."

I enter. Bianca Thompson is standing by the window. "Don't worry," she says, not turning around. "I'm not thinking of jumping."

"That's reassuring to hear." I advance into the room. "You're probably wondering who I am and why you're here."

"The second part is perfectly obvious. You saw me, you wanted me, you took me." She finally turns. She's blonde, like Kiera, but her face is thinner, and her eyes are harder. Life hasn't been kind to Bianca Thompson, and her eyes wear the proof. "Whoever you are, you've just signed your death warrant. Luis will hunt for me."

"I'm quaking in my boots." She doesn't trust me, and that's okay. I don't expect her to. "You're safe from Martinez here. My name is Nolan Wolanski. I'm in a relationship with your sister."

"Kiera?" Shock slaps her face. "What have you done?" Her voice rises. "Luis will find her, and he'll hurt her."

Her fear is real and palpable. We were right; she isn't with Martinez by choice. "I promise you that he won't." I sit down on a spindly chair that creaks under my weight. Knowing Xavier, it's probably a priceless antique. "I know who Martinez is. I know what he's capable of. Your sister is protected, Ms. Thompson. She's safe, and so are you."

"No, we're not," she says flatly. Her voice doesn't betray her emotions, but she can't conceal the tremor in her hands.

"Luis is obsessed with me. He'll never let me go; I will never be safe. If I disappear, he'll make Greg find me."

"Greg Dratch is no longer relevant," I reply. "He can't help Martinez find you. He's in jail."

"That's never stopped him before," she says bitterly.

"It will this time. Have you heard of a man called Anton Nekrasov?"

Her head snaps up. "The Russian."

Anton's reputation saves the day. If I tell him, he'll be impossibly smug. "We gave Dratch a choice. He could either go to prison, or we'd surrender him to Nekrasov's custody. You understand what that means."

The first sign of hope dawns on her face, but it quickly smothers out. Bianca Thompson has gone through too much to believe in happy endings. "You don't know what you're dealing with," she insists. "Luis... he will go after Kiera." She wipes her palms on her dress. "Greg told me Kiera was dead, but the night Luis bought me, he showed me pictures. Kiera wasn't dead; she was in witness protection. The detective who was supposed to be protecting her identity had sold her out." Her voice turns lifeless again. "He swore to me that if I ever tried to leave him, he'd make my sister pay. I believe him."

"When Mandy gave you Kiera's note, you told her you didn't want to see Kiera. Are you angry with your sister?" I'm being blunt, but I don't want to see Kiera heartbroken tonight.

"That was you?" She shakes her head. "I was terrified. Luis is... jealous. Wildly possessive. He has me watched around the clock. He flies into a rage if a man even looks at me. I'm not allowed to have friends. He wants me alone, isolated, completely dependent on him."

"That's why you never visited Kiera?" I persist. "You

knew where she lived, yet you never once called her to let her know you were alive."

Her eyes narrow. "Is this an interrogation, Mr. Wolanski? I don't know where Kiera lives, but even if I had, it wouldn't have mattered. If I gave Luis the slightest sign that Kiera's well-being was important to me, I would have been putting her in even more danger. My love for my sister is the weapon Martinez has used on me for three years."

"You don't know where Kiera lives? That's not what you told Mandy."

"I don't remember what I told the woman. I just wanted her gone before my bodyguards entered the washroom."

She's telling the truth.

"Luis doesn't know either," she continues, answering what would have been my next question. "I'm sure of it. If he knew where Kiera lived, he'd have taken me outside her house. He'd have taunted me with that information. He would have told me that if I behaved myself, then maybe I'd be allowed to see my sister."

Miles Armstrong never gave Luis Martinez Kiera's precise location. I'll be damned. Did the detective have a belated attack of conscience?

"But he'll find out," Bianca finishes. "So far, he hasn't needed Kiera's location. But now I've disappeared, and he needs leverage. One way or the other, he'll get it from the detective."

Armstrong's life could be in danger. Too bad. Crooked detectives who take bribes from criminals are not my concern.

I stand up. The chair creaks alarmingly. "Your sister is the most important person in my life," I tell Bianca. "And you're important to her. I meant what I said. You're safe now.

Martinez won't touch you again. Let me help you. Please. For Kiera's sake."

I've helped people before, but it's always been anonymous. But this time, I'm helping Kiera's sister. This time, I get to see the joy on Kiera's face when she lays eyes on Bianca.

It won't undo what happened to Lina and Stephan. Nothing will do that. But for the first time in years, I feel at peace. I can have love and happiness now, because I finally deserve it.

"What can you do?"

I smile. "For starters, I can tell you that Kiera is downstairs. Would you like to meet your sister?"

37

KIERA

It's been eight years since I saw Bianca.

For eight years, I thought she was dead. For eight years, I wrestled with my failure to protect my younger sister. For eight years, there was a gaping wound in my heart, one that never healed.

But she's alive, and even more incredibly, she's here at Club M.

There are tears, of course. I turn into a weeping faucet as I hug my baby sister, and she's not much better. I cry for the wasted years, I weep for the horrors that Bianca has had to endure, and I mourn the irrevocable loss of her childhood.

But there's also joy, and a profound gratitude. *This is a miracle.* If someone told me three months ago that my sister was alive and I would be reunited with her, I would have laughed bitterly and wondered what sort of mind-altering drugs they were on.

We talk for hours. Bianca doesn't want to talk about her life, so she asks me questions about mine, and I fill her in on what I've been doing in the last eight years. I tell her about going into witness protection, changing my name, and moving across the country to start over. "I was so naive," I say bitterly. "Detective Armstrong told me you'd died in the bar fire. The body I saw was charred beyond recognition. I was such a fool."

Bianca shakes her head. "You weren't the fool. I thought Greg loved me. He promised me a better life, and I believed him." Her eyes are bleak. "Then it went to hell, but by then, it was too late. I thought I was all alone."

"You were fifteen," I tell her fiercely. "Nothing that happened to you is your fault."

Two people did this to us. Greg Dratch, motivated by lust and greed, preyed on a child. Miles Armstrong wanted the head of the Kitai Bratva in jail. He'd lied to me. He made me believe that I was all alone, that my sister was dead. All of this to ensure I testified at Vladimir Sirkovich's trial.

She gives me a small smile. "You're always on my side, Ki. I don't deserve your support."

"Yes, you do." I keep talking before she can protest again. "Anyway. I moved around a lot at the start, and then I came here, and I started working at Club M."

"My straitlaced big sister working in a sex club." She smiles wryly at my look of surprise. "I have heard of it, Kiera. It's pretty well known in the right circles."

"Yes, well. It paid well, and that's all I cared about at the start." I always needed the money. Moving was expensive. Apartments I could rent on a short-term basis weren't cheap. I needed a cash reserve so I could run at a moment's notice. "It was eye-opening though. On my first day, there was a wax play demo on the main floor. I didn't know where to look." My cheeks heat. Less than an hour ago, Nolan and Caleb had dripped wax over me, and I'd come harder than I've ever come in my life.

"The guy who was here earlier, he said he was dating you."

I blush harder. "Nolan. Yeah." Oh God, this is awkward. "There are two of them, actually. Nolan and Caleb. I met them at the club. They were the ones that found you."

Her eyebrows climb. "Two guys? You?"

"I'm not as straitlaced as you think I am," I say defensively.

Bianca chuckles. "I'm just teasing you. I'm grateful to them. I never thought I'd see you again." Her expression sharpens. "Membership here isn't cheap. They're rich, I assume. Do they respect you? Do they treat you well?"

"They're pretty great."

"How did they find me?"

"It started with a photo of Greg Dratch on Caleb's computer." I tell her the rest of it. How one of Caleb and Nolan's friends had remembered seeing Bianca in a party in Colombia. She'd had a photo. That picture had led to Caleb's analyst locating Bianca in New York. "Nolan's been after Martinez for a long time," I finish.

Fear flashes across Bianca's face when I mention Martinez. "Kiera, listen to me," she says urgently. "I warned Nolan already, but he didn't take me seriously. I understand Luis better than anyone else. I had to; knowing every single one of his moods has kept me alive. Luis is..."

Her voice trails off. She swallows hard. "When Luis gets angry, he goes cold, and he gets even. I was his possession; I got away. In his world, there's no forgiveness for that kind of betrayal. Luis is smart, cunning, and obsessive. He'll kill the crew that rescued me. He'll kill Caleb and Nolan, and he'll murder their families. He'll slit your throat, and he'll make me watch, because that's who he is. And then he'll take me back to his condo, and I'll never sleep again, because I'll know it's only a matter of time before he kills me too."

She's terrified. I put my hand on hers, and her skin is cold. Icy. "Listen to me. Caleb and Nolan will protect us."

"For how long, Kiera?"

"As long as it takes. They'll find Martinez. Nolan's amassed evidence of his wrongdoing. He'll go to jail, and we'll be safe."

Bianca stares at me, stunned into silence. "You've never been a fool," she says at last. "Kiera, Luis owns the cops. Even if he goes to jail, you don't think he can reach us from there? Vladimir Sirkovich was in jail serving a life sentence, and you still changed your identity and ran for your life."

She's right. I spent eight years looking over my shoulder, waiting for my past to catch up with me. I don't want to spend the rest of my life that way.

Then there's Nala, Caleb's niece, who is still plagued by nightmares. If something were to happen to her...

"We'll think of something." I make my voice reassuring. "You're not alone. Eight years ago, I should have done a better job protecting you, and I didn't. I won't fail you again."

At some point in the night, Henri wheels in a room service cart, filled with food and drink. At two in the morning, when my eyes are beginning to shut from exhaustion, there's a knock on the door. It's Nolan and Caleb. "Hey," Caleb says. "You doing okay?"

Warmth blooms in my chest, and a tidal wave of love overwhelms me. "Yeah. Thank you so much. I don't know how I can ever..."

Nolan tilts his head to one side. "Were you planning on finishing that thought, Kiera?" he asks, his voice silky.

Oops. They don't like me keeping score. "No." I turn around and wave my sister forward. "Come meet Caleb."

Caleb shakes Bianca's hand. "It's so good to finally meet you." He gives her an apologetic look. "I know it isn't ideal, but for the next few days, it'd be safest if you stay here in your room."

"Of course," my sister replies. "I completely understand."

Her tone doesn't betray her, but she wraps her arms around her waist, hugging herself. Her fear is palpable, and I hurt for her.

I need to make this better.

Caleb sees it too. His expression is worried when he turns to me. "Do you want to spend the night here, or head home?"

They're so considerate. I'm so lucky. "Here, please. If that's okay?"

"Of course." He hands me a key card. "For the room next door."

"Will you stay too?"

"We'll be happy to."

WHEN BIANCA IS FINALLY ASLEEP, I make my way next door. It's almost four in the morning, but Caleb and Nolan are awake, talking to each other in low voices. "Hey." I sit on the couch between them. "It feels like ages ago, but I had a really good time tonight. Downstairs, I mean."

Nolan puts his arm around my shoulders, and I lean into him. I've had time to think. I've reached a conclusion, and Caleb and Nolan aren't going to like it. "So, Luis Martinez. Be honest with me. What are the chances that he disappears?"

"Fifty-fifty," Nolan admits, his voice weary. "He'll be off-balance tonight, but tomorrow, he'll start investigating who snatched Bianca." He runs his hands through his hair. "I talked to Aydin, the leader of the team that got Bianca out. They had to move quickly—your sister was running out of time. She was supposed to go to Cancun with Martinez, but at the last minute, her plans were changed. Martinez has his eye on someone else."

My skin goes cold. "He's tiring of Bianca."

Nolan nods soberly. "Bianca knows too much about Martinez for him to let her live. Omer's instructions were clear. Bianca's safety was the priority."

"But," Caleb says. "Shots were fired, and one of Lockhart & Payne's team was injured. Martinez's guards saw Rachel take a bullet. They'll be looking for the hospital to which she was taken. From there, they'll find her identity, and figure out who her employer is. Lockhart & Payne provide private security services, and they never divulge their client list. Martinez will go underground until he identifies his adversary."

"Bianca says he won't let this go," I tell them. "He'll come after us."

Nolan sighs. "He's already tried. He called Detective Armstrong a couple of hours ago, demanding to know your location."

"And?"

Caleb's smile doesn't reach his eyes. "We're not going to let Miles Armstrong answer his phone, Kiera. Nolan and I are fanatical about your safety, and the corrupt detective is a weak link. We have a team on him. He's not going to get an opportunity to talk to Martinez."

"What if he does?" I lean forward. "Hear me out. I spent eight years in fear. I don't want to repeat that experience, and I don't want that for Bianca either. She needs to feel safe, and the only way for that to happen is if Luis Martinez is put away." They're *really* not going to like this. "He's off-balance tonight. We need to strike while the iron's hot."

"You have an idea." Caleb sounds resigned.

"What if Armstrong were to tell Martinez where I am? Then he'll come here, right? Right now, Martinez doesn't know we took Bianca. As far as he's concerned, I'm just a bartender who works here. Club M is a controlled setting. We could set a trap for him."

"No," Nolan says flatly. "It's too risky."

I lift my chin in the air. "Tell me what the alternative is."

"We'll figure something out."

"Nolan, you searched for this man for years, and you had no idea what he looked like. If he goes underground, has plastic surgery, changes his appearance, how long will it take you to find him again?"

His lips tighten. He doesn't reply.

I take his hand in mine. "I won't be in any danger. I'll be in the club. It's safe, otherwise they wouldn't have brought Bianca here."

"It is a good plan," Caleb admits reluctantly. "Luis Martinez is off balance now. As soon as he finds out Lockhart & Payne is involved, he'll go on high alert. Our best shot is to get him before that happens."

Nolan grimaces. "I hate this."

The two of them exchange a long glance. I hold my breath. They're on the verge of giving in.

"Fine," Nolan says, his voice unhappy. "We'll get Armstrong to give up your location."

38

CALEB

Most of the year, Club M is closed on Sundays. Just our luck, this Sunday is not one of them. Over a hundred members from Rafael's club are visiting Club M, and Xavier's determined to put on a good show. There's a masquerade ball that kicks off at midnight. Floor demos run all night long. It's a security nightmare.

"Tell me again why you can't cancel tonight's event." I give Xavier Leforte a death glare.

It bounces off him. "We've beefed up our security," he says calmly. "Adrian and Brody's teams are patrolling the perimeter. There's only one entrance into the club grounds. Every vehicle entering tonight will be searched. Nobody who isn't on the guest list will enter the club."

We're in Club M's control room. It's ten at night; the club's been open for an hour. There are banks of monitors here, and more than a dozen people, all of who have their eyes glued to the screens in front of them.

"It's dark," Nolan says grimly. "It won't take a lot of effort to climb a fence between patrols."

"The fence is electrified. The teams patrol with dogs. If anyone approaches within twenty-five feet of the castle, motion-sensitive lights will flood the lawn."

He surveys the two of us with a disapproving frown. Nolan looks as awful as I feel. Neither of us got much sleep last night. I lay awake a long time after we made the call to Miles Armstrong and explained to the corrupt detective exactly what we needed him to do.

I've lost people I've loved; I know exactly how much it hurts. Nolan couldn't prevent Lina from dying. Right now, he's feeling helpless and so am I, and it isn't a good sensation. This situation is both our worst nightmare come to life.

"You look like ass," Xavier says finally. "You're too close to Kiera; you care too much. Sit this one out and let the pros handle it."

"The pros?" Nolan snarls. "Are you fucking kidding me with this shit?"

"No," I say flatly. "We're not walking away from this."

A woman next to us raises her hand. "Mr. Leforte," she says. "I think you need to see this."

We crowd around the monitor. A van pulls up at the gate. The window rolls down, and a woman sticks her head out. The guard says something to her. She nods and gets out of the van.

She's dressed in a red dress that hugs her curves. "She's not a delivery driver," Nolan says, pointing out the obvious.

"We shut down deliveries for the next couple of days," Xavier says. "That's Elise Gordon. She's been a member for a year. She works on Capitol Hill. For obvious reasons, she wants to keep her membership secret."

"So, she drives a delivery truck?"

"She told me she's afraid of being followed."

Seems rather paranoid to me, but hey, it's not my life. I

watch the screen. The security guards at the booth shine a flashlight into the front seat. Then they open the back, and finally give Ms. Gordon the all-clear.

"What am I missing, Tina?"

The woman rewinds the video to before the van showed up. "Look here," she says, tapping the screen and enlarging the image. "It's a dark spot on the driveway. It hasn't been raining, so it's probably an oil slick."

"Okay."

She forwards the video to just after the van rolls away. "Look at the slick now."

I stare at the enlarged image, the hair on the back of my neck prickling. "It's smudged."

Nolan swears out loud. "Somebody rolled through it."

"That was my deduction as well," Tina confirms. "False bottom on the van, in all likelihood." She taps the screen, and the van is back in front of the security booth. "We can't see the passenger side. It's possible that someone could have lowered themselves to the driveway, and then, when the guards were checking the back, rolled to the tree cover."

"How long ago did this happen?"

"Ten minutes, Mr. Leforte. Something kept bothering me about the footage, so I went back to review it."

"Where's Kiera?"

"Working," I reply.

"Why?"

Strangling Xavier isn't the solution. "She works here, Xavier," I remind him pointedly. "You're throwing a masquerade ball tonight. Henri's had her on the schedule for months."

Tina's already pulling up the bar cameras. I see Kelli and Farid pouring drinks, but Kiera's nowhere to be seen.

I have a very bad feeling about this.

I grab my gun and break into a sprint, Nolan at my heels. "Text me if you find her," I yell over my shoulder. I dial her number as I run for the elevator. *Damn it, Kiera. Pick up your phone.*

But there's no answer.

39

KIERA

I thought I'd be a nervous wreck tonight but working at the bar calms me down. Even though it's early, the club is already much more crowded than usual. Well-dressed people gather around the floor shows.

This year, Xavier's recruited what appears to be members of an erotic circus. Near the bar, a naked woman, her entire body coated in gold paint, juggle a half-dozen flaming torches. The ceiling is covered with rigging, and a pair of trapeze artists soar from one side of the room to the other. There are jugglers, ballerinas, acrobats, strolling musicians—everywhere my eye lands, there's a new wonder to be seen. Club M is on display tonight, and it's pulled out all the stops.

I've just finished mixing a martini for Eric Kane when Diane James hurries up to the bar. Diane has been a member for about five years now, though she's rarely here. A few months ago, she confessed to me that the only reason she joined the club was to keep an eye on her younger sister, Heather. "She has terrible taste in men," she'd slurred after one too many margaritas. "She keeps dating these assholes who hit her and call it BDSM. Now she's joined a sex club so she can meet more of them. She's an adult. Why doesn't she act like one?"

I could relate to Diane's desire to protect her baby sister. I'd cut her off and called her a cab, and that night, I'd gone home and cried about my failure to take care of Bianca.

Diane looks terrible. She's not wearing a mask, unlike most of the people on the floor. Her eyes are red, and her mascara is smudged, which is extremely unlike her. I smile at her automatically. "Ms. James, what can I make you to drink?"

"Kiera, thank heavens you're here. I need help."

Her hands shake. There's a tremor in her voice. I frown in concern. "Of course. What can I do for you?"

"Heather's boyfriend," she spits out. "He beat her. She's badly hurt, Kiera. We were both going to come to the club tonight. When I walked into her apartment..." Her eyes fill with tears. "I didn't dare take her to the hospital. Paul is a Secret Service agent. I drove straight here."

Oh God. "Where's Heather?"

"In the car. She can't walk; her ankle is sprained. I didn't want to make a scene."

No, no matter what the situation, Diane James would never want to draw attention to herself. I doubt that Paul is a serious threat; Diane probably just didn't want to take Heather to the hospital where people were bound to ask questions. Heather is an actress; it'll end up in the tabloids.

"Xavier knows how to keep this quiet," she continues. "Can you help me get Heather upstairs, Kiera?" She looks around. "Please? Heather's new movie comes out in two weeks."

I could tell her that any of the club security staff would be happy to help her, and all of them can be trusted, but she didn't ask them; she asked me. She thinks I'll be discreet. Diane isn't a friend, but I still can't say no to her. I've felt what she's feeling right now, the helplessness that comes with being unable to protect someone from themselves. "Sure," I say, taking off my apron. "I'll be happy to."

We hurry to the parking lot. Diane's BMW is parked in the north-eastern corner. My phone beeps as I follow her, and I glance down at it. It's Caleb. I'm about to pick it up when a hand grabs my wrist.

"I don't think so," Luis Fernando Martinez says. "Hello, Kiera. Where's your sister?"

40

KIERA

Well, fuck.

Martinez has one arm wrapped around my throat. He holds a gun in his right hand. He's strong, and I'm not going to be able to free myself. Not without risking getting shot.

I stare at Diane, stunned at her betrayal. "I'm really sorry," she whispers, backing away from the two of us. "He threatened Heather."

"Drop your gun, Martinez," a familiar voice barks.

My heart leaps. It's Nolan. He's got a gun in his hand, and murder in his eyes. Caleb moves to the right of him, also armed. A trio of Adrian and Brody's soldiers fan out in front of us. A pair of Xavier's security guards walk out of the shadows.

"You're surrounded," Caleb says. "There's no way out. Drop your gun. Give us the girl and I'll let you live."

Martinez backs up against the car, dragging me with him. He is ringed by soldiers with weapons, all pointed at us. "It will take me less than a second to break her neck," he snarls. "Are you ready to take that risk, Wolanski?" There's a sneer in his voice. His arm tightens painfully around my neck. "Tell me where Bianca is, and I will let her go."

He's cutting off my breathing. Spots swim in front of my eyes. But the instant he says Bianca's name, a cold clarity fills me. We are not trading my sister's life for mine.

I will never let that happen.

I'm surrounded by crack shots. I just need to buy them a second.

I bite down on Martinez's forearm, hard enough to draw blood. He screams in anger, and his grip on me slackens. I wrench free and twist away.

Nolan jerks his gun up and fires. He's not the only one. Behind me, Martinez fires as well.

I brace myself for agony; it doesn't come.

Luis Fernando Martinez drops silently, a bullet between his eyes, dead before he hits the ground.

It's finally over.

Then my eyes take in a slumped body in front of me.

Martinez didn't fire at me. Acting on pure instinct, he fired on the greatest threat.

Nolan.

Oh God no. He's been hit.

41

NOLAN

Kiera bends over me, her face etched with fear, the pink strands of her hair glittering in the light from the parking lot. "Nolan," she whispers, lacing her fingers in mine.

All I see is her face, her eyes shining with tears. I don't want to see her cry, ever again. Kiera's precious to me. I want only happiness for her.

Dimly, I'm aware of one of Xavier's security guards kneeling next to me, putting pressure on my chest. People swim and out of existence. Then I'm loaded on a stretcher, Caleb and Kiera jumping into the ambulance along with me.

Her hand is still laced in mine.

I look up at Caleb, a question in my eyes. *Am I going to die?*

Because I don't want to. I want to live. I want her, I want a house, filled with warmth and laughter. I want vacations with Kiera. I want to show her the world. I want it all.

Caleb doesn't need to be a mind-reader to understand what I'm asking. "The paramedics think you're going to make it," he says. "I told them you're too stubborn to die." He's badly worried. "The bullet just missed your heart. You'll be spending a few weeks in hospital." His eyes narrow. "This time, you better be seeing visitors."

This isn't Mogadishu. I'm done holding myself apart. Kiera and Caleb are the two people I care about most in the world. "Absolutely." I fix my gaze on Kiera, who gives me a tremulous smile. "It's over," I tell her as the world once again drifts into darkness. "Martinez is dead. Your sister is safe. You're safe."

The last thing I hear before I black out is Kiera's voice. "It's not over," she says. "The really good stuff is just beginning."

EPILOGUE

KIERA

Ten months later...

They whisked Nolan into surgery as soon as he arrived. It took seven hours, the longest seven hours of my life. I sat next to Caleb, clutching his hands for warmth, unable to stop shivering. At some point, I remember apologizing for going to the parking lot. "This is all my fault," I'd whispered. The tears had finally stopped falling, but my eyes were red and itchy. "I should have never left the club."

"Diane James was a member in good standing," he'd replied, pulling me onto his lap and wrapping both arms around me. "You had no way of knowing. This is not your fault."

Bianca, who had ridden with Xavier to the hospital, had fetched me a cup of hot chocolate. I'd wrapped my fingers around it, but it had brought me no comfort. It wasn't until the surgeon had stepped out into the hallway and told us that Nolan was going to be fine that I finally felt like I could breathe.

Nolan spent four weeks in hospital. His recovery was slow and painful, but three months after he was shot, he was back to normal. "Never again," he'd promised me. "No more risks. I'm going to live a life so boring that it'll be like watching paint dry. You'll be sick of me in a month."

Ten months later, I'm not sick of him, not even a little. I'm the happiest I've ever been in my life.

Miles Armstrong, the corrupt detective that had been the source of so much pain in my life, didn't get away with his crimes. There was a sting operation, and he was caught giving out the location of someone in witness protection. The bribery trial made national news. Last month, he was sentenced to ten years in prison.

Less than a month after Nolan killed Martinez, Greg Dratch escaped from jail. We'd barely received word when Nolan and Caleb got a phone call from Anton Nekrasov. "Thank you for finding Gregory for me," he'd said. "I have him now."

"Damn it, Nekrasov," Caleb had sworn. "I promised him he'd go to jail."

"And he did. You kept your part of the agreement. My priorities are different."

But it wasn't all good news.

Bianca's recovery wasn't quite so easy. How do you find your way back from eight years of exploitation, especially when the damage started when she was only fifteen? She tried. She really did. She didn't want to work in Club M; the scenes of sex disturbed her. She went to work at the grocery store, and for a couple of weeks, I thought that maybe things would work out.

Then her manager forced himself on her during a break, and he'd kissed her, sticking his tongue into her mouth.

Bianca's been through a lot, but I think that was the

thing that broke her. For a couple of months after that, she'd been too depressed to get out of bed. Finally, I'd given her Hunter Driesse's card and insisted she talk to him. "He specializes in PTSD," I told Bianca.

"We can't afford it," she'd replied.

"We can," I said firmly. I don't really like taking money from Caleb and Nolan, but for Bianca, I would have done it. But I hadn't needed to; Hunter had generously offered to see her *pro bono.*

I don't know what Hunter told her, but it helped. Within a month of her first appointment, she'd been online, researching flights to Russia. "You're going to see Nekrasov?" Nolan had guessed.

"Yes." She'd tilted her chin up. "You're going to tell me he's a dangerous criminal, and it's a bad idea."

"On the contrary, I think Anton's exactly the person you need right now. And whatever Nekrasov's other failings, he won't take advantage of you. That's a line he won't cross."

I hadn't really been thrilled at the idea, but the prospect of joining Anton Nekrasov's shadowy, clandestine organization was the only thing that Bianca had shown any interest in. Nolan had paid for her air ticket, and right after Christmas, my sister had flown to Moscow.

I miss her terribly. But she calls me every week, and she seems cheerful and happy. In the end, that's the only thing that matters.

Farid comes up to me. "So," he says, a wide smile on his face. "It's your last day here. Are you excited?"

"I'm trying not to freak out," I reply honestly. "But yeah. When I remember to breathe, I'm very excited."

For many years, Club M has been my home and my shelter. But it's time to step outside the nest, spread my wings, and learn to fly.

For the last ten months, Nolan and Caleb have been nagging me to accept financial help from them. "Did you grow up wanting to be a bartender?" Caleb had asked pointedly.

I'd rolled my eyes at his question. Rich people—they're not like us. When I was growing up, if I dreamed, it was that we'd have enough to eat. If I got lucky, maybe I'd find a backpack in decent shape in the thrift store at the start of a new school year.

The future was never something I thought about. All I had energy for was surviving the present.

"I'm not with you for your money," I'd replied to Caleb.

They had both looked exasperated. "Yes, Kiera," Nolan had said with an exaggerated note of patience. "That's obvious. Listen, you can work the bar if that's what you want. But if you ever want to do something else, we're here for you. We will support you completely."

Their words had stuck in my mind. Things are different now. I have space to dream. To think about what I'd like to do if I'm not fighting for survival.

In January, the week after Bianca had flown to Russia, I'd gone online and bought an SAT study guide. For three months, I'd prepped, and then, in March, I'd taken the exam and scored in the 95th percentile. "What'd I say?" Dixie said smugly. "Of course, you were going to ace it."

This fall, I'm going to college. I don't know what I want to do yet. I enjoy talking to people, and I like feeling like I'm helping them out. There's a tiny part of me that thinks that eventually, I want to become a therapist like Avery and Hunter. The thought of spending more than ten years in school is a little daunting, but I don't necessarily need to earn a PhD to work in the field.

Nolan and Caleb couldn't have been more supportive. Not just about my college plans, but about everything.

I live with them now. It's amazing. I thought I'd miss my space, but it's really nice to wake up next to them. It's wonderful to get back home at the end of a long shift to a hot meal. Sometimes, we're all busy with work, each of us on their own laptops. Sometimes, we eat dinner together, and relax on the couch with wine and Netflix. Sometimes, we head to the city. Whatever we're doing, it just feels right, because I'm with them.

There's an influx of people at the bar, and for the next thirty minutes, I'm kept busy making cocktails. When I can breathe again, I look up, and my mouth falls open.

It's Dixie, who only shows up to Club M when she's worried about me. She's dressed in a lacy black cocktail dress that clings to her bodice and flares at the waist, falling to her knees in soft folds. Four-inch high heels add to the look. She teeters over to the bar and sits down.

"Tell me everything," I say, slapping a glass of white wine in front of her. "What are you doing here?"

She gives me a sheepish look. "It's a complicated story. The simplest version is that I lost a bet."

My eyes widen. "You're going to play at the club? In public?"

"In private."

I pinch myself. "With who?"

Before she can answer, Hunter Driesse and Eric Kane walk up to the bar. Hunter offers Dixie his hand. "Ready, Dix?"

Dixie blushes. "I'll be along in a minute," she murmurs. "As soon as I'm done with the wine."

"Just the one, okay?" Eric says, putting a key card on the counter. "I don't want you tipsy."

A guy telling Dixie what to do. I wait for her to rip him a new one, but to my everlasting shock, she nods. I remember to close my mouth. Once they're out of earshot, I turn back to my friend. "Are you okay?" I demand. "They're not coercing you into this, are they?"

"No, of course not," she says at once. "Don't worry. Xavier's already given me the third degree." She takes a sip of her wine. "Can I tell you something?" She leans closer to me. "I might even be looking forward to it." She slides off the barstool, tucking the key card into her clutch. "See you later, Kiera."

I barely have time to recover from my shock when Caleb and Nolan enter the club and walk over to me. "So," Caleb says. "It's your last day. Are you sad?"

"A little," I admit. "What about you? Are you sad the cocktail games will come to an end?"

He grins. "None of our games are coming to an end, Kiera."

Nolan winks at me. "When you're done with your shift," he says. "I thought we'd play here tonight."

Anticipation pulses through me. We haven't played at Club M for almost three months. SAT prep, college applications... I've just been really busy.

"What do you have planned?"

Nolan's lips tilt up. "What's your pleasure, Kiera? What would you like to experience tonight?"

What's your pleasure? That had been the first question I'd ever asked Nolan.

"That's an intriguing question to ask in a place like this," I reply, repeating his answer of that day back to him. I look up at the two men that I love and trust more than anyone in the world. "Surprise me."

THANK you for reading Keeping Kiera I hope you love Kiera, Nolan & Caleb as much as I do.

Dixie's book will be next in the Club Menage series, and it will probably be released in the second half of 2020. If you'd like to be notified when it's available, please sign up to my newsletter and I'll send you a note when it's live.

THE DIRTY SERIES

If you enjoy menage romances, may I suggest my Dirty series? The series is set in the small town of New Summit. Each book features a smart and sassy heroine, and a pair of men who fall in love with her, and each book in the Dirty Series is a standalone MFM Menage romance.

Flip the page for an extended preview of Dirty Therapy, the first book of the Dirty series.

Dirty Therapy - Mia, Benjamin & Landon
Dirty Talk - Cassie, James & Lucas
Dirty Games - Nina, Scott & Zane
Dirty Words - Maggie, Lars & Ethan

Or, buy the collection for a discount...
Dirty - the Complete Collection

A PREVIEW OF DIRTY THERAPY BY TARA CRESCENT

My O is missing. Two therapists are going to help me find it.

Two hours after Dennis proposes, I find my fiancé with his d*ck buried in Tiffany Slater's hoohah, and he has the nerve to suggest it's my fault.

Because I'm frigid.

Sure, I've never had an orgasm with him, or with anyone for that matter, but relationships are about more than good nookie. (Not that it was ever good. Adequate is more like it. Okay, who am I kidding? ***Dennis couldn't find his way down there with a flashlight and a map.***)

Now I'm determined to find my missing O with the help of two of the hottest men I've ever set eyes on. Therapists Benjamin Long and Landon West. If these two men can't make me come, then no one can.

I shouldn't sleep with them. I shouldn't **succumb** to their sexy smiles. I shouldn't listen when their firm voices **promise** me all the pleasure I can handle.

I can't get enough. But when a bitter rival finds out about our forbidden relationship, ***everything will come crashing down.***

CHAPTER 1

Mia:

I'm going to sum up the suckitude of my life with a three-point list.

1. Though I haven't had sex with my boyfriend for over a month, he proposed last night in an extremely crowded restaurant, and I said yes. Because everyone was looking at me and I didn't want to be the girl that broke his heart in a public setting. Even though I wasn't really sure I wanted to marry Dennis.
2. Once I got back home, I started thinking about whether we were doing the right thing. So, I went over to his place to talk to him, and I found him plowing his dick in Tiffany Slater's willing pussy. That wasn't good.
3. I started yelling. Instead of groveling, he yelled back. "You're frigid," he accused me. "I've never been able to make you come." Right. As if it's *my* fault that I have to draw him a map to my clitoris.
4. (Okay, I lied. This is a four-point list.) Worst of

all, when I threw his stupid engagement ring at his pasty-white butt, I missed. Big dramatic moment—ruined.

"So there you have it," I finish reciting last night's humiliating events to my best friend, Cassie, while unpacking a new shipment of cocktail dresses. "Can my life get any worse?"

It's eleven in the morning, or as I like to think of it, 'Treat Time.' Usually, this is my favorite part of the day. The store is quiet, and I can arrange the clothing neatly on hangers, organizing them by color and function. I can fiddle with the display cases of costume jewelry and make sure that everything is perfect.

Cassie, who runs the coffee shop next door, is my supplier of treats. She's watching me now, her eyes wide. "Dennis never made you come?" she asks, honing in unerringly to the most embarrassing part – the lack of orgasms. "Mia, the two of you dated for a year."

"I know."

She takes a bite of her muffin. Chocolate chip, if I know my friend. "Why on Earth did you keep going out with him?" she demands. Crumbs fall on my ornately tufted vintage velvet loveseat. Normally, I'd shoo her out of the way and bust out my hand-vac, but today's not a normal day. "The guy's not a looker, and he has the personality of a wet towel."

I feel strangely compelled to defend my ex-boyfriend, but then I remember Tiffany, and I clamp my mouth shut. "I tried to tell him what turned me on," I mutter, my cheeks flushed with humiliation. "At the start. He called me a pervert."

Cassie's eyebrow rises, and she gives me her 'what-the-fuck' look. "He called you a pervert?" Her voice is dangerous. "And you still dated him after that?"

Worse, I almost married him.

I avoid Cassie's gaze. This situation would never happen to my friend. She's bold and uninhibited, and she has every guy in our small town wrapped around her finger. Me? I'm the boring one in the corner, grateful for any scrap of attention that comes my way.

"Anyway." Cassie dismisses Dennis with a shrug of her shoulder. "Forget Dennis. You dodged a bullet there. Let's get you back on the horse. Friday night happy hour at The Merry Cockatoo?"

Normally, even the mention of The Merry Cockatoo would get a giggle out of me. The newly opened bar is on the same block as my clothing boutique and Cassie's coffee shop. My landlord, George Bollington, has been waging a low-grade war with the woman who owns the bar, trying to get Nina Templeton to change the name.

"We're a family-friendly town," he grouses every time he sees me. "What kind of woman calls her bar that name?" Mr. Bollington is so uptight he can't even say Cockatoo out loud. Because I'm the town's resident good girl, he thinks he's got a sympathetic audience in me. I get to hear him grumble about Nina, about the sex therapists who've just opened a practice in town, about people who chew gum and listen to loud music, about people who litter... you name it, and my landlord probably disapproves of it.

I agree with him on the litter, but the rest of it is Mr. Bollington being a grouchy old man. Except for the sex therapists. That's professional jealousy. Mr. Bollington is a psychiatrist, and he's grown accustomed to being the only option in town. He now has competition, and he doesn't like it.

Speaking of Mr. Bollington, the door bells chime, and my landlord walks in. When he sees Cassie sitting in my store, he frowns. Cassie is another person Mr. Bollington doesn't approve of. "Mia," he says, ignoring my friend, "I just saw your window display." His forehead creases with disapproval. "It's very unsuitable. This is a family-friendly town."

Last week, I'd received some incredible hand-made silk lingerie from a small French manufacturer. Each piece was so gorgeous that it should have been in a museum. I'd spent most of Saturday setting up a window display for the bras, panties, and slips. I should have known Mr. Bollington would get his knickers in a knot about it. (Ha ha. See what I did there?)

"Mr. Bollington, I run a clothing store." I try and keep my voice firm. "Window displays are an important part of my marketing strategy."

He's unmoved. "Need I remind you about the morality clause in your lease, young lady?" he demands. The threat is unmistakable. Take the offending display down, or my landlord will make trouble.

Cassie snorts into her muffin once he leaves. "One day," she gripes, "I wish you'd stand up to him and tell him his stupid morality clause isn't legally enforceable. You're going to take the lingerie down, aren't you?"

"Probably." I'm a people-pleaser. I want everyone to like me. And it seems easier to give in to Mr. Bollington's demands than fight him. It's just a window display, after all.

Cassie lets it go. "Back to more important things," she says. "Friday night. We'll get drinks, get tipsy, and go home with unsuitable men." She winks in my direction. "The kind that will have you screaming with pleasure. The sooner you forget about limp dick, the better."

I feel my cheeks heat. "Yeah, about that," I mumble. "Dennis might be right."

She frowns. "Right about what?"

Oh God. It's mortifying telling Cassie the truth. "I've never had an orgasm with a guy in my life."

Her mouth falls open. Thankfully, she's finished chewing her muffin. "With any guy?" she asks, her voice astonished.

I think back to the three men I've slept with. Brett, my high-school boyfriend, who I went out with for two weeks before he dumped me to date Gayla, a big-breasted blonde cheerleader. Tony, my college crush, who slept with me *once* before confessing that he preferred men. And of course, Dennis, who buried his cock in Tiffany's twat less than two hours after proposing to me. "Nope." I lower my voice. "There's something wrong with me, isn't there?"

"Apart from your horrible tastes in men, no." She gets to her feet and muffin crumbs cascade to the floor. "Friday. Meet me at six. Prepare to party your brains out."

Once she leaves, I stare blankly at the rack of beaded and glittering dresses and think about my ex-fiancé. Even at the beginning of our relationship, I'd never felt the kind of passion for him I read about in books. Maybe he's right. Maybe I am frigid.

Cassie isn't going to tell me the truth. The best-friend rules clearly state that she's supposed to say supportive things.

But there's another way to get the truth. As I vacuum up chocolate chip muffin residue, I make a decision. I'm not the kind of girl who sleeps with a guy she picked up at the bar. Even if I wanted to have sex with a stranger, they never tended to notice me. That kind of attention is reserved for Cass.

No, I'm going to solve my orgasm problem the responsible, adult way. I'm going to see a therapist. Not just any therapist. I'm going to see the sex therapists that Mr. Bollington hates. Benjamin Long and Landon West. Maybe they can figure out what's wrong with me.

~

CHAPTER 2

Benjamin:

It's been two months since Landon and I opened our practice in this small town, and I can't say that I'm enjoying it so far. While the pace of life is a lot more peaceful than Manhattan, I'm used to the anonymity of the big city. In New Summit, everyone has their noses in our business all the time. Given what we do, that's a problem.

Landon, my partner and best friend, comes into my office at ten in the morning. "I need to talk to you about Amy," he says without preamble, taking a seat opposite me and propping his legs up on my desk.

I give him a pointed look, one that just makes him laugh. Landon knows I like my office tidy and organized, and he takes delight in messing with me. "Make yourself at home," I say dryly. I look him over. His hair is tousled, he hasn't shaved, and his eyes are red. "You look like hell by the way. Late night?"

He grins. "Samantha came over," he says. "She's a tiger, that one. She kept me up all night."

It's far too hard to keep up with Landon's dating habits, but I could have sworn he was seeing someone else. "Weren't you sleeping with Claire?" I ask him.

"Not anymore," he replies with a shake of his head. "She was getting clingy. Talking about clingy, how's Becky?"

I gave him a puzzled look. "We broke up. Didn't I tell you?"

A faintly hurt expression flashes across his face. "No," he says. "You forgot to mention it. When did this happen?"

I do the math in my head. "Three weeks ago."

"Why did you break up with her? The two of you seem to get along well enough."

Landon knows me pretty well, so he's guessed, correctly, that I initiated the break-up. I think about the lawyer I dated for six months. Landon's right—Becky and I got along just fine. We never fought, we never argued, and we never even bickered. It had been an amicable, adult relationship, and it had bored me to tears.

"She wanted to move in," I explain.

Landon raises an eyebrow. "Let me guess," he says, his voice amused. "That suggestion filled you with horror. You thought about Becky's stuff all over your place, her toothbrush next to yours, her pretty lingerie in your closet, and you ran for your life."

"You don't need to psychoanalyze me," I tell him. Landon and I have been friends since college. He knows my flaws, and I know his. After a childhood filled with chaos, I'm almost pathological in my desire for calm. Landon's father cheated on his mother and slept around like a randy tomcat, and as a result, Landon avoids relationships, convinced he wouldn't be able to stay faithful. "I'm quite aware that I'm a little stuck in my ways."

"That's not what I was going to say," he replies, his expression serious. "I was going to tell you that you only pick women that you aren't truly attracted to, so it's easier to walk away from them when you're done."

I glare at my friend. That assessment is a little too close to the truth for comfort. "Didn't you say you wanted to talk about Amy? What has she done this time?"

Amy Cooke is our receptionist. She's new; the receptionist we had in Manhattan hadn't wanted to leave the city. She's still on probation, and at the rate she's going, she's not going to last very long.

"She outed Natalie to her sister-in-law." Landon's voice is angry. "Nat called me in tears this morning. It seems that Amy ran into Doris in church, and proceeded to ask her if Nat's husband knew what she did in our office."

I see red. Our practice specializes in sex therapy, and Natalie is one of our best surrogates. We use her to help clients who are having issues with their sex lives.

Unfortunately, surrogacy is still considered similar to sex work, and while Natalie's husband knows what she does for a living, the couple would prefer that no one else does.

Now Amy has outed Natalie to her family.

"We should fire her," I say flatly. "Amy knows how important confidentiality is. If she can't respect the most basic rules of our profession..."

Landon winces. He's kinder than I am. "Give her a warning," he says. "Tell her that she's out of second chances."

I frown. "You do it then," I tell him. "I'm too angry."

"Not a chance," he says promptly. "She has a crush on me. She'd be more terrified if you yell at her."

"Fine." Amy has to realize how important discretion is in our profession. Otherwise, she is going to get herself fired. Already George Bollington, the psychotherapist in town, is gunning for us. We don't need any more hassle.

My intercom buzzes just then. "Dr. Long? Dr. West?" Amy's voice sounds in my office. "Your ten thirty appointment is here. Mia Gardner."

"Thanks Amy." I put the phone on mute and grin at Landon. "I hope you're ready to put your thinking cap on."

"New patient?" he asks. Landon and I see new patients together, at least until we have a treatment plan in place. "Let's go."

~

Landon:

There's only one word I can use to describe the woman who waits in my office. *Hot.*

She's in her mid-twenties. Her eyes glitter like green emeralds. Her hair is dark and lustrous, cascading in long, loose waves down her shoulders. Her body is the kind that a man dreams of, curvy and lush.

Except she's a prospective client, for fuck's sake. And though Ben jokes that I'll screw everything in a skirt, I have some boundaries. Clients are always off-limits.

"Ms. Gardner," I greet her with my most professional smile. "I'm Dr. West. This is Dr. Long. Please, sit down."

I wave toward the deep burgundy couch, and she perches on the very edge of it. Her fingers are clenched into fists, and she's yet to say a word.

"What brought you in today, Ms. Gardner?" Ben asks encouragingly.

She bites her lower lip. My cock takes note of the way her teeth indent the flesh, and I stir in my armchair, trying discreetly to adjust myself. God, this is embarrassing. I'm a sex therapist. I've watched people get fucked in this office, and I've never yet had to fight off an erection.

Fuck me. My dick hardens even further at the thought of seeing Mia Gardner naked.

Okay. Focus, Landon. She's here for help.

"Ms. Gardner." I lean forward. "It's okay. You can tell us what the matter is. Everything you say in this office is confidential. We're here to help."

She nods. "I have a problem," she says, her face flushed. Her voice is barely a whisper. "I don't think I enjoy sex."

"Why do you think that?" Ben asks her.

Her eyes drop to her lap. "I never orgasm," she mumbles. "My fiancé thought I was frigid."

She has a fiancé? I don't know why that bothers me as much as it does.

Ben is more helpful than I am. "It's pretty common not to orgasm with a partner."

"It's not just Dennis," she confesses, her hands worrying the fabric of her skirt. "I've never been able to come with any partner."

"Couples sometimes fall into a rut," I suggest. "They find it helpful to tell each other about their fantasies. Role play, kink. Whatever jolts you out of your rhythm."

Her face turns fiery. "Have you tried telling him what turns you on?" I continue.

"What turns you on, Ms. Gardner?" Ben's voice drops an octave, and his eyes glitter with heat. Whoa. Benjamin Long is interested in this girl too. Well, well.

"It's too embarrassing." She can't look at us.

"If you don't tell us, we can't help you."

"I just can't," she wails.

I have a brainwave, which is a miracle, given that most of my blood has pooled in my dick. "Sometimes, when our clients are having trouble relaxing, we use hypnosis."

"Good idea, Dr. West," Ben says, giving me a sidelong look. He turns back to Mia. "Would you like to try that?"

She bites her lower lip again. I can see her debate it in her head.

"We record the session," I assure her. "So you don't have to worry about what you say."

She appears to reach a conclusion. "Yes," she nods. "I really want to solve this problem of mine, and if that's what it takes, let's do it."

Ben's the hypnotist. "Lie back on the couch," he instructs Mia, while I set up the recorder.

She gulps, but obeys. She stretches out on the red burgundy velvet, her skirt riding up to mid-thigh. Her skin looks creamy and soft and very touchable.

"You have nothing to worry about," Ben assures her. "Despite what you hear, we can't make you do anything during hypnosis that you won't do otherwise. It's just to get you to calm down."

He looks deep in her eyes, the lucky dog. "Relax," he says, his voice low and soothing. "Let your muscles sink into the couch." He draws out his sentences, the syllables slow and smooth. "Breathe in. Fill your chest and lungs with air."

She complies, and her breasts strain against her shirt. I want to adjust myself but can't. Until Mia goes under, sudden movements will startle her and pull her out of her trance.

"Good," Ben continues. "Now breathe out slowly. Empty your lungs."

After several steadying breaths, Ben proceeds to the next step. Despite what you see in pop culture, you don't need a swinging watch to hypnotize someone. Just a focal object.

Unfortunately, Ben picks me. "I want you to look at Dr. West's face," he instructs. "Focus on him. Don't move your eyes away from Landon, Mia."

Her pretty green eyes meet mine. There's a hint of

nervousness there, but as Ben goes through each step, it disappears. After five minutes of slow, patient encouragement, her eyes grow heavy, and her breathing evens out.

Ben nods at me. She's good to go.

"We were talking about sex, Mia," I say. "Tell us what you want."

"Dennis was tentative," she murmurs, her voice soft. "Sometimes, I wanted him to take charge."

"Take charge how?"

She hesitates. "I wanted him to push me against a wall," she whispers. "Pull my hands above my head and hold them in place. I wanted him to be forceful. I wanted to be taken."

Stay calm, Landon.

"What else?" My voice is strained. "What do you fantasize about?"

"I want to be spanked," she replies. "I want to be dragged over a man's lap." Her expression turns dreamy. "He'll pull my panties down, and he'll order me to take my punishment like a good girl. And if I don't obey, he'll tie my wrists up so I can't move."

Oh my fucking God.

Even hypnotized, her cheeks go pink. "Then, once the spanking is over, he'll push me down on my knees, and he'll thrust his cock into my mouth."

Ben makes a strangled noise in his throat. Thankfully, it doesn't stop Mia Gardner, because she keeps talking. "Sometimes," she whispers, "I even dream about more than one cock. One in my pussy, one in my ass. Taking me hard."

This girl will be the death of us. Her fantasies are dirty and kinky, and I want to fulfill them.

She's a prospective client, asswipe. Keep your dick in your pants.

Ben's heard enough. He pulls Mia Gardner out of her

hypnotic trance. When she's sitting on the couch again, her back straight, her hands clenched in her lap, he continues gently. "Do you remember what you told us you want?" he asks her.

She shakes her head.

I swallow. Mia is an irresistible combination of good-girl on the outside, and hot kinky vixen when her inhibitions are down. Following procedure, I copy the recording on a flash drive and give it to her. "If you want to listen to it later," I say in explanation.

Ben takes a deep breath to steady himself. "It sounds like you want to spice up your sex life," he says. "Perhaps your orgasm problems are tied to that. Have you tried talking to your fiancé?"

Her fiancé. What a douchebag that guy must be. If I had a woman like Mia in my bed, I'd make damn sure I please her.

Ben says *tied*, and I think of Mia stretched out on the couch, her arms above her head, bound together with a tie. Not mine; I never wear one. Ben's tie would work nicely, though.

"I can't. We broke up."

An unexpected surge of triumph runs through my blood. Yes. She's single. *Tell me more about your fantasies,* I want to urge. Ben and I have shared women in the past. We haven't done something like that in a long time, but for this woman, I'll be happy to make an exception.

"We have some other options," Ben says. "If you'd like, we can explore using sexual surrogates to help you climax during sex."

She sits up. "A surrogate? You mean someone will have sex with me while you watch?"

"We're trained professionals," I reply. "I know it sounds awkward, but it isn't as bad as it sounds."

She jumps to her feet, her palms pressed against her cheeks. "I can't," she says, her eyes wild. "What was I thinking? Oh my God, I need to get out of here."

She rushes out of my office. I stare after her retreating back. "Well, that went well," Ben mutters. "Now I get to go and yell at Amy. What a fucking day."

Start reading Dirty Therapy, book 1 of the Dirty series today! Each book is a standalone MFM menage romance with a guaranteed HEA!

ABOUT TARA CRESCENT

Get a free story from Tara when you sign up to Tara's mailing list.

Tara Crescent writes steamy contemporary romances for readers who like hot, dominant heroes and strong, sassy heroines.

When she's not writing, she can be found curled up on a couch with a good book, often with a cat on her lap.

She lives in Toronto.

Tara also writes sci-fi romance as Lili Zander. Check her books out at http://www.lilizander.com

Find Tara on:

www.taracrescent.com

taracrescent@gmail.com

ALSO BY TARA CRESCENT

MÉNAGE ROMANCE

Club Ménage

Claiming Fifi

Taming Avery

Keeping Kiera

Ménage in Manhattan

The Bet

The Heat

The Wager

The Hack

The Dirty Series

Dirty Therapy

Dirty Talk

Dirty Games

Dirty Words

The Cocky Series

Her Cocky Doctors

Her Cocky Firemen

Standalone Books

Dirty X6

CONTEMPORARY ROMANCE

The Drake Family Series

Temporary Wife (A Billionaire Fake Marriage Romance)

Fake Fiance (A Billionaire Second Chance Romance)

Standalone Books

Hard Wood

MAX: A Friends to Lovers Romance

A Touch of Blackmail

A Very Paisley Christmas

Boyfriend by the Hour

BDSM ROMANCE

Assassin's Revenge

Nights in Venice

Mr. Banks (A British Billionaire Romance)

Teaching Maya

The House of Pain

The Professor's Pet

The Audition

The Watcher

Doctor Dom

Dominant - *A Boxed Set containing The House of Pain, The Professor's Pet, The Audition and The Watcher*

You can also keep track of my new releases by signing up for my mailing list!

Made in the USA
Columbia, SC
19 August 2020